The Hemlock

1 pretty little town

1 picturesque inn ove

2 talented sisters bett
they are at their day jobs.

1 (or more) murders . . .

A WINNING RECIPE FOR MYSTERY LOVERS!

Don't miss these Hemlock Falls Mysteries . . .

A Taste for Murder

One of the year's biggest events, the History Days festival, takes a deadly turn when a reenactment of seventeenth-century witch trials leads to twentieth-century murder. Since the victim is one of their guests, the least Sarah and Meg Quilliam could do is investigate . . .

A Dash of Death

The Quilliam sisters are at it again, this time trailing the murderer of two Hemlock Falls women who won a design contest. Helena Houndswood, the celebrated expert on stylish living, was furious when the small-town women won. But mad enough to murder?

A Pinch of Poison

Hendrick Conway is a nosy reporter who thinks something funny is going on with a local development project. But nobody's laughing when two of his relatives turn up murdered. For Hendrick and the Quilliam sisters, this could be one deadline they'll *never* meet . . .

Murder Well-Done

Big-time politics come to the little town of Hemlock Falls when the Inn hosts the wedding rehearsal dinner of an ex-senator. While politics makes strange bedfellows, the dead fellows turning up are what worry the Quilliam sisters—because their rehearsal dinner could end up being someone's last meal . . .

A TOUCH OF THE GRAPE

CLAUDIA BISHOP

BERKLEY PRIME CRIME, NEW YORK

A TOUCH OF THE GRAPE

A Berkley Prime Crime Book / published by arrangement with
the author

PRINTING HISTORY
Berkley Prime Crime edition / July 1998

The Penguin Putnam Inc. World Wide Web site address is
http://www.penguinputnam.com

ISBN: 0-425-16397-0

Berkley Prime Crime Books are published
by The Berkley Publishing Group,
a division of Penguin Putnam Inc.,
375 Hudson Street, New York, New York 10014.
The name BERKLEY PRIME CRIME and the BERKLEY PRIME CRIME
design are trademarks belonging to Penguin Putnam Inc.

PRINTED IN THE UNITED STATES OF AMERICA

10 9 8 7 6 5 4 3 2

For Helen Stanton
With love and admiration
for your eighty-three years of talent

CAST OF CHARACTERS

The Inn at Hemlock Falls

Sarah "Quill" Quilliam . . . owner/manager
Margaret "Meg" Quilliam . . . her sister, the chef
John Raintree . . . business manager
Doreen Muxworthy-Stoker . . . the housekeeper
Dina Muir . . . the receptionist
Kathleen Kiddermeister . . . a waitress
Nate . . . the bartender
Bjarne . . . the *sous*-chef
Ellen Dunbarton . . . vice president, the Crafty Ladies, a guest
Freddie Patch . . . secretary, the Crafty Ladies, a guest
Robin Robinson . . . treasurer, the Crafty Ladies, a guest
Fran Grimsby . . . member, the Crafty Ladies, a guest
Mary Lennox . . . member, the Crafty Ladies, a guest
Rocky Burke . . . Burke's Insurance, a guest
Paul Pfieffer . . . of the governor's Budget Office, a guest
Thorne Smith . . . an investment counselor, a guest

The Hemlock Falls Chamber of Commerce

Elmer Henry . . . the mayor
Adela Henry . . . his wife
Dookie Shuttleworth . . . minister, the Hemlock Falls Church of the Word of God
Harvey Bozzel . . . president, Bozzel Advertising
Marge Schmidt . . . owner, Hemlock Home Diner
Betty Hall . . . her partner
Esther West . . . store owner

Villagers in Hemlock Falls

Myles McHale . . . a private investigator
Andrew Bishop . . . a physician
Hugh Summerhill . . . a vintner
Selena de la Vega Summerhill . . . his wife
Davy Kiddermeister . . . the sheriff
Denny Webster . . . chief, the Hemlock Falls
  Volunteer Fire Department
Howie Murchison . . . a lawyer

A TOUCH OF THE GRAPE

CHAPTER 1

The dog peered around the corner of the garden shed. It was a large dog. Sort of a yellowish brown, with large lop ears and big feet. He cocked his head at the three women facing him, whined, and ducked back out of sight. Sarah Quilliam, known as Quill, had called the Humane Society when she'd noticed the dog had left blood on the fountain in the center of their herb garden.

"Somebody kicked it, undoubtedly," said Selena de la Vega Summerhill. "Right over the kidneys. My guess is that the damage is there." She sighed. "I've seen too many abused animals since I've started working at the shelter. It's terrible the way they treat animals." She was a lovely woman in her late thirties. Her Spanish accent was slight.

"The way who treats animals?" Meg Quilliam demanded. She nudged her sister affectionately. "Quill's been feeding it. She doesn't think I've noticed, but I have. My beef Marengo, if you can believe it. So it isn't terrible the way Quill treats animals. Not when this particular animal gets a stew that's been rated the best in fifty states."

"Meg got the third star back from *L'Aperitif,*" Quill

said to Selena. "After that trip to Florida earlier this year."

"So we heard." Selena smiled. "And you heard, I think, that our Summerhill Chardonnay took second place in the winegrowers' competition this year." Her warm olive skin took on a rosier glow.

"No!" Meg said. "That's great, Selena. Who says Upstate New York's in a depression? Award-winning wines. Award-winning chefs." She scowled suddenly. "So how come neither of us has any business? How come you, Selena, as part owner of one of the largest wineries in central New York, has to take a job as the town dogcatcher to help make ends meet? How come Quill has to—"

"Because Upstate New York's in a depression," Quill said abruptly. "Come on, guys. What about the dog?"

She whistled. The dog stuck its head through the azaleas planted to the right of the shed door and barked once. Then he flopped over on his side and yawned. One scarlet petal drifted down from the bush and settled over his right eye. It didn't add anything to his looks. He was still the most unprepossessing mutt Quill had ever seen.

"I have this leash sort of thing," Selena said. "It's a collar attached to a pole. I'll get it. You, Quill, get some of Meg's stew. Meg, talk to it so it will stay here while we fetch these things."

"Talk to it?" Meg ran one hand through her short dark hair. "Talk to it? What sort of things do you say to a dog?"

"Call him *querido*," Selena suggested. "Talk to him of lady dogs. *I* don't know."

"You're the dogcatcher," Meg said. "If you don't know, who does?"

Selena shrugged. "I've only had the job a few days. I'm in training."

"So where's the person that's supposed to be teaching you how to catch dogs?"

"Laid off," Selena said. "Budget cuts, they said."

"How much does it pay?" Quill asked, thinking catching dogs might be a far easier job than catching nonexistent guests in a depressed economy. The dog growled.

"Not enough," Selena said, her voice quivering slightly. "But I got there first, Quill."

"Selena! I didn't mean . . . I mean, we're not that desperate."

"Well, we are," Selena said grimly. "Hugh? He is most unhappy that I have this job. But we cannot sell enough wine. And you know the people that bought his clothing business?"

"I didn't know Hugh had a clothing business."

"Oh, yes. Not very fancy clothes, you understand. The more inexpensive lingerie, and the women's pantsuits of . . . what do you call it? It is fake."

"Polyester?" Meg said.

"Polyester. This is where I met Hugh, of course. I was a runway model. As I said to Hugh, a woman who has been a runway model for cheap lingerie does not mind being a dogcatcher. He did not seem to like that much." She giggled.

"Um," Quill said, floundering. She didn't know Hugh Summerhill very well, but she had heard his family was from upper-class Boston. He looked the part, that was for sure.

"About this dog." Selena pushed a tendril of black hair from one eye. "You must keep its attention, Meg. While Quill obtains a bribe. It is the way of the world. Even dogs must be bribed. I will sneak up on it and be ready to pounce. But first I will get the catch collar."

"I'll sing to him," Meg said. "It's very soothing. I've tried it on the *sous*-chefs."

"Which is why we go through so many," Quill said. "Keep it sotto voce, Meg. You don't want to get bitten."

"Very funny." Meg crouched on her heels, facing the garden shed. The dog raised himself at the sudden movement and regarded her for a long moment. "*How much is that dooo—oogy in the window?*" Meg sang. Her voice, Quill always thought, was reminiscent of very small trains changing tracks. "*The oooonnnee with the waaagyly ta-a-a-a-il.*"

"It's going to howl," Quill predicted.

It did.

Selena muttered something in Spanish.

Quill bit her lip to keep the giggles back. "I'll get some food or something," she said steadily. "I'll be right back." She made her way up the flagstone path to the Inn at a rapid clip. It was a Monet-ish sort of morning in spring: a misty rain settled like silver mesh over the newly green grounds surrounding Hemlock Gorge, blurring the lilacs into soft lavender and muting the pale yellow of the jonquils. The Inn occupied the highest point of the cliff over the waterfall. Usually, the sound of falling water in spring was one of Quill's pleasures, an aural painting surrounding the visual beauty. At the moment, Meg's off-key crooning denying the desire for goldfish or a parrot mingled unfavorably with the dog's counterpoint tenor, and the natural music of the Falls receded. The view, today, wasn't the pleasure it usually was.

Maybe it wasn't the dog and the singing. Maybe it was the fact they were going broke.

Quill shook off the thought and entered the Inn through the back. She shut the door on the noise. It didn't help the volume much. The Inn was solidly built—most of the structure dated from the mid-18th century, and parts were even older—but the double-hung windows facing the perennial gardens had been opened to the fresh spring air and the ululation found its way through with the persistence of a collection agent. Quill went through the short hall leading to the kitchen. Mid-morning was one of the few times of the day when the kitchen was empty; the breakfast crew was on break in the dining room, and preparations for lunch wouldn't start until eleven. With luck, she could grab the stew and escape outside without having to deal with questions about the canine/three-star chef chorus or the endless other minutiae that were part of her days as manager of the Inn.

Like how to pay this month's gas bill.

Or how to keep out of filing for Chapter Eleven. "It's not bankruptcy, Quill," their attorney Howie Murchison had said. "It's protection from bankruptcy."

She headed for the glass-fronted refrigerator where Meg kept her leftovers.

"What'n the double-dyed *heck* is all that noise?" Doreen, Quill's head housekeeper, chief nemesis—and, Quill freely admitted, one of her best friends—banged through the double doors leading to the dining room and addressed Quill, one hand on an aproned hip, the other armed with a mop. There were days that Doreen looked more like a rooster than others, and this was one of them. Her sparse gray hair spiked over her head like a cockerel's comb, and her eyes were narrowed into birdy black beads.

"Meg and the dog," Quill said briefly. She opened the refrigerator door and began to search the shelves.

"Why are you out playin' with that damn dog when all we got stayin' here at the Inn is that ladies organization? And *they'll* be gone as soon as that president of theirs shows up for their meeting. You should be out bangin' the bushes for business." Doreen leaned back and addressed the ceiling. "Who was that damn fool

Eye-talian who played the fiddle while the whole place burned down around him? Nero. That's the one. Nero." She lowered her gaze.

Doreen's stare was so accusing, Quill could feel it through her back. She ignored it and continued her search through the refrigerator. The glass bowl containing stew was gone. There was a huge mound of tenderloin for the steak tartare scheduled for that evening's Crafty Ladies dinner; two loaves of chicken liver pâté shaped like dollar signs for the Association of Insurance Agents banquet; and a casserole dish filled with an unidentifiable green goo that turned out, on a quick taste test, to be pesto. Quill muttered, "Dang," shrugged, and scooped up a handful of raw tenderloin.

Muttering, Doreen filled her mop bucket at the sink and set it on the floor with a bang. "Insteada dog tricks, you oughta—" She broke off, and gasped. "You ain't gonna feed that good meat to that DOG!?" Outraged, she advanced like Patton on Inchon. Or was it MacArthur? Quill could never get military history straight.

"Missy?!"

"What?!!" Quill closed her hand defensively on the meat. That was a mistake. She patted futilely at the red oozing over her knuckles.

"That meat's a hunnert dollars a pound—"

"It's nowhere near a hundred dollars for *twenty* pounds, much less one pound—"

"—and in Times-Like-These-Here you're gonna feed a damn dog that there meat? What, you're gonna put it on his bill? In Times-Like-These-Here, you gotta watch the bottom line. That means cash flow, missy, in case you don't know it."

"I don't," Quill said tightly, "want to hear another word about Times-Like-These-Here. As for the dog, I called the people at the pound. Selena Summerhill's come to take him away."

"That's a sign for you," Doreen muttered darkly. "The wife of one a the best winegrowers in central New York takin' a job as a dogcatcher. I ask you, what are things coming to when—" She stopped herself in midflow. "She's takin' the dog?"

"That's right. I think it's been hurt, Doreen, and I just couldn't stand watching it mooch around here. It won't let anyone near it."

"You know what's gonna happen to that dog once it gets to the shelter, doncha?"

"Probably," Quill said with a sigh. "But it's a stray, Doreen, and it needs a vet, and we can't afford to help it. Besides, what do you care? I thought you hated that dog."

"Ugliest damn thing I've ever seen," Doreen agreed with suspect belligerence. She thought a moment, her jaw working. "What you should do is, you should tell Mike to get out the shotgun and just . . ." She cocked her forefinger.

"Why don't *you* tell Mike to get out the shotgun and shoot him?"

"You're the boss. You do it."

"The only time you agree that I'm the boss is when there's something horrid to do that you don't want to do and I'm not going to do it. Like try to get more business here at the Inn. I don't notice you standing by the side of the road flaggin' down tour buses . . . oh, no. You just come in here and nag on at me." Quill shook her head, exasperated and ashamed that she'd lost her temper. "Never mind. There's a very nice vet that volunteers at the shelter, Selena says, and there's a chance the dog can be treated and adopted. So. Good-bye. I'm going back to the garden shed and help Selena get the dog into her pickup truck." Clutching the beef, Quill marched toward the back door. She heard Doreen marching after her. Quill skidded to a halt and turned around. "Why are you following me?"

"I'm goin' out to he'p you. Scrawny thing like that'd soon as bite you as look at you."

Quill looked at her suspiciously. She was carrying her mop like a rifle. "Okay. You can help. But don't scare it."

Doreen gave an indignant sniff.

"And don't even think of bashing it. Leave your mop in the kitchen."

Doreen set the mop against the side of the long birch worktable that dominated the kitchen, raised her eyebrows at the meat in Quill's fist, and said truculently, "You better ditch that meat and get some Doritos."

"Doritos?"

"Doritos," Doreen said flatly. "Damn dog like that, it ain't used to meat. Used to eating out of garbage cans. You wanna catch it, you get yourself something it's used to. Like Doritos."

"Doreen, this is a three-star gourmet restaurant attached to a two-star hotel. We don't have any Doritos. Meg wouldn't let a bag of Doritos within sixty feet of the Dumpster out back, much less in the pantry itself."

"Bjarne's got himself a stash right next to the stockpots."

This didn't surprise Quill at all. Bjarne was a young Finn from the Cornell School of Hotel Managment (as were all of their *sous*-chefs), and he thought no one knew about his addiction to junk food. He was wrong. When Quill regretfully laid off all the others due to the desperate state of the business, it was the first thing they told her.

Doreen tramped to the shelving underneath the long windows and rummaged among the pots. After a prolonged bout of clanking (an unwelcome addition to the cacophony still drifting in from the garden) she emerged with a familiarly marked cellophane bag. "See?"

"Do you think we should just take it? I mean, those are Bjarne's, not ours."

"Finns are a bunch a damn Socialists anyways. They don't believe in ownership."

Quill tried to keep the beef from dripping out of her hand and onto the floor, and decided not to clarify the distinction between communism and socialism. She rather hoped the dog preferred Doritos to beef. The dog looked as if he might be a very good biter if he had the inclination, and you could just scatter Doritos in front of it. "Come on. Let's get this over with."

Outside, the mist had turned to a fine rain. Quill ignored the damp air and the puddles forming under her feet, and strode purposefully back to the azalea bushes. The dog was sitting bolt upright near the shed, clearly anxious. Whether this was because Meg had switched from "Doggie in the Window" to "Old Shep"—in which, Quill recalled, the dog died—or because Selena Summerhill had returned from her pickup truck armed with a long pole and capture collar, Quill wasn't entirely sure. She brandished her fistful of beef. "Here, boy. Here, boy."

The dog looked alertly at Quill. His tongue lolled. He licked his lips.

Selena flourished the catch pole. "You go up to him, Quill. I'll be right behind you." He looked at Selena. His lips curled back from his teeth. He growled. It was a low, nasty growl, entirely ferocious. Meg stopped singing, rose to her feet, and backed carefully away. "Ah, Quill . . ."

"I've got this side covered," Selena said bravely. She was wearing a long flowered skirt and a gauzy blouse that hung limply around her slender figure. She was getting very damp in the misty rain. She didn't look like any dogcatcher Quill had ever seen. "You take the other."

Meg shrieked. "Are you *crazy*, Selena? He'll bite her hand off! He'll bite all of us!"

"Be quiet, both of you!" Quill said. "Here, boy. Here, boy." She advanced slowly, her hand outstretched, palm up to display the beef. The dog extended his neck and sniffed. Quill took two steps forward. The dog sneezed, shook his head, and backed up. "Easy, boy. Whoa, boy."

"He's not a horse," Meg said.

"Well, 'stay' then, boy. Or sit. Can you sit?"

The dog barked and ran under the azalea bush. Quill could hear him panting. Doreen, gazing skyward, pursed her lips in an "I told you so" whistle.

"Do you think I should crawl in after him?" Selena asked.

"I do *not*," Meg said.

"I can't believe that four intelligent women can't get a little old dog out from the bushes," Quill said. She clucked in what she hoped was a dog-tempting way.

"Three intelligent women," Meg said. "Not four."

"Speak for yourself."

"I was."

Quill glared at her.

"For heaven's sake, Quill. What kind of lunatic is going to go after a stray sick dog with a fistful of meat? You're nuts."

"It's just a dog, Meg. Not a wild boar."

"That dog's a hundred and twenty pounds if it's fifteen," Meg said. "It might as well be a wild boar. Did you see those teeth? I think we'd better get the guys. This could be dangerous."

"Crimney's *sake*," Doreen said. She rattled the Doritos bag, then shook all the chips onto the ground. The dog emerged from the bush flat on his belly and inched forward. Grasping the catch pole in both hands, Selena moved to the dog's left. Meg began a series of ducklike squawks as what Quill presumed was an encouraging diversionary tactic. Suddenly, the dog jerked his head back and stared over Quill's left shoulder. Distracted, Quill turned, saw the group approaching the garden shed, and groaned under her breath. Five middle-aged ladies gathered under three brightly colored umbrellas were strolling in a clutch on the path through the gardens. Headed straight for them. That many people were bound to scare him off. Quill turned back to the dog. All she could see was a tail thumping at the perimeter of the azalea bush. The rest of the animal was nowhere in sight. The Doritos were gone. "Damn," Quill said.

Doreen smoothed her apron and greeted the approaching group with a toothy grin. The largest umbrella, the one with the Cinzano label on it, dipped forward and a voice cried, "Miss QUILLL-I-yam."

"Oh, yippee," Meg muttered. "It's the crafty ladies."

"*Qué pasa?*" said Selena. "This name-calling does not suit you, Meg."

Meg looked startled. "It's what they call themselves. Their organization is the Crafty Ladies. They're into . . ." She waved her hand vaguely. "You know—crafts. They stuff things. They booked into the Inn for a week. As a matter of fact, they're the only guests we've got booked for the entire summer."

"That's not true," Quill said. "Two of the insurance brokers are staying overnight after their banquet this evening."

"The Crafty Ladies do more than stuff things," Doreen said indignantly. "I've been talkin' to that Ellen Dunbarton all about it. They're artists. They make things. Quite a bit a money innit, or so she says."

"And so there is," said the Cinzano umbrella. The canvas tipped up to reveal a cheerful woman with a comfortably plump figure, bright orange-red hair, and a startling pair of earrings. The earrings appeared to be made of bottle caps. All of the Crafty Ladies seemed to be on the far side of sixty. Quill admired the verve for life that resulted in their colorful clothes and attention-grabbing (if peculiar) jewelry.

"Ecology-minded, too," Doreen added. "Them are caps from Coke and like that."

"We recycle," said the red-haired woman. "Have you forgotten, Quill? The tour?"

"Madonna," Selena said.

Quill, not knowing whether this was an imprecation or an attempt to seem saliently hip, abandoned her contemplation of the dog's tail and made a guilty face. "Oh, dear. I had forgotten we had arranged to tour the Inn."

"That is a very ugly dog," Ellen Dunbarton observed pleasantly. "OOPS! It went back into the azaleas again."

"I am attempting to catch it," Selena explained. She waved her catch pole. "I am the dog warden. Warden Summerhill." She smiled in a pleased way.

"Sorry," Quill said, "I'm forgetting my manners." She began introductions. "Selena, I'd like to present some of our guests."

"Our only guests," Doreen added, "on account of somebody here'd rather play with dogs than get any more of 'em."

"Hush, Doreen. Selena, this is Ellen Dunbarton."

"Vice president, the Crafty Ladies." Ellen smiled graciously at Selena. "And these are all the members of our group but one. We're ladies-in-waiting, you see. Our group has assembled to meet our president, which brings our total organization to six. Fran Grimsby's there in the hand-painted muumuu. Right beside her are Robin Robinson and Mary Lennox; Robin's the sequin sweatshirt, Mary's the pink twinset—hand crocheted. And that's

Freddie Patch, under the yellow umbrella. Short for Frederica. She's our craftless Crafty Lady.''

Selena raised one slim black eyebrow. "But this Mary Lennox is a lady-in-waiting! I study history, you see, when I am not catching dogs and helping my Hugh press grapes. I am getting an associated degree at the Hemlock Falls Community College. My Hugh wishes me to be more conversable. Right now, we are studying the American labor movement.''

"Associated with what?'' Ellen asked.

"Associates,'' Quill said. "She's getting her A.A. And you're right, Selena. Mary Lennox was a lady-in-waiting. To Mary, Queen of Scots.''

No one seemed especially interested in this, and Quill went back to considering the dog.

"How come you called Ms. Patch the craftless Crafty Lady?'' Doreen asked.

Ellen winked. "'Cause she's not wearing anything handmade. All store-bought.''

"Just call me an oddball,'' Freddie said. She had soft, rose leaf cheeks and very pure white hair that floated around her head like cotton. "I can't find anything I really like to make. And I've tried it all. I'm all thumbs, too.'' She held out her hands, which were a little swollen with arthritis. Quill felt a tinge of pity. "I'm hopeless at needlepoint, lousy at wood carving, terrible at cross-stitch. I can't even do plastic forks and glue.''

"Fans,'' Ellen said, by way of explanation. "You make fans by gluing plastic forks together. You line them up, parallel to each other, with the tines facing *in*.''

"You could try rag work,'' Doreen said unexpectedly. "I seen some pret' good work done out of just rags, like.''

"You mean like rag rugs?'' Robin said. Her hair was dyed a pinkish-blond somewhat at odds with her wrinkles and bright red lipstick. Her sweatshirt displayed her expertise with sequins: a vegetable garden of red radishes, emerald lettuces, and carrots spread from bosom to bosom. Or maybe the radishes were tomatoes; Quill wasn't certain. "Now there's something for you, Freddie. Rag work is fun, inexpensive, and you can do it in the privacy of your own home."

"Money innit, too," Doreen added, with a significant look at Quill. "Be happy to show ya. If you are innerested."

"Really?" said Freddie. "I'd like it if you did. It sounds like something I'd like to try."

"What I do is, is I run a class," Doreen said. "Twenny bucks an hour; takes maybe five, six hours to learn it. I don't earn twenny an hour myself," Doreen added. "This rag class is part of the entertainment offered by the Inn."

"Since when?" Meg demanded.

"Since we're broke," Doreen said flatly.

"Stop," Quill said. "You guys, honestly!" She laughed in what she hoped was a lighthearted and careless way. "Ha, ha."

"We are broke," Doreen said remorselessly. "And if we don't walk right . . ."

Ellen intervened with an executive-style firmness, which demonstrated just why she had been elected her organization's vice president. "Maybe we should discuss it after the tour of the Inn?" She turned to Quill. "We thought we were to meet at ten-thirty? It's way after that now."

Dismayed, Quill looked at her watch. "My goodness, I'm so sorry. I had no idea. . . ." She gave the azalea bush a quick glance. The tail was gone, and so presumably was the dog. "Selena, can you excuse me? Ellen and her group particularly asked to see each of the suites in the Inn. I developed a little speech to go with the tour. I'm sorry to get you out on a rainy day like this, and we couldn't even catch the poor thing. . . ."

"It's not a problem at all," Selena said with an absentminded air. "I'm sure Meg and Doreen and I can take care of it. Tell me, is there a fee for the tour of the suites?"

Quill felt her cheeks flush. If the village of Hemlock Falls had any criticism of the two women who ran their internationally renowned Inn and restaurant, it was that they were too "highfalutin." Quill, the first to demur becomingly when accused of elitism, was self-consciously aware she was also the first to wince at the thought of paid tours of her Inn. The second rule of good innkeeping was that guests were, well, guests. (The first rule, laid down after six months in business eight years ago, was that you didn't belt the guests. Unless severely provoked.) Guests, as Nero Wolfe would have put it, were to be treated as "jewels on the cushion of hospitality." Specifically, one didn't charge guests to take tours of a home away from home they'd already rented in the first place. On the other hand, Nero Wolfe never seemed to have significant money troubles, and Quill certainly did. "Yes, I do charge a fee, Selena. A slight one, only. I add a little lecture to each of the stops on the tour, and I demonstrate our remodeling plans and show the original architectural drawings. It's very informational, very historic."

"Good for cash flow, too," Doreen said with approval.

Selena clasped Ellen's hand between both her own with a great deal of playful charm. "Señora Dunbarton, perhaps you and your group would like a tour of our vineyard, too? It is called the Summerhill Winery and it is about twenty minutes from here. My Hugh knows a great deal about wine. And he is so handsome! Like Richard Gere, only a little older. Yes, there is a fee. But it is a slight fee, only. Much less, in fact, than the fee for the tour of the Inn.''

"Well!" Doreen said, with a competitive glitter in her eye. "I must say we was the ones who—"

"We'd love to take all the tours," Ellen said, with a shrewd glance from Quill to Doreen. "We've brought our crafts with us, of course, and we have our business meeting coming up as soon as our president gets here, but we still have a lot of free time on our hands. And we're happy to pay a reasonable fee We love to learn new things. I've never been to a winery. I'd love it. What about it, Robin?"

"Well, if the fee was reasonable, like this Selena said," Robin Robinson said. "Hemlock Falls is such a pretty village, and we haven't even begun to explore all its nooks and crannies. The more we know about a place, the more we love it."

"The more people work together, the easier it is to show off a place like Hemlock Falls," Quill said with a significant look at Doreen. "We've had very good luck with sponsoring wine tours in the past, and I think you ladies would enjoy seeing Summerhill. Selena's not being prejudiced, you know. Hugh is very good-looking and very knowledgeable."

"Tomorrow might be very good," Selena said. "I will check with my Hugh, and let you know. I will take this dog, now, and then come back in an hour to let you know, okay? I, myself, will probably not accompany you, however, on the tour of Summerhill. There are a great many dogs to catch in Hemlock Falls."

"Great," Quill said heartily, already beginning to dislike "my Hugh." "We'll start this tour right now." She found herself making shooing motions to drive the Crafty Ladies toward the Inn, and away from any more revelations of their financial plight by blabbermouth Doreen. She took Ellen Dunbarton by the arm, and drew her along the path; the other ladies followed like baby ducks. "I haven't really had time to get to know you all, and this will be a wonderful opportunity for both of us, I hope. The tour will take about an hour, and then we'll have lunch on the terrace. Meg's prepared something wonderful. It's new. Quiche á la Quilliam. Fresh fruit in a cheese custard. Perhaps at lunch we can plan your trip to Summerhill Winery. Or would you prefer to wait until your president comes in?" She linked her other arm companionably with Freddie's and led the whole group down the flagstone steps leading to the front door.

Behind her, she heard Doreen methodically kicking the azalea bushes, in an attempt to flush out the dog. Meg whistled, a piercing soprano note that used to bring their old collie at a run, back home in Connecticut, when neither she nor Meg had to worry about whether or not they were going to make payroll.

"Well!" Quill said, coming to a halt in front of the old oak door at the Inn's entrance. "Here we are. The Inn at Hemlock Falls dates back to the mid 1700's, when it was a small hostelry frequented by trappers on their way to the fur trade in Canada. . . ."

She gave them the whole history, from the Inn's first hostess/owner (Turkey Lil, who sold her favors to the trappers along with homemade gin) to the present.

"And you paint, don't you?" Mary Lennox asked abruptly. She was tall and angular. Her hands were as work-roughened as Doreen's.

"Yes, I do. Or did. In the past."

"There's some of her stuff in the bar, Mary." Freddie looked up at Quill with bright eyes. "You're quite famous in places like New York City."

"Hmm," Quill said, embarrassed. "Do you get to New York often? I thought you were all from Trenton."

"We retired to Trenton," Fran Grimsby said. She was

tall, with an unflattering haircut and an eager, aggressive walk, rather like a hen's after corn. Quill had noticed that she was conscious of speaking through her nose. She took a deep breath and said, rounding the syllables carefully, "We found this cute little apartment complex, and we all took one-bedrooms. It's just adorable." She stopped at the archway to the dining room. Quill had selected an exuberant mixture of cream, maroon, yellows, and greens to celebrate the view of the Falls. The archway faced the south wall, which was almost entirely of glass. Beyond the windows, the water leaped in the sunlight. "You'd love our place," she said doubtfully.

"She'd hate it," Mary Lennox said with cheerful brutality. "It's nothing like this. This place has class."

Quill took them through the Provençal suite, with the blue and yellow tiles she'd purchased in France, and the Shaker suite, with its stark, clean simplicity. She also showed them the rooms on the top floor, where they were converting two of the suites into four rooms. "To accommodate the extra bookings we have in the summer," Quill explained. Ellen, charmed with the view, asked if she could be moved to 310, which opened almost over the Falls themselves. The room she was in, she explained, was lovely. But the Falls! Selena, slightly breathless, joined them as the tour ended two hours later with a small party in Quill's own suite, where she still painted, when she had the time and energy.

They admired the view of the perennial gardens from her balcony, and clustered around the fruit and breads Quill had set out in the small living room.

"Well, this *is* nice," Mary said. "A little party, too!"

"We should have brought something!" Ellen said. "I know! I've got a little something in wine I picked up the other day, in my room. I'll get it, shall I?"

"It's awfully early," Quill said doubtfully.

"It is never too early for wine," Selena said grandly.

"And my Hugh is happy to host you all at our vineyard, whenever you wish. I would very much like some wine, if you please."

"We really shouldn't," Fran said. "Thin edge of the wedge. First thing you know, we're all old soaks."

"Heavens! This is a vacation!" Ellen trotted out and soon returned with a well-worn silver flask; Quill, reminded irresistibly of bathtub gin, bit back a giggle.

"Aren't we naughty," Fran said with relish. Ellen poured with abandon, and they settled themselves around the room.

"It's quite different from the rest of the Inn," Ellen said. She pushed her toe along the pale Berber carpet, then sat down on the semicircular couch in front of the French doors to the outside.

"What's this?" Fran pointed at the painting on Quill's easel. "It's not finished."

"That's the ocean at night. Meg and I were in Florida a few weeks earlier this year." Quill drew her thumb lightly across the blue-green swirls of acrylic.

"It is?"

"We go every year to Florida. Fort Meyers," Ellen explained. "We just love it. There's a mahjong club we joined, and when the ladies get together, well!"

"We have such a good time there!" Robin said eagerly. "Did you enjoy your stay?"

"The weather was wonderful," Quill said carefully. She had, in fact, had a terrible time in Florida, which, like Hamlet, she found "flat, stale, and unprofitable."

"Now, Miami," Freddie said eagerly. "You want to see some action, Miami's the place to be."

"Freddie!" Fran said. "Quill's going to think we're . . . we're . . ."

"The Loose Ladies, rather than the Crafty Ladies," Ellen said. They all laughed heartily at this. "This tour was just wonderful, Quill. I don't know how you bear to leave this place, even for Florida.''

"So did you get a chance to get them all straight?'' Meg asked some hours later. They were both in the kitchen. The lunch concluding the tour had been a great success. Meg's fruit quiche was a keeper. ''I mean Grimsby, Dunbarton, Lennox, Robinson, and Patch. Sounds like an Idaho law firm. They checked in so fast, and all in a big lump, that I wasn't at all sure who was who.''

"They're such sweeties, Meg. And they've worked so hard for so little all these years! Ellen Dunbarton, the one with the bottled red hair? She was a clerk at Tracey's Department Store for thirty years, Meg. Raised three children. Salt, as Dad would say, of the earth. The others have all had similar kinds of jobs—pink-collar. Freddie Patch got to assistant bank manager, at least. And Fran Grimsby, the woman who talks through her nose, had a pretty decent career as a customs agent at LaGuardia. Mary Lennox 'had a career in real estate,' she said. They've been friends forever. They even had a little craft business together for a while. Remember Tupperware parties and Mary Kay cosmetics? Stuff like that. But by and large, these are women who've put husbands, home, and kids first. They've all had to work to supplement the family income. Robin lived on a farm, before she became a paralegal, and I'll bet she worked herself to a frazzle. She's tough, Meg. Oldest one of the whole group, but I'd put my money on her in a marathon. She'll outlast us all.''

"Then how the heck can any of them afford this place? Our regulars don't seem to be able to afford this place anymore.''

Quill picked moodily at a piece of leftover bruschetta. ''I don't know. I didn't care to ask. If I were to engage

in wild surmise''—she looked up at Meg with a smile—
"I would say that craft business of theirs is doing pretty
well. Do you know what they're really here for?''

"Not murder, I hope." Meg shuddered slightly, re-
calling several past cases.

"I don't *think* so. No, they're designing their new
spring line of craft kits. For not this year, not next year,
but, get this, the year 2000. They've got some sort of
mail-order consortium going. It's great business, I guess.
They sell craft kits. The plastic forks to make fans kits,
kits to use safety pins and plastic beads to make dolls
that sit on your telephone. That sort of thing.''

"Oh," Meg said thoughtfully.

"Can you imagine? After years and years of these low
paying jobs, clerking at Tracey's, going through other
people's luggage, their own business takes off and ka-
boom. Success.''

"Speaking of success," Meg said. "John needs to
talk with you. As soon as you're free, he said. Anytime
today, he said. No rush.''

Quill had known John for almost the entire time the
Inn had been open. He was their business manager, a
minority stockholder, a wizard with the books. No rush,
from John, meant more bad news. And lately, the news
had been very bad, indeed. "Would you like to sit in?''

Meg shook her head. "No way. Just let me know how
bad it is.''

"Maybe I should get Doreen. She owns a few
shares.''

"She drove to Syracuse to see if we can get the grocery credit extended another ninety days. She won't be
back until after dinner.''

Quill looked hopeful. "Are there a lot of reservations
this evening?''

"Two tables, if the ladies don't end up at Marge's
diner for their supper. Otherwise? Just the insurance

guys. And there's only six of them. I don't know why they call it a banquet. A banquet is twenty people. Forty people. Smoked salmon appetizers. Lamb *en croutè*. Strawberry coulis. I would,'' Meg said a little wistfully, ''have been happy to make all that just for six. But they didn't want it.''

''Not any of it?''

''I talked them into the liver pâté. But they want chicken for the main course.''

''You make a terrific chicken terrine, Meggie.''

''Barbecued chicken.''

''I see.'' Quill sighed and got to her feet. ''John's in the office?''

''He was there all morning, looking grim. Kathleen took his lunch in there, so I expect he hasn't left.'' She reached up and rubbed Quill's cheek. ''It'll be okay.''

''Not this time. I wish I hadn't taken Ellen and her friends on the tour. Normally I'm too busy to think about how the place looks, its impact. If we lose it, Meg, I just want to leave everything, walk out the front door, and not look back. It's too hard seeing everything we've accomplished through other people's eyes.''

''Hey. We'll just both get married—you to Myles, finally. Me to Andy, finally, and . . .''

''And what?''

''Don't ask me what. I'm a chef. A good chef. Don't ask me what's next because, Quill, I really, really don't want to know.''

Quill paused on her way out the door to the dining room. ''Did you ever find that poor dog?''

''Nope. Selena took her catcher's mitt—''

''Catch pole.''

''Whatever, Selena went on home, dogless. She was in a good mood, though. I told her it'd be fine with us if she called Ellen Dunbarton to arrange a winery tour.''

''Ellen said Kathleen gave her a fax this morning. The

prez has been delayed a few days. So they'll have time.''

Meg brightened. ''Maybe the whole group will stay on, then. Through next week.''

''Maybe.'' She shoved the door open. ''I sure wish you'd found that poor dog.''

Quill was a little fuzzy about the particulars, but she knew there was a psychologist's term for her worry about the lost and wounded dog. Deployment? Deferment? Displacement, that was it. She was displacing her anxieties about the future—not to mention the bill-filled present—onto a stray dog. She bit her lip. The poor dog looked like he'd had nothing but a handful of Doritos for weeks.

She crossed the dining room, waving to the Crafty Ladies They were scooping up crème brûlée and Meg's chocolate walnut mousse with a happy disregard for calories.

She was depressed. She'd just taken five very nice middle-aged ladies through her Inn, and shown them what she and Meg had built so laboriously and with such enthusiasm over the years. The Provençal suite, with the blue and yellow print material they'd found in Provence. The Shaker suite, with its pale wood floors, beautifully polished wood trim, and quietly elegant furniture. The Tavern Bar, with its teal walls, and her own acrylic paintings on the walls.

She stopped as she crossed into reception. The old oak door was open to the soft air, and spring blew gently over the cream wool Oriental rug. Even the foyer and the cobblestone fireplace dating from the earliest period of the Inn's history were painful to look at. She'd seen all these things, shown off all these things, she—perhaps—was about to lose them, and she'd spent the best part of the morning trying to save the dog instead of her sister and her friends.

"Woof," said the dog, coming out from behind the mahogany reception desk. He limped heavily. He'd been down the Gorge to the waterfall; his paws were slimed with moss and his coat knotted with teasel left over from the winter. He put his head almost to the floor and wriggled, a painful wriggle, the classic posture of submission.

"Will you *stop*," Quill said.

The dog waved his tail frantically.

"See that?" Quill pointed to a discreet sign, tucked under the rim of the front desk in as unobtrusive a way as possible. It was teak, with small brass letters that said, "We will be happy to make accommodations elsewhere for your pet."

"That's because of the Iditirod winners last year," Quill informed the dog. "They made reservations for sixteen. What they didn't say was that the sixteen were the winner, her husband, and a team of fourteen huskies." She sat down on the floor, on the softest part of the rug, and patted the wool invitingly. "We had to make other arrangements. It was," she added, "the start of this decline in business, come to think of it. The first indication that we were going to the dogs. What do you think of that?"

The dog pawed at the floor. His nails, long, untrimmed, left scratches in the polished wood. "No," Quill said without heat. "No clawing or pawing. If Doreen sees you do that, she'll have your guts for garters."

The dog crept nearer, sideways, shyly, quivering with a kind of terror Quill couldn't imagine. "Hey," she said softly. "Hey."

"If you give him a name, it's all over," said a quiet voice behind her. The dog looked up, cringed, then made a rush for the front door.

"John," Quill said. "Darn it!"

The dog turned at the sound of her voice, gave one

more "woof," and limped out the door and across the lawn at a run. Quill got to her feet, brushing at her skirt, and started out after him.

"Want some help?" John closed the office door behind him, and stepped into the little area behind the reception desk where Dina used to sit before they had to lay her off. "I'll be happy to track him. Use some of the knowledge passed down to me by my ancestors."

"Oh, ha." John's coppery skin and coal-black hair would have identified him as Amerind anywhere, even if he weren't fond of bringing it into the conversation. "No. Let him go. I called the Humane Society this morning to see if they could catch him. He needs some help, John. Selena Summerhill's taken the Animal Control officer job and she says he may have kidney damage." To her absolute amazement, she felt tears prickling behind her eyes. She coughed heavily into her hand.

"From a kick?"

Quill nodded, unable to speak.

"Then let him alone. He'll either get better on his own or he won't."

"That's cruel!"

"Quill." John's tone was patient. "If you did get hold of him and did get him to a vet, what do you think the vet would do? A kidney transplant?"

"Don't be silly."

"The treatment for this kind of thing is to leave the animal alone. Let it rest, and let nature take its course."

"But he needs food and water."

"Then I guess he'll just have to get it near the garden shed, where you've been putting out food for the last three nights. Truly, Quill, my guess is that he'll be fine. We, on the other hand, are not."

"Do you want to go into the office?"

"Let's walk, instead. Maybe we'll find the dog."

They walked out the front door onto the lawn. The rain had cleared, and a brilliant sun spread light over the daffodils, the early tulips, the crocus. In silent agreement, they headed toward the Gorge, the sound and the rush of the water drawing Quill, as it did at least once a day, to the brink of the precipice.

She was conscious of John beside her, in a way she hadn't been before. Quill was tall for a woman, close to five eight, but John towered over her. His physical presence was strong, but quiet. Unlike Myles, who was just as tall, and as broadly built, she never felt challenged with John, but relaxed, almost content, as if there were no need to tap into the kind of energy that suffused all her closest relationships. There was no relaxed feeling now. Just tension.

They stood looking at the water for a long moment. "So how bad is it?" she finally asked.

"We need to make more cuts."

"But we've already made deep ones. We've laid off practically everyone, and cut the remaining staff's hours to zero. Meg's about to collapse from handling that kitchen all on her own. We've closed the boutique at the mini-mall. Meg's been specializing in charcuterie, just like we did when we opened eight years ago, because it's cheaper cuts of meat. We've tried that Advanced Menu Reservations thing, where people order their food before they come, so we don't have to keep inventory as high. We've switched almost entirely to New York State wines, and cut the cellar budget for the imported wines down to almost nothing. I don't know what other cuts we can make, John. If we cut breakfasts and lunches, we'll lose our double star rating from the Caravan Association. If we cut the menu, Meg's going to lose that third star for sure. What more can we do?"

"I've done the numbers . . ."

"You always have the numbers." Quill rubbed her

forehead. Her hand still smelled faintly of the raw beef she'd tried to feed the dog earlier that morning. She shoved her hand rather guiltily into the pocket of her denim skirt. "So, what's the next round of cuts? Gruel for the staff? It'll be hard on the *sous*-chef. He hates gruel."

"The next cut is me. You have to fire me, Quill."

She stared at him, openmouthed.

"I'm serious. If I could take a pay cut, Quill, I would. You know that." He looked away from her.

Across the Gorge, a doe and her fawn picked their way carefully down the sheer stone to the water. Quill knew why John couldn't live on any less. His sister. Quill knew better than to ask about her. The Institution where she stayed was one of the most expensive in the state. And John wouldn't give her up. Quill would never ask him to give her up.

"I'll take more of a pay cut," Quill said steadily. "Meg and Doreen will take pay cuts."

"That's already in the emergency budget. And I'm afraid it won't wash, Quill. Just to keep the Inn open, the lights on, the water flowing, the taxes paid, the dishwasher and refrigerator running costs you more than fifteen thousand dollars a month. The mortgage is—"

"I don't want to hear any more numbers," Quill said. "There's got to be a way. What is it, John? Why isn't anyone coming to the Inn anymore? It can't just be the recession. We never drew our paying customers from around here, anyway. They're all from downstate. And a lot of them are from out of state."

"If you want to hear a why, all I can give you are guesses. The number of rooms you have is too—"

"We," Quill interrupted crossly, "the number of rooms *we* have."

"Sorry. We have twenty-seven rooms. Even if we ran at one hundred percent occupancy every single day of the year and charged two hundred dollars a night, we wouldn't make it. It was the last tax reassessment that did it. Two hundred a night is stiff, Quill, even for an internationally known inn, and you still couldn't make the budget. Do you see? You can't charge any more than you do. And there aren't enough rooms to carry the expenses of living in this state.''

"Let's get a bank loan and build an addition, then.''

"Quill, you can't manufacture pens for a dollar and sell them at ninety-nine cents, and then make it up in volume.''

"So what do we do?''

"Well, we've always known that the rooms carry expenses and the restaurant makes the profit, right?''

"Right.''

"And now we've come to a point where the rooms aren't going to carry expenses.''

"We figured we'd run a seventy percent occupancy eleven months of the year,'' Quill protested. "You said that would work.''

He was losing patience, something he'd never done before. "That was *last year*. We have been reassessed this year. The reassessment is fair. My protest didn't work. We cannot afford to run the Inn anymore. I will not borrow to put us into debt when the chance of repayment is slim to nonexistent.'' He took her by both shoulders and stared hard at her. "I told you this last month. You didn't want to hear it. I am telling you again.''

"And I told you,'' Quill said with spirit, "the New York State Winegrowers' Association is planning a lot of large events for this region. I think you should hook up with Hugh Summerhill. He's the P.R. for the local W.G.A. this year, and there's a lot of business potential there.''

He let her go.

Quill looked at him, her eyes steady. "You've already made up your mind we're going to fail." His eyes flickered, and Quill drew a deep breath. "You made up your mind. And, dammit, John, you've found another job!"

CHAPTER 2

John looked tired. "I've found another job, yes." He sat down on the verge of grass overlooking the Gorge. "We've been over the financials for months now, Quill."

"It's the insurance thing, isn't it?" Quill said, stricken. "That check that bounced, and then the policy getting canceled. I'm sorry about not writing down the amount of those checks I write, John. You know my style. Slapdash. Once in a while I stop to think about how hard it must be on you, and I feel so guilty." She sat down next to him. He moved slightly away from her, taking his warmth with him.

"I've made some calls about the new policy. And Prudential will cover any property casualty losses until tomorrow. When they cancel a policy for nonpayment of premium, they don't cancel it boom, like that. You have thirty to sixty days to find a new insurer. And I've found one; there's a guy coming in with the broker's banquet tonight who'll have a binder policy for you. I want you to sign it."

"Why won't you sign it? You're not leaving now, are you?"

"No. I've got a meeting in Syracuse tonight. I'll be back late. But insurance is one thing you don't want to screw around with, Quill."

"What am I going to do? What are all of us going to do?"

"We've been over this before, as well. We've cut back on everyone's hours. You and Meg are going to have to go without paychecks for a while, and it'd be best if you two do as much as you can yourselves. I've talked to Myles . . ."

"He's in Germany on that E.C.U. thing. When did you talk to him?"

"He hasn't dropped out of sight. I called him last night. Grounds maintenance is going to be a problem. He can help with the larger items, but he's gone so much and there's so much to do, it's a stopgap measure. He's willing to keep paying Mike's salary for a while, but that's only a temporary solution—"

"You asked Myles for money?"

"I asked Myles to help out a bit."

"Why don't we ask the bank for money?"

"The line of credit's gone, Quill. They won't give us any more. I told you that. I also told you I'm not going to be responsible for borrowing more. You owe enough already. Now, I've left a list of the customers we want to book this summer. You keep up the phone calls to them—just once a week, and don't let them talk you into any more discounts, okay? And there's enough in the account to keep things going through the summer. You have any questions, call on either Howie or Myles—"

"For God's sake, John. I *told* you not to involve anyone else. It's our business. It's my responsibility. Our responsibility. I can't believe you've gone behind my back."

"I've never once gone behind your back. But when

you won't pay attention to the financial, Quill, this is
the sort of thing that happens.'' He touched her arm,
then withdrew his hand with an abrupt, almost angry
gesture.

Quill blinked back tears. "I'm sorry. I'm really
sorry."

"Me, too. About my shares in the business . . ."

"I'll pay you out," she said tightly.

"There isn't anything to pay out, Quill. What we have
is debt. I'll take care of my portion of the debt."

"You will not."

"You should have a C.P.A. handling the paperwork
from here on in. There's a small business on Main called
PayFor. Do you know it?"

Quill nodded her head, not trusting herself to speak.

"They have a computerized service that will handle
the General Ledger and the payroll until Labor Day. You
do what they tell you to."

"Then what?"

"Then the money runs out. If something doesn't happen this summer. But that's still not going to solve the
long-term problem. You know what the solution there
is, don't you?"

"I am not going to sell. You heard that. I'm not going
to sell."

"You're kidding, right?" Meg's eyes, gray, narrowed, and suspicious, stared at Quill over a pile of *petit
choux* pastry. "More layoffs?"

Quill, delaying the really bad news, made a stab at
humor. "It's a good thing I took that seminar in 'Termination.' The first rule—did I tell you?—is empathize.
Tell the employee how much she or he has contributed
to the job."

"How the heck are we going to operate this place
with no people?"

"We'll just have to handle as much as we can by ourselves."

"Quill, I can't handle three meals a day by myself. I just can't." She ran her hands through her short, dark hair. She was half a head shorter than Quill, brunette, where Quill was red-haired, gray-eyed to Quill's hazel. Quill wondered sometimes if they were truly blood relations, or if she'd been adopted as a child.

"QUILL!"

Quill jerked to attention.

"You're doing it again."

"Doing what?"

"Displacing. You always go vague and think about other stuff when the stress level gets too high. It's called displacement. You must have heard of it, you do it all the time. Anyhow, you shouldn't be displacing over layoffs. We've had to lay off people temporarily before. It's worse, whatever's bugging you. So spit it out. Forget the termination formulas, which always sounded too grisly anyhow. What is it?"

"John's taken a job on Long Island."

"John *quit*?!"

"He didn't quit, exactly. He said he started looking for another job about a month ago, when he realized that we wouldn't be able to afford him after the first of July. Actually, we haven't been able to afford him since Christmas. He said."

"And he's going to work where?"

"For a bank. The headquarters are on Long Island. So he's going to move."

Meg punched the pastry with two vicious jabs of her knuckles. I may displace, or whatever the correct verb would be, Quill thought. At least I don't punch defenseless pastry. "I don't believe it."

Suddenly, Quill was too tired to respond to this with other than a shake of her head. Her feet hurt. She needed a nap. She'd walked for hours in the land surrounding the Gorge, looking for the stupid dog, and all she had to show for it was a blister on her left heel. She'd come back to the Inn just before the dinner hour, hungry and depressed. A quick check of the dining room had depressed her even further. The Crafty Ladies were cheerful and noisy over drinks which seemed to be made of rum and various kinds of juice at table seven; otherwise the place was empty. She'd walked into the kitchen to find Meg, alone, working on desserts, made herself a cup of latte, then sat at the high counter surrounding the center island to give her the news about the current lack of money. The other news—the sell-the-Inn-because-it-will-never-make-it news—could wait for another time.

Meg stuffed the warm *choux* into a pastry bag, then reached for the first in the pile of aluminum cookie sheets stacked to the right of her worktable. She grabbed the top one, set it aside with a clatter, grabbed a second, cursed, and slammed the sheet onto the marble pastry board with an exasperated "Tcha!"

"What do you mean, 'tcha'?"

"I mean 'goddammit,' that's what I mean. I said 'tcha' instead. I'm too polite to say 'goddammit' when you're under all this stress. And the reason I went 'tcha' is that the cookie sheet hasn't been prepped. You know, buttered and floured. I keep forgetting we laid off Bjarne." She bent over and searched the shelves under the counter, muttering. She reemerged with the flour shaker and cast a wild glance around for the small canister of warm butter the *sous*-chefs used to prep pans. If, Quill thought, there had been any *sous*-chefs to prep pans, which there weren't. At least when the chefs were laid off, they simply went back to the Cornell School of Hotel Management—where they all had come from in the first place—and looked for another co-op job. There wasn't going to be any comfortable, reassuring co-op job for Doreen. Or Kathleen Kiddermeister, their waitress. Or for Quill herself, for that matter.

"I'll get the butter." Quill got up from the stool—a little stiffly because of her long walk—and retrieved a jar of cold butter from the refrigerator. She set it carefully by Meg's elbow and sat down again. Her coffee was getting cold. She wondered what her chances were of getting some soup and several large chunks of Meg's fresh breads when her sister was in this kind of mood.

"It's not that I mind prepping pans myself," Meg said. She broke off a piece of the butter and rubbed the cookie sheet energetically. "Not a bit. Nossir. I only studied for three years in Paris, in a language I only partly understood, and took another year as an apprentice in that hellhole restaurant in New York just so I could PREP PANS!" She sifted flour over the cookie sheet with a fine disregard for her face, hands, and blue jeans, tossed the sifter aside, then took her twenty-inch stir-fry lid and used it to trace a circle on the floured sheet. "We have to lay off Kathleen, too? 'Cause if we do, forget it. I didn't study that hard, then work my buns off to be a waitress." She grasped the upper part of the pastry bag in her right hand, and, with her left, guided the tip of the bag around the circular guide on the sheet.

"That's one of the largest cream puffs I've ever seen, Meggie."

"One of?" Meg looked up with a reluctant grin. "It's going to be the biggest. As a matter of fact, that's what I'm calling it. The Largest Cream Puff in the World au Chocolat. It's for the Crafty Ladies. Sugar and a touch of the grape. Those women love both. Did you come in here by way of the dining room? Did you see how many Hurricane drinks those ladies have had already? If I don't get this pastry out there soon, they aren't going to remember eating it."

"What's in it?"

"The usual cream puff stuff. Just a lot more of it."

"I'm sorry we had to lay off all the *sous*-chefs."

"Well, I'm sorry that I told you I'd rather eat a rat than be a waitress. I'll waitress if we need it. I'll scrub my own pans, scrub my own floor, and yours, too, Quill. I refuse to believe that this is anything other than a temporary condition." She slid the cream puff ring into the oven with a slam. "It's this business with John that has me so huffy. I can't believe he's deserted us like this. What a jerk! What kind of loyalty is it, anyway, to just go out and get another job right under our noses?"

"Slavery went out in 1862."

"What do you mean?"

"I mean that we don't own him. We don't own anyone. I think it's pretty remarkable that he's stuck with us this long. And when you think about it, Meg, he's always put us and his poor sister before his own needs. What kind of job is this for a talented guy with an M.B.A.? He hasn't had a date in ages, since there's no one in Hemlock Falls to date, except maybe Marge Schmidt and she's not all that keen on guys. Plus she's older. Plus she's *mean* . . ."

"Got all the personality of an attack tank," Meg agreed.

"He hasn't had a steady relationship with a woman in all the time I've known him here. It's more than an hour's drive into Syracuse to the theaters and the clubs and any kind of social life at all. . . ." Quill trailed off. She told herself that it had been a terrible choice for John to make. That he loved the Inn, and the job, as much or more than she did. That he was moving to Long Island out of loyalty to them. "It's not the better pay that's forcing him to take this job, Meg, although it's considerably better. And I don't think it's because they're offering him better opportunities, although he'll have three employees working for him. And it's not because it's a more interesting job, either. I mean, this bank wants a strategic plan for the year 2000. John's going to visit most of the two hundred branches this bank has all over the world. A couple in Australia, if you can believe that."

"So if it's not all that horribly boring stuff—a lot of money, great travel, and a short train ride away from the greatest city in the known universe, which is to say, New York—why is he taking this horrible job?" Meg asked. Both eyebrows were raised almost to her hairline. She placed both hands onto the counter, leaned over, and shouted, "I mean to say, QUILL! Earth to QUILL!! If that's not why he's taking the job, what is it?"

"It's me," Quill said miserably.

Meg looked at her sharply, then said with a deceptively casual air, "Oh?"

"I'm a terrible partner. I forgot to write down the amount of a couple of checks. . . ."

"Again?"

"And this time, the insurance company canceled our policy."

"They what?"

"The check John wrote bounced because he thought there was more in the account. Oh, he's fixed it, as usual, but honestly, Meg. I must drive him crazy."

"I don't think *that's* the reason," Meg said thoughtfully.

And so, Quill thought, Meg knows more than she's letting on.

She knows John won't stay on in a business that couldn't—according to the numbers at least—make a profit no matter how successful it was. Wrong place, wrong time, wrong state, John had said. Even if you could run a hundred percent occupancy all year round, you still couldn't make expenses, John said.

Sell the Inn, Quill.

She'd have all her teeth pulled and then eat glass before she told Meg John's solution.

"So why do you think he's leaving us?"

"I don't think he's gone because you're driving him bananas. You drive everyone bananas. He's an M.B.A. A good one. This job never offered the kind of scope he can have with a good company. The reason he stayed in a dead-end job with an improvident partner all these years is the same one he's leaving."

"It'd be nice if you would try and make some sense, Meg. Given the kind of day I've had, and all."

Meg unhooked the copper whipping bowl from its place above her head and filled it with heavy cream. She whipped vigorously with her hand beater for a moment, then said casually, "If you ask me, he's stayed because he's in love with you. And he's leaving because he's in love with you."

"For heaven's sake, Meg!"

Meg shrugged. "This *temporary*—and by that I mean I don't care what John says, it's temporary—this business slowdown of ours has forced his hand. If he could afford to take a pay cut he would. Just to stay near—"

"Shut UP, Meg!"

"—you, but he can't. Because of his sister." Meg stopped beating, tested the whipped cream with a critical air, then resumed her vigorous whipping. "Another thing is Myles. If you hadn't agreed to marry Myles, John would have taken a second job to make ends meet, rather than leave you. But" —Meg set the copper bowl down with a satisfied *thunk!*— "there you are."

"You are a complete and utter idiot."

"I have a sixth sense about these things."

Quill was so annoyed, she barely registered the opening and closing of the dining room door. "You have NO sense about anything. You've been a complete and total idiot since you were six years old. No. No. Pardon me.

It came much later than that. And I remember the exact precise time.'' Quill stood up and leaned over the whipped cream. "It was after you read *Gone With the Wind*. What kind of woman with any pretensions to adulthood takes Scarlett O'Hara as a role model?!''

Meg flicked a handful of whipped cream in her face. Furious, Quill scooped up the butter (now somewhat liquid in the warmth of the kitchen) and drew her arm back for the best overhand pitch she'd made since the Connecticut Intramural Girls Softball Tournament in her freshman year.

"Ladies? Am I interrupting?''

Quill froze, her arm upraised, butter dripping onto her hair. The voice was male, with a smoker's rasp, and quite unfamiliar. She turned to face him. He was just shy of middle-aged. About forty-five, she thought. He wore a pale blue sports coat with gold buttons, gray linen trousers, and a dark blue cotton, button-down, Oxford cloth shirt with white collar and cuffs. She was pretty sure she'd glimpsed a gold chain around his neck. She was very sure about the white patent leather loafers, since they winked in the overhead lights like a street-walker's eye.

"May I help you?'' she asked coldly.

"I wish somebody would. Name's Burke. Rocky Burke, owner/president of Burke's Central New York All-inclusive Insurance Agency. The Rocklike Broker for Rocky Times.'' He gave Quill an appreciative look, beginning at her ankles, traveling up her hips, waist, and breasts, and ending with her nose. "You can call me Rock, Cookie.'' Then, "I *like* a feisty woman.''

"Here, sport,'' Meg said. She tossed Quill a damp towel. "Insurance? You must be part of the broker's dinner booked for this evening.''

"Banquet. Broker's banquet. Little celebration for my five top salesmen this year. Yes, that's what I am. Came a little ahead of time to check on the arrangements and couldn't find a perishing soul out there except a lot of very drunk old biddies in that bay window table. They get all that booze here?''

"Please don't call them old biddies," Quill said.

"Golden-agers, then. Whatever. They're sure drunk, though. Like I said, if they're going to drive somewhere, I hope you didn't sell them all that booze."

"What business is it of yours?" Quill demanded. The butter seemed to have gotten all over her. She dabbed futilely at her hair. "They've had some rum, to be sure, but . . ."

"Dramshop Law," Mr. Burke said darkly. "Nasty sidelight to doing business in the great state of New York. See, that's a law which holds you, the bar owners—" He stopped. "You are the Quilliam sisters, aren't'cha? Thought so. The Dramshop Law, or Act, holds you, the bar owners responsible for the amount of liquor served to invitees on the premises. This law . . . "

"We've got insurance," Meg said. "Quite a lot of insurance."

"Actually, we don't," Quill reminded her.

Mr. Burke addressed an invisible companion. "I know they have no insurance, don't I? And aren't these the ladies who are supposed to sign my binder policy?"

"Oh! You're that Mr. Burke. I'm sorry there was no one to greet you, sir." Quill tucked her hair behind her ears and took a deep breath.

"Yeah, well. S'all right. Okay with you, we'll take care of the business tomorrow. Your current policy's good till then, right?"

"Right."

"So what I came back here for is about the banquet."

"Would you like to check on the arrangements for your dinner, I mean banquet? You know already that Meg is one of the finest chefs on the eastern—"

"That a fact? Nah. Screw the food. All the boys will care about is the booze. And it looks like the booze is okay, from the way those broadies out there are slurping it up. What I wanna know is, what about the entertainment?"

There was a short silence. Quill looked at Meg. Meg opened her mouth, shut it, then went to the oven to check on the World's Largest Cream Puff.

"Entertainment," said Quill, just to be certain she'd heard correctly.

"Yepper. Thing is, I wasn't quite sure what you got here."

"We have dog duets," Meg said to the World's Largest Cream Puff, "or maybe the Quarreling Quilliams? Whipped cream and warm butter All-Girl Wrestling? Take your pick."

"Huh?" Mr. Burke said, with a worried geniality that undoubtedly served him well on the claims end of his business.

"Why don't we go into the Tavern Bar, Mr. Burke? We can discuss the issue there, over—er—some booze." Quill took his arm, and, with the expertise born of years of dealing with guests who were unimaginably rude, unforgettably snide, and ridiculously bellicose, she steered him out of the kitchen across the dining room, and down the short corridor to the Tavern Bar.

"Very nice place you have here," Mr. Burke offered as she pulled him briskly along. "Very historic."

"Very," Quill agreed. She tugged him over to the mahogany bar. Here, at least, were customers. Not many, but a few. She signaled Nate the bartender with a lifted forefinger and a smile. The sight of Nate, stolid, dark, reassuring in his familiar stance behind the long mahogany bar, lifted her spirit. She smiled brightly at Rocky Burke, then said, "Um . . . name your—er—poison, Mr. Burke. Rocky, I mean. On the house."

"That right? Double V.O. Gibson on the rocks. And a Kleenex."

"I beg your pardon?"

Nate gave the bar in front of them a graceful swipe with his cloth. "He means a pickled onion, Quill. Shall I pour the usual for you?"

"Thanks, Nate."

"No problem. By the way, you got some time later, I'd like to talk to you. No rush. No biggie."

Oh, *shit*, Quill thought. Another no rush. Another no biggie. Another ex-employee. "Of course," she said. "Anytime. My office is always open."

Rocky Burke grasped his Gibson with the air of a man coming home. He tested it. Smiled. Said, "A drink this good, may be all the entertainment we need."

"As a matter of fact, Mr. Burke, we really don't have any entertainment. As such."

"As such? As such what?"

"Well, there's the pianist, of course, but he only comes in for special occasions. For example, we had a banquet for a group called the Savoyards. They're from New York City, and they're devotees of Gilbert and Sullivan—"

"*I am the very model of a modern major gen-er-al!*" Mr. Burke sang in a creditable baritone. "Sure. I know Art and Bill real well." He winked. "Course, at our little banquets, we kind of change the words to fit, you know. Make it all about insurance."

"All about insurance?"

This put Mr. Burke on his dignity. "Of course all about insurance. You know the 'Policeman's Song' from *Pirates*?"

"I don't think—"

"Sure you do. Only we sing, *When a broker's not engaged in his employment, (his employment) or maturing his annuity's little plans (little plans)*. Like that. Or

'Buttercup's Song' from *Pinafore. Hurrah for commissons,/ three cheers for commissions/ there's no need at all to decry/ the cash from commissions/ tho' it's quite an omission/ if the insured one refuses to die.''

"Aagh," Quill said and took a long sip of her red wine.

"So a pianist would be just fine."

"Really?" Quill brightened. Their pianist was a retired concert artist from Cornell, usually available, and very good. "I'll make the arrangements right away. Of course, there's a fee, quite reasonable, considering."

Mr. Burke hunched forward in a confiding way. "Tell you what I'm gonna do."

"What are you going to do, Mr. Burke?"

"I'm gonna write you a fire policy you won't believe." He patted his breast pocket and looked at her in an appealing way. "Mind if I smoke?"

"Not at all."

He lit up, flicked the match into the ashtray and sipped his Gibson. He exhaled luxuriously. "I wonder what the poor people are doing tonight!"

Sitting watching you drink my mortgage money, Quill thought.

"What about this fire policy?"

"Not just fire. No, Cookie. Includes wind, rain, floods, and other acts of God. Vandalism. Malicious mischief. The works. It's your policy, you get me?"

"Sort of."

"See, the deal is this. How much does it cost for this pianist?"

"Three to five hundred dollars, depending."

"Depending on what?"

On how many times he has to play "New York, New York" and the Macarena, Quill thought, but she said, "Whether the group wants requests, or a concert—he's

one of the world's best known interpreters of Mozart—
that sort of thing.''

"We're a sing-along bunch of guys, that's for sure.''

"Then for sure he's going to want five hundred.''

"And you just guess how much a two-month straight
fire policy on this old Inn is from the Rock's agency?''

"How much?'' Quill asked warily. "Not . . . five hundred?''

"You betcha!'' He swallowed the remains of his
drink and signaled Nate with an exuberant, "My *man*!
Another!''

Quill had the very distinct feeling that she wasn't the
one getting the advantage here.

"Now. This will be on a binder. Two months. With
a slight, very slight rise in the premium after we do the
inspection thing.''

"How much of a rise?'' Quill asked.

"It's *de minimis*. Which is to say, not to worry. You
get a hell of a deal on your fire policy. I get a new
customer. And the boys get a terrific pianist tonight.''

"Well,'' Quill said. "We already—''

"No, you don't. Checked on you, of course, before I
came out. Had a little talk with your business manager—
bright guy. He asked about lower rates from me than
from the boy you were buying from before. I said I'd
check it out—never let an opportunity pass you by,
Cookie. You're going to be canceled, if you haven't
been already, for nonpayment of premium. Now. You
need a policy. I need a pianist. Bingo. Bob's your uncle.
Deal?''

"What's that expression mean, anyway? Bob's your
uncle?''

"Can't say as I know for sure, Cookie. Have we got
a deal?''

"I . . . you say John asked about rate fees from you?''

"He did. Yes, ma'am.'' He took the cigarette out of

his mouth and eyed her through the smoke. "He here, still? Heard he had a new job."

"How did you . . . never mind. Yes, he's still here. But he won't be back until quite late."

"Uh *huh*. Well, you tell the old boy, if he questions the amount of the *quid pro quo*, that rates were a little higher than I thought."

"I see." Quill began to understand how the poor got poorer. Mr. Burke seemed to know she didn't have the cash on hand to pay him—and take care of several urgent bills tomorrow—but that Signor Bellasario, the pianist, would wait for his fee. So she ended up paying more, because she couldn't afford to pay now. "John thought it'd be okay to go with your company at a five-hundred-dollar premium for two months?"

Mr. Burke shrugged.

"Then I guess it would be okay." Quill tapped her thumb nervously against the side of her wineglass. She'd defer a five-hundred-dollar payable for two months. Anything could happen in two months. "You wouldn't have any paperwork with you right now, would you?"

"Sure would. In the old briefcase. Left it in your foyer. You show me where my room is; I'll haul out the old laptop and bingo! Barb's your aunt. Ha!"

Nate set the second double V.O. Gibson (with Kleenex) in front of Mr. Burke. He swallowed it, slapped Quill on the back, and rose to take his leave. "You got a key?"

"You're booked into 212. The key's on the board behind the reception desk. But I'll—"

"Don't you worry your—"

Pretty little head about it, Quill thought.

"—pretty little head about it. Sit there. Finish that touch of the grape. And I'll see you in a while."

There was quite a bit of Burgundy left in the wineglass. Quill swirled it around, took a sip, and closed her eyes. She could see every detail of the room around her: the long shining sweep of the bar; the rows of wine-glasses hanging from the beech wood racks, bell down; the round tables and the comfortable lounge chairs. She and Meg had traveled to all five boroughs in New York looking for lounge chairs a customer would love to sit in sober, but wouldn't encourage too much consumption. They'd never actually found one.

"You have a minute, Quill?"

She opened her eyes. She'd hired Nate on a snowy afternoon in January five years ago. They'd decided, John, Doreen, Meg, and Quill herself, that maybe, by spring, there'd be enough business to hire a bartender full-time. John, a recovering alcoholic, hadn't liked the work, Quill had known that from the beginning, but he'd insisted on tending bar while the business was building.

Nate had come to the back door, hat twisted between his hands, not too certain he wanted to work for two women, but in need of a job and willing to try. He stood in front of her now, head turned a little sideways.

"So who made you an offer you couldn't refuse?"

Surprise and relief gave him a slightly comical look. "The Croh Bar," he said readily. "Stewie Harrelson had to quit. Heart, the doc said. Tips are pretty good there. I hope there's no hard feelings."

"No. Of course not." She reached out and clasped his hand briefly, as warmly as she could. "I'm just sorry we couldn't keep you in work. I feel awful."

He shrugged. "Hey. Times get good again, I'll be right back. If you want me." He hesitated. "I suppose John'll be taking over?"

"No. No. The thing is, Nate, John's found a great opportunity in Long Island. He thought he might give it a go. As they say."

"Hm. Wouldn't have figured that would have happened. But then—"

A man's gotta do what a man's gotta do, Quill thought.

"—a man's gotta do what a man's gotta do."

Quill, whose memory of nonfinancially related facts was almost eidetic, recalled a relevant section of Termination. When you terminated, (although, granted, Nate had terminated himself) you were supposed to be positive, upbeat, and sincere. "You've been the best, Nate, just the best. We couldn't have done it without you."

Nate nodded. "It's been a pleasure."

"It's been more than a pleasure. I'll always feel that you had a big part in our success, Nate. When we were successful, that is."

"Thank you very much. Now, who's going to take care of her?" He indicated the long sweep of the bar.

"I thought I'd ask Kathleen. Tips in the dining room are even worse than in here. Not that she'd be a tenth of the bartender you are, Nate."

"Thank you. Thank you very much. Who's going to take over for Kath in the dining room?"

"We'll figure it out. Me, probably."

"Yeah? Just like the old days."

"Just like the old days."

"I thought I'd work out the week. Maybe start at the Croh on Monday. Tell you what, Quill. You get a special party in, like that Swamp Engineers Group, I'd be glad to sub for you. Anytime. All you gotta do is ask."

"That's a good idea." Quill sat up a little straighter and took a healthy swallow of her wine. "That's a very good idea. I wonder if we could do it all with part-timers. I mean—we've always felt it was important to offer salaries and health benefits, but part-timers don't care about that, do they? And they work cheap."

Nate nodded.

"You don't think it's a good idea, Nate. I can tell you don't think it's a good idea."

"You've been a good boss, Quill. Hate to see you start the nickel-and-dime stuff, that's all."

"Well, maybe if I'd paid more attention to the nickel-and-dime stuff, you wouldn't be looking for a job at the Croh Bar."

"Could be."

Quill waited until the heat in her cheeks subsided. "Sorry."

"S'all right. Times are tough."

"Times aren't that tough. People like Marge Schmidt never seem to go through tough times." She thought a moment. "Nate?"

"Yeah, Quill. Still here."

"Marge Schmidt's run the Hemlock Home Diner for how long?"

"Long as I can remember. I think she bought that place with the money from her high school graduation party, I swear to God. And she's never looked back."

"I've heard she's the richest woman in Hemlock Falls."

"Richest citizen in Tompkins County," Nate said. "And that's saying something, with all the wineries."

"I wonder." Quill beckoned Nate closer, and leaned forward until her curls tickled his cheek. "You don't think . . . you don't think she'd like to buy out John's share in the Inn?"

"John's got shares in the Inn?" Nate frowned.

"Fifteen percent. Of course, at the moment, that fifteen percent isn't worth a bucket of warm spit, as they say in Fargo, but still. She's a successful woman, Nate. A woman who knows her way around a bank."

"When did you give ol' John fifteen percent of the Inn?"

"We didn't give it to him, he earned it. It's called

sweat equity. He deferred part of his salary every year, or something. I'm not entirely sure. Howie Murchison handled it for me.''

"How come I didn't get a chance at these shares?"

"You?"

"Me." He tapped his chest. "Nate. Guy that's standing right here in front of you. I mean being such a valuable employee and all."

"Oh." She thought a moment. "Well, everyone got a chance to participate in the boutique when it opened."

"Thanks a lot."

"I detect a little sarcasm here, Nate."

"Well, the dang thing went bust, didn't it? So much for all that profit sharing."

"Who knew Mr. Sakura was going to make it into a car wash and miniature golf course?"

"Anyway."

There was an awkward silence. Quill cleared her throat. "I'll be getting along then." She glanced at her watch. "Myles usually calls about now. He's in Europe, you know. That German thing And I've got to give Signor Bellasario a call. The brokers want some music."

"See you around, Quill."

"See you."

She walked briskly out of the Tavern Bar with, she hoped, an attitude of purpose and confidence. The foyer was empty, the front door closed. No noise at all came from the dining room, and when she looked, she saw it was empty. The Crafty Ladies had finished their dinners and gone—who knew where. The silence was deafening.

A note from Kathleen was taped to the room ledger: 214, 216, 218 checked in. So the other brokers must have arrived. A second note taped to the telephone was from Doreen: SORRY. So the wholesaler wanted his money up front. "Damn," Quill said. The answering machine light blipped red; she punched the Play button:

Myles, his voice hollow and tinny on the line from Frankfurt. Love and he'd call in two days.

Selena Summerhill, offering dates for a wine tour.

Two calls from the obnoxiously cheerful, nastily firm credit card people.

Marge Schmidt, inviting her to the Hemlock Home Diner (Fine Food and Fast!). No rush. Anytime. Just to talk. Thought she might be interested in doing a little business.

Marge's number at the diner was easy to remember: all the village telephone prefixes were the same, 597. The diner was 597-FOOD. Quill dialed before she lost her nerve.

"Diner, 'lo."

"Hello, Marge. It's Sarah Quilliam. Up at the Inn."

"How's it going, up there at the Inn, Ms. Quilliam?"

"Fine!"

Marge didn't say anything to this, although the quality of the silence was of the "what am I, stupid?" variety. Then, "You got some bonehead insurance guy named Burke stayin' up there with you, Quill?"

"Rocky Burke? Yes. Why?"

"I hope he chokes to death on one a Meg's chicken bones, that's why. Creep comes in here at lunchtime with his round little stummick stickin' out, tries to hit up the whole damn town for new policies. Threw the bugger out."

"Good grief," Quill said.

"Thing is, Quill. I'm kinda startin' in that line myself."

"Insurance?"

"Good hedge against bad times."

Quill made an attempt to sort this out before Marge said anything more. Was she trying to sell Quill a policy? Did she leave the call just so she could rub it in that half the village was eating lunch at her diner, rather than at the Inn? Was there a hidden message (Marge could be subtle) in the phrase, ''bad times''?

''Quill?''

''Yes?''

''Wondered if you might want to talk about selling the Inn.''

So much for subtlety. ''No,'' Quill said, and hung up. ''Hell.''

''Speak of the devil and he appears!'' Rocky Burke bounced ebulliently down the stairway. ''My guys down yet?''

''Not yet. And if you'll give me a moment, I'll give Signor Bellasario a call. What time would you like to start?''

''Where's the piano?''

''In the Tavern. We can serve your dinner in there, if you like.'' At least, she thought, there were a couple of customers still there. The empty dining room would seem oppressive.

Burke peered shrewdly at her. ''Kinda quiet for a Saturday night, isn't it?''

''It's usual this time of year,'' Quill fibbed. ''Why don't you come and sit down in my office while I call Signor Bellasario?''

''Fine, fine. I've got the binder right here.'' He drew a sheaf of papers from his breast pocket, and followed her into the office. ''Your business manager still around or has he left already?''

''He's in Syracuse tonight. It's his night off.''

''I see. He said that nonpayment of premium was a mistake; drew the check from the wrong checking account or something.''

''It was my fault,'' Quill said, because it was. ''I forget to list the checks I write sometimes, and I didn't tell John about a couple of them, and then I forgot to make a deposit.''

"Good thing you had him running the financial end for you."

"It certainly is."

"Too bad he's leaving."

Quill didn't answer him.

Her desk was piled high with the paperwork John insisted she had to review. She sat down at her desk and glanced at the paper at the top of the pile: it was the spreadsheet for the year's revenues. The numbers at the bottom of the income column were in the dreaded parentheses. The parentheses, John had explained more than once, did NOT mean profit. It meant, in the memorable phrase of Hudson Zabriskie, the former manager of the Hemlock Falls Paramount Paint Company, negative profit. A deficit. A loss.

A failure.

For the benefit of the clearly suspicious Mr. Burke, Quill smiled at the spreadsheet with delight, then took the whole pile of papers and stuffed them in the top drawer. "There," she said brightly. "I'll have time to go over those later. You should have a seat, Mr. Burke, and I'll make that call."

She had to disabuse Signor Bellasario (who was eighty-six, and going just a little deaf) of the notion that she was selling house siding before he agreed to have his daughter-in-law drive him to the Inn. "Bad line," she said to Mr. Burke before he could question the entertainment value of a deaf pianist. "But he's delighted to help out. He'll be here within the hour." If his arthritis medicine kicks in, she thought. "Now. About this binder."

"Right here." Burke spread his papers carefully on the desktop and looked at them with possessive pride. "Burke's is an insurance agency that can meet all your liability and casualty needs, Miss Quilliam. Like I said, our motto is Rocklike Security in Rocky Times. Now,

Mr. Raintree seemed to feel that the value of your buildings here was over eight hundred thousand. That fit with your assessment?''

"Yes," Quill said recklessly.

"Good. 'Cause that agrees with your tax assessment. And now Mr. Raintree gave me your revenue numbers from '95. Hell of a business you've got here, Miss Quilliam, if I do say so myself.''

"Ninety-five," Quill recalled, "was a very good year.''

"Part of this insurance plan provides for interruption of business due to fire, flood, famine, or other acts of God. Now, I'll need your numbers for the past year to verify the actual amount of business you'd lose if your beautiful Inn here were to burn down, but based on Mr. Raintree's word, I'm gonna go with the flow for '95. We'll reassess when you get me the 96–97 numbers, of course, so don't worry that you're underinsured. You get me? I mean, if you stand to lose more from an interruption of business than the '95 figures show, we'll take care of you.''

"It'll be fine," Quill said.

"Mr. Raintree seemed to know what he was doing. You got his figures for this year around anywhere? 'Cause I'll be happy to write in the figures for those, even if the statement's unaudited.''

"I'm not sure exactly what you mean, Mr. Burke." Which, Quill figured, wasn't as blatant a lie as it sounded. She was picking up the nouns and verbs in Mr. Burke's spiel, but the insurance jargon was beyond her.

"Well, we'll go with the '95 figures, then. Chances of anything happening in the next sixty days while the binder's in effect are slim to nonexistent. Not," he added hastily, and with an earnest expression, "that you can do without this, Miss Quilliam. Insurance is important.''

He took a pen from his breast pocket, rose, and stood behind her. "You sign right here."

Quill signed.

"And here."

Quill signed again.

Mr. Burke sighed happily. "There you are, Miss. Quilliam. This binder's good for sixty days, as I said, and your formal policy will come through the mail. You just sign it and send it right back to me. And now . . ." He clapped her on the shoulder. "Now you can sleep easy."

CHAPTER 3

Quill dreamed of rain. She stood at the tip of the Gorge under a thunderous sky. Lightning flashed and flashed again. She smelled ozone. The rain felt at odds with the bleak and cold landscape: it was soft, warm, and somewhat sticky.

"Woof," came a bark in her ear. "WOOF!"

Quill sat upright in bed. Red eyes glared into hers. She yelped, fumbled for the light next to the bed, and switched it on. The dog stood at her bedside, tail wagging frantically. He backed up, the woofs escalating into short, high barks. He dashed to her bedroom door, then back to the bed again.

"How in the heck . . ."

The dog roared. Quill gasped, shrank back, and pulled the covers up to her chin. She coughed. Smoke. The ozone smell in her dream was smoke.

Her head cleared. She reached for the phone at her bedside, hand steady. She dialed 911, spoke curtly, quickly to the volunteer fireman at the other end of the line, then leaped out of bed, headed out of her bedroom and through her small living room. Her set of master keys hung by the coffeepot in her little kitchen. She grabbed them and raced into the hall. The dog followed, frantic with impatience to be out and gone.

It was quiet. The night lighting along the edges of the ceiling shone into air just slightly tinged with smoke. Alarms were placed throughout the Inn; the age of the building and the sprawling layout made quick access to them essential. There was an alarm and fire extinguisher between her suite and Meg's. She grabbed the extinguisher with one hand, and pulled the alarm with the other, then ran to Meg's door.

The *whoop!whoop!whoop!* of the alarm struck the air like a brass knuckled fist. Quill pounded on Meg's door with the extinguisher, opened it, and almost tumbled into her sister. Andy Bishop stood behind her, hastily knotting his bathrobe around his waist.

"Where?" Meg demanded tersely.

"I don't know. There's smoke. No burning. You take this floor. I'll go up."

"I'll take the up—"

Quill was already gone, the dog at her heels. The alarm was shrill, insistent, terrifying. She ran up the stairs and rounded the landing to confront confusion and shouts. The Crafty Ladies had five of the rooms on the third floor. The smoke was heavier here, and there was a smell of burning. Robin Robinson, hair in curlers, dressed in a shabby chenille bathrobe, raced into the hall from her room and slapped the door to 314. "Fran!" she cried. "Fran!" Mary Lennox emerged from the door to 316, hair wild, her bedspread clutched around her.

"Fire escape at the end!" Quill ordered. "Quick! Quick!"

"My purse!" Fran shrieked. "I've got to get my—"

Quill grabbed her by the shoulders and shoved her forward. "Out! Out!"

Fran Grimsby opened her door and tumbled into

Robin's arms. "Ellen?" Fran said. Her voice was thin and high. "Where's Ellen?"

"Three-ten!" Robin screamed. "She's in 310. I'll get Mary. She's at the other end."

"Get out!" Quill said. "All of you get out now!" Three-ten was behind the landing and faced the Falls. It had a balcony, thank God.

The smoke was thicker there. Quill found herself at the door, the dog leaping at her side. She tried the handle. It was hot. The door was locked. Smoke seeped in thick, ugly waves from beneath the door. Quill hoisted the fire extinguisher to her hip. She used the master key in the lock. The door flew open, sucked inward by a hot draft.

The room was blazing. Thick fingers of flames twisted drapes, crawled up the walls, reached for the ceiling. It was intensely, incredibly hot. Something grabbed Quill's nightgown and pulled her off balance. "Not NOW, dammit," Quill said to the dog. "Beat it! Beat it!"

The dog ran halfway down the hall and back again, his barking colliding with the yell of the alarm. Quill snapped the extinguisher nozzle free of the clamp. Thick foam spurted out like evil-smelling Redi-Whip. She sprayed in a slow, smooth arc, the thick gush of foam smothering the flames. The nozzle sputtered; the foam trickled to nothing. Quill threw the empty canister away with a curse. The smoke cleared for moment. The bed in this suite faced the balcony. The balcony doors were open. Quill didn't know much about fire, but she knew that the fresh air coming in would fuel whatever smoldered in the room. When the fire reignited, it would come back with a blast. She could make out a huddled figure beneath the spread.

She didn't stop to think. If she had, she would have run away, down the stairs, out the door, to the safety of the lawn. She took a breath and held it. Ran into the room. Grabbed the figure in the bed by the hair and screamed. The hair came off in her hands like masking tape from a wall. She clutched the shoulders and was briefly aware of heated, crumbling, greasy flesh. She pulled. The weight was incredible, an anchor, a deadweight, immovable.

She pulled, hard. Near the open French doors, a white-orange pillar sprang for the open air, a giant cat after prey. Quill sobbed, pulled, and pulled again. The fire resurrected with a roar and a bellow that set her hair crackling. She heard the dog barking with sharp hysteria. Fear drove her like a blow. There was a moment of heat, of huge strain. She heard herself scream.

And she was in the hall, the body of Ellen Dunbarton at her feet.

"Move! Move! Move!" John, beside her, lifted the blackened lump with no effort at all.

"So where . . ." Quill gasped, "were those muscles when I needed . . ."

"MOVE!" Ellen's body over his shoulder, John propelled Quill forward with one hand.

"The dog!" Quill said. "Where's the . . . ?" Sharp teeth nipped at her hand. The dog bounced ahead to the landing, then scrambled first down the steps. Quill followed, John behind her, stumbling down the flight to the second floor, then to the first, and to the blessed welcome sight of the open door, and beyond that, the lawn crowded with people.

The air was cool, too cool. Quill shivered. She wrapped her arms around herself, and discovered she couldn't stop. In the distance, she heard the wail of the fire trucks. "Meg?" she shouted. "Meggie!"

"Right here." Meg's hair was standing up around her head. She was wearing her purple nightshirt. "Andy grabbed the guest register. He's counting everyone off. I don't think there's anyone left in there. Here. You've singed your hair. And you're shivering, Quill. I'll get you a blanket.''

"I don't think it's spreading," John said. He faced the Inn calmly. "See? The fire's confined to the upper floor. I shut the door at the top of the stairs, so with any luck—Quill, no.''

Quill knelt in front of the bundle at his feet. "Oh, my God,'' she said. "Oh, my God.''

"Don't look,'' he said quietly.

"Where's Andy?''

"Right here, Quill.'' He emerged from the crowd of exclaiming, excited guests. Like John, his voice was calm and unruffled. "Everyone's out, unless you had some unregistered guests? No? Just the rats?''

"There aren't any rats,'' Quill said indignantly.

"Always are in a building this old.'' He knelt beside her, quick fingers light and capable. "Well,'' he said. "Well.''

"Is she dead, Andrew?''

"Poor woman. I don't think . . . where the hell's the ambulance?'' He rocked back on his heels. The driveway up the hill to the Inn was filled with the beams of darting headlights, goldfish in the black night's bowl. The oncoming sirens were raucous. Meg reappeared with a blanket, and Quill huddled gratefully into warmth. She wished she could stop shivering. John's arm went around her and she leaned against him.

"What in the name of all that's holy,'' he asked, "happened to the sprinkler system?''

"Turned off?'' Quill said, bewildered, fifteen hours later. "How could the sprinkler system have been turned off?''

"Little valve in each of the rooms,'' the fire chief said in a helpful way. "Easy enough to turn it on, turn it off. You got a good system, I'll give you that. Could have been a lot worse than just the one room.''

Meg sat at Quill's left, Doreen was on her right. She felt a bit like the captain in the *Charge of the Light Brigade* after the survivors left the valley. "I know *how*, Denny. I meant who. And why?" They were sitting at table seven in the dining room. The afternoon sun made burnished gold of the Falls. In the rose garden, the first buds of the *rosa pastura* were beginning to unfold in the soft spring air. The dog, who'd accepted a heavy meal of bacon, hamburger, and rice, lay outside next to the koi pound. He'd refused to come into the building when the food was offered, and had waited patiently for Quill to back away from the bowl before he'd plunged in. At this distance, it wasn't possible to see the singe marks or the matted coat, and he looked as if he belonged there. Quill watched this innocent and beautiful scene without really seeing it.

Denny the fire chief was a stocky man in his late forties, with grizzled hair and an amiable smile. He took a huge bite of chicken pâté and swallowed it with an appreciative grunt. "This here's the best liverwurst I ever tasted," he said. "The guys at the station want to thank Meg for the hamper. Me? I could eat it all day. This'll be my third serving since last night." He waved at the pile of fruit Meg had placed in the center of the table. "And them strawberries . . . delicious."

"You're welcome," Meg said.

Doreen sniffed. "But it ain't liverwurst, you toot. That there is liver pâté."

"Patties or spoonfuls, my stomach thanks you just the same."

"You can have a fourth and fifth serving if you want," Quill said warmly. "You saved the Inn! I can never thank you enough."

"No, I didn't. I mean, the boys and me, yeah, we did a good job. But that fire was set in that room and it kept itself to that room. Didn't even get the wiring or nothing. Amazing.''

"And thank you for letting us keep the Inn open." Meg took two slices of sourdough bread from the basket in the center of the table and set them on Denny's plate with a smile. Quill kicked her in exasperation. "I—ow! What'd you do that for?!"

Denny set his fork down with a stern expression, a man on a mission. "No, don't you thank me for that, Meg. You thank that interfering lawyer Howie Murchison. I told him and I'm a-telling you. . . ."

"*That's* why!" Quill hissed.

". . . s'not right to keep the premises open when the origin of a suspicious fire has not yet been determined."

"That's why I kicked you," Quill said.

"And it's going to take a whiles to determine what happened, too. You heard from Sher'f McHale yet, Quill?"

"I called him about the fire this morning, Denny. And he's not sheriff anymore, you know."

"I don't know that you could call Davy Kiddermeister a sheriff," Denny grunted. "Just a kid. Don't seem to know his ass from a hole in the ground, if you'll excuse the language, ladies. Thing is, Myles is good at this sort of stuff. I mean, it's the kind of thing he gets paid for now, right? Investigations. I was just wondering when he was headed back this way. Sher'f McHale, he wouldn't have let no lawyer bamboozle him into keeping the scene of a suspicious incident open. Nossir. He would have kep' this place closed up right and tight. Like it should be."

Quill looked around the dining room. It was late, after three, but the lunch crowd had been substantial, and they had had to turn people away even after the third sitting. The remnants of the crowd, including the four remaining Crafty Ladies, were still eating. She'd had to call in all the help they'd laid off the month before, and more. None of her employees had turned down the opportunity to be included, however peripherally, at the scene of the tragedy. Quill doubted that their willing responses were due to the effectiveness of her Termination techniques. Quill's own reaction to disaster had always been to retreat to a discreet distance until the fuss was over; everyone else's seemed to be to crowd in and watch. Human beings—and their curiosity—never failed to amaze her.

"Myles offered to come home, of course," Quill said. "But I told him I don't think it's really necessary."

"You let me talk to him next time he calls," Denny said. "I'll let him know how necessary it is. We got ourselves a murderer here, plain and simple. That fire was set, sure as I'm the volunteer fire chief of the Hemlock Falls Volunteer Fire Department, and that poor lady murdered in her bed."

"Why didn't she just get up and get out?" Quill asked. "That's what's been bothering me. Was she that heavy a sleeper?"

"Andy said the autopsy wouldn't be finished until tomorrow." Meg ran both hands through her hair. "We won't know cause of death until then, and until we do—maybe it was just vandalism or something. Maybe the murder part was unintentional."

"Ladies, Chief." Rocky Burke approached the table, unsmiling, rumpled, his briefcase clutched in his hand. "Rocky Burke, Burke's Insurance. Mind if I sit down for a bit?"

"Siddown right here," Doreen said, pleased. She hitched her chair over to provide room for him. He sat down primly, holding his briefcase in his lap. "You got a check for us, mister?" Burke frowned. Doreen shook an admonitory finger in his face. "Now, you look and look smart—"

"Doreen," Quill said.

"—I got experience with you bozos, and I know how you all like to weasel outta your commitments."

"Doreen!" Quill said.

"You wrote us that fire policy last night, and it's as good as gold. I talked to Howie Murchison myself this morning and you owe what you owe. So pay up." She turned to Denny with a grim smile. "We can sure use that check for payroll this week, I can tell you. This is going to he'p cash flow quite a bit. Quite a bit."

"DoREEN!" Quill shouted.

"I've done a preliminary estimate," Mr. Burke said stiffly. "But I have to tell you, Mrs. Stoker, that I am advising my company to withhold payment until the investigation is completed. The circumstances surrounding the taking out of this very expensive policy, and the discovery I've since made that your Inn is in a great deal of financial trouble have created suspicions. Yes, I have grave suspicions."

"You what?" Fortunately, Quill thought, Doreen's mop was safely stowed in the kitchen. By the time she went to retrieve it and came back, Quill could have the hapless Mr. Burke safely out of the way.

Doreen bent her head and gave Mr. Burke the full benefit of the Glare. "You try any tricks, Rocky Burke of Burke's Insurance, and you're gonna see your puss spread all over the front page of the *Hemlock Falls Gazette*. And you ain't gonna like what you read."

"What?!" Mr. Burke—who'd looked rumpled and exhausted after a sleepless night calculating his losses— now looked rumpled, exhausted, and pissed off.

"My husband. Third husband. Axminster Stoker. Publisher and editor-in- chief of our newspaper. And I," Doreen said grandly, "have bin named special correspondent to the Inn. Just this morning. So you watch yourself, smart guy. When the media's on the trail, the buck stops here."

"And other mixed metaphors," Meg said cheerfully.

"Suspicions?" Denny said alertly. "Of the girls, here?"

"Wimmin, you bozo," Doreen said. "Watch your tongue, or I'll get the Ax after you, too. For harassment."

"That," said Quill, rising to her feet, "is bloody well enough. Doreen, I want you to supervise the cleaning on the third floor . . ."

Denny pounded his fist on the table. "Oh, no, *oh,* no. Don't you touch that room."

". . . and stay out of the room in question."

"Huh," Doreen said belligerently.

Quill turned conciliatory. "Doreen, we've got the backup cleaning crew in, and you know what they're like."

"Bozos," Doreen said darkly. "You're right. They don't know shit from shinola, those girls. I'll git my mop and git up there."

"Good. And thanks. Oh, and Doreen?" she called after the housekeeper's retreating back. "Don't hit them, okay? They're doing the best that they can."

"You should keep a better handle on your help, Cookie," Mr. Burke said sulkily. "That attitude of hers is going in the report, too."

"Just what sort of information do you need for this report of yours, Mr. Burke?" Meg popped a strawberry in her mouth and regarded him with wide eyes.

"That's for me to know, and you to find out." He reached for a strawberry. Meg slapped his hand away. "Hey!"

"For guests of the Inn, only."

"You gave the fire chief all he wanted. He's making a pig of himself. Just look at him." Denny grinned through a mouthful of strawberries. "And I'm a guest at the Inn."

"You've extended your stay?"

"You bet your"—he searched for a less belligerent word—"bippy I extended my stay. Until I know for sure this is a fraudulent claim. Preliminary estimates on this little caper of yours add up to a good fifty thousand." He scowled. "All those damn antiques. And labor. You know what even a half-assed carpenter costs these days? And we're required to pay the union rate even though"—he lowered his voice and hissed fiercely— "even though I know *darn* well your basic type of insured gets his uncle Al to do it for minimum wage."

"We don't have an uncle Al," Meg said. "But if we did, I can assure you we'd pay the going rate. Okay. If you're staying, have a strawberry. Have," Meg said generously, "two."

"Is there any help we can give you, Mr. Burke?" Quill rubbed the back of her neck. She was tired. She was really tired. She wished that she'd given in to impulse and said to Myles: "Please, yes, come home NOW." "I know it looks suspicious. But honestly. We didn't set that fire. You can't believe my sister and I would do anything like that for any kind of money."

"You'd be surprised at what people will do for money."

Denny grunted agreement.

Quill thought about this, then said, "No, I guess I wouldn't. I've seen a lot of people do a lot of horrible things for money. All I'm telling you is that this isn't that kind of town. And we're not that kind of people."

Meg squeaked irrepressibly in a high falsetto, "Daddy! Clarence got his wings!"

"What the hell?" Burke said in a tired voice.

Quill made a face. "I guess I *was* sounding Pollyannaish. It's a line from Frank Capra's movie, *It's a Wonderful Life*. Meg hates that movie. Every time I start to sound a little, um . . ."

"Jimmy-Stewart dorkish?" Meg asked. "Donna Reedish?"

". . . *noble* is a word I like. Anyhow, she likes to poke a pin in me. So she quotes. Worse yet, she sings."

"That so?" Mr. Burke looked at Meg, and grinned suddenly. "You know what? I hate *It's a Wonderful Life*, too. It's not an especially wonderful life, if you ask me. Look at crime in the cities. Look at the people who think AIDS victims should be shunted away to a camp. Look at Arab terrorists. They are all people like you and me—which is to say, mean, rotten, and dirty as dogs."

Meg grinned back and slid him the entire fruit bowl.

Quill shook her head, covered her face with her hands, and muttered, "I get it, Mr. Burke. You don't know us from Arab terrorists. We could be bad guys in innocent young women suits, for all you know. So. Stick around. Poke your nose into anything you want. We'll be right behind you. Because if the fire chief is right, and this was a deliberate murder, somebody set that fire to burn poor Ellen Dunbarton to a crisp. And somebody should find out who."

A slender young girl with brown hair and big eyes sidled softly up to the table. "Quill? I'm sorry to interrupt. There's quite a few people from town to see you."

Meg leaped to her feet with a whoop. "Yes! Dina Muir, returned from the world of the laid-off, downsized, and unemployed. Returned to her job as receptionist. It's good to see you." Meg grabbed Dina in a hug. "Are you glad to be back? I'm sure glad to see you. And I don't know how long the business generated by these curiosity-seekers is going to last, but I'm sure happy to see you now. Was it horrible, being unemployed?"

"Um," said Dina. "Not really." She was growing her hair long again, and she wound a piece around her finger. "I, like, was getting unemployment, you know?

And, like, the check? Almost the same as my pay here. And I didn't have to, like, work for it. I got a lot of work done on my thesis. Anyhow.'' She turned to Quill. ''It's the Reverend Mr. Shuttleworth? And like that? They said if you were busy or harassed or whatever, they'd come back later. I said you were eating lunch.''

''You should have asked them to come in.'' Quill got to her feet. ''I'll go see them. Unless you need me anymore, Mr. Burke? Denny?'' Rocky Burke shook his head. Denny, who had retired to the silent and efficient disposal of his lunch, shook his head and grinned. Bits of pâté fell on his shirt. ''Where are they, Dina?''

''I stuck them in the conference center. It looks like it's the whole darn Chamber of Commerce.''

It wasn't the entire Hemlock Falls Chamber of Commerce—which numbered twenty-four—but it was the regulars, plus one new member Quill was very glad to see: Selena Summerhill. Quill smiled at them all: Mayor Elmer Henry; Dookie Shuttleworth, the Minister of the Church of the Word of God; Miriam Doncaster, the librarian; Esther West, owner of the West's Best Dress Shoppe; Harvey Bozzel, president of Hemlock Falls' best (and only) advertising agency. She was even glad to see Marge Schmidt and Betty Hall, co-owners of the Hemlock Home Diner.

Selena Summerhill, glowing and elegant in a dark olive linen pantsuit, her black hair knotted in a smooth chignon in the back, clasped her hands and murmured, ''Terrible, Quill. This is just terrible. I said that to my Hugh this morning, and he thought I should come to offer help.''

''I'm glad you did.''

They were seated in their old, familiar spots around the conference room table. When Quill walked to her own place at the far end, they all stood, and one by one shook her hand as she passed by.

"Hey, guys." Quill accepted an embrace from Harvey, resisting the impulse to muss up his careful blond hair. She shook hands with the mayor, kissed Dookie on the cheek, hugged Miriam with genuine affection, and squeezed Betty Hall's shoulder. She exchanged significant looks with Marge.

"Siddown, everyone," Marge growled. Even if Marge didn't have the personality of General Sherman's younger (and meaner) brother, her massive jaw, column-shaped figure, and steely eyes would have made her a commanding presence. When Marge told you to "siddown," you did. Especially Mayor Henry, who felt (not wrongly) that the moment Marge decided to run for mayor, he might as well pack up his Samsonite and retire to Zolfo Springs, Florida, where his older brother ran a trailer park. The mayor sat. Everyone, including Quill, sat, too.

One of the most important adjuncts to the mayoral office was the gavel, which the mayor carried in a custom-made case in his sports coat pocket. With all due solemnity he withdrew it now and rapped it on the mahogany surface of the conference table. "This meetin' is called to order."

"Use the *rest*, Elmer," Marge snapped. "You're going to dent Quill's table yet."

Elmer chose not to gavel again at all. He put the little hammer back in its case and said kindly, "We're here to apologize, Quill. And to he'p you if we can."

"Apologize? What for?"

"Kinda let you down," Marge said gruffly. "Switching the Chamber meeting to the Legion Hall, and all."

"I knew why," Quill said. "And I understood completely. Lunches here were getting very expensive."

"We can find the money. You can always find the money." Marge drummed thick fingers on the table. "Thing was, I was kinda thinking maybe you didn't need the customers, know what I mean? That maybe we should give somebody else a chance at the income. And the Legion's a good cause.''

"That's okay, really.''

"Thing is, we didn't know how tough things was for you. Not that our once a week lunches dropped all that much to the bottom line.''

They helped, Quill said silently. Paid a good portion of poor Dina's salary for the day. Quill was alert, last night's fatigue gone. Marge was up to something, and she wanted to know what. She had engineered the switch to the Legion; why the change of attitude now?

"Anyways. What's done is done. Thing is, we wanna start meetin' here again—right, folks?''

There was general assent among those present.

"And we thought as how you might wanna be seketary again. Although Betty don't mind it, do you, Betty.'' This wasn't a question, just as the decision to make Betty secretary had nothing to do with what Betty wanted. Betty, the thin, silent partner to Marge's bulky voluble one, cast Quill a look of appeal. Quill resisted it. She hated being secretary.

"Gosh,'' Quill said. "Well, actually, you might as well know by now. In addition to the—the—'' She searched for an appropriately diffident word. Hemlockians were notoriously diffident. ''. . . ah—fuss here last night, John's had to take another job. In Long Island. With a bank. It's a great opportunity for him,'' she added unhappily. "He'd be crazy not to take it.''

To her surprise—although given the nature of the Hemlock Falls bush telegraph, she shouldn't have been— her announcement of John's departure didn't seem to be news to anyone at the table. "Anyway, that means I'll be taking over the accounting function.''

"You kiddin'?'' Marge demanded. "Now *that's* a mistake. No offense meant, Quill.''

"None taken. At any rate, I'll be a little too busy to pay the right kind of attention to the Chamber minutes that they deserve. So, Betty, if you don't mind."

"She don't," said Marge, although Betty clearly did. "So that's items one and two. We're gonna start havin' meetings here again, and Betty here stays seketary. Okay. Item three."

The mayor pulled his gavel out of the case and whacked the table. "Who's mayor here anyways, Marge Schmidt?"

Fortunately for the mayor's manly feelings, no one answered that question. "I am, right? So here's item three, Quill. We got a volunteer work crew lined up to do the cleanup on that room that burned, soon as that damn-fool Denny completes his investigation. So don't you worry about that. You take what ever that saves you from that insurance money and use it to tide you over, just till business gets better again."

"Oh, my." Quill wasn't sure what to say. Cleanup was going to be an awful job, smelly, dirty, and exhausting. "I really appreciate it. It's extremely generous."

"Phuut," Marge said dismissively. "Now. The last thing. And the biggest. We're gonna work all together to do something about the state of business in this town. And that, Quill, is gonna involve the Inn. Big time. The person who's got the best idea I've heard of in a long time is Ms. Summerhill here. Selena? You wanna give the folks a rundown on your idea." This last sentence, in typical Marge style, wasn't a question, but a command.

Selena stood and slid both hands down the sides of her pantsuit in a nervous gesture. Her accent, which Quill almost never noticed, except in the way she selected her words, became marked. "Thank you, friends," she said formally, "for the opportunity to speak to you here today."

"Here, here," said Harvey, apropos of nothing in particular, except, Quill suspected, Selena's undeniable elegance. The effect of this was to throw Selena momentarily off stride. She began again. "Thank you, friends. I come to talk to you today about the chance to put our town on the map. Not just the map it is already on, which is the New York State map, you understand, but the Map of Success." She sent Harvey a questioning glance.

He nodded benign approval, then, in his Harveylike way, added, "Good. Snappy. Very snappy."

"And so," Selena continued, "I thank you." She sat down.

"Huh?" said the mayor. He looked around accusingly, as though someone had swiped Selena's speech when he wasn't looking.

Selena, flustered, stood up again. "So. I didn't say it, did I? Harvey, you will not speak when I am speaking, *comprende*? And I will say what I have come to say." She steepled her hands and tapped her chin with her fingertips. "I am not accustomed to speaking in public. Which is what Hugh does, usually? *Mi esposo*. Of course, I am not accustomed to catching wild dogs, either, and can do that, so here it is. You will excuse the nerves.

"You all know that New York is the premier grower of wines in the United States of America. California is nice, of course, but"—she flung her hands out dramatically—"*we have better whites!* Now. How many people know of this? Not enough. Not nearly enough. And how many people drink wine? Many, many, many. Although not so many as in Spain. Not yet, anyway. We, the winegrowers of New York, would like all wine drinkers to know about this. White wine drinkers especially. Therefore, we are declaring this year, beginning now, the Year of the Grape!'' She paused. It was an applause pause, clearly. But since Harvey's intervention had thrown her off stride before, no one wanted to discompose her again.

Quill, finally, said firmly, ''Hooray!'' which Selena received with a grateful look.

''The Year of the Grape,'' she repeated. ''What will this mean for Hemlock Falls? First, a gala fair to celebrate the harvest in October. The place? The Inn at Hemlock Falls. The people? All the tourists who will come when we begin to advertise this oh so significant event. I have many, many ideas to celebrate the Year of the Grape. The fair is only the first of them. We have Ice Wines, to draw celebrants and wine drinkers in winter. In spring, all of the boutique wineries around our Finger Lakes will begin their testing and tasting of the year's previous harvest. I have many, many ideas. Harvey, he, too, has many, many ideas. And we have set up a calendar of events—just a proposed one—which I will distribute to you at the end of this meeting.

''Now. The money part. Who will fund this oh so brilliant idea? I have been in touch with our governor. I have asked him, Sir, do you wish all people to leave New York because of high taxes and bad business? He does not, he says. And does he wish upstate and central New York to stop being depressed? Does he want happy voters who will drink our wines and be even happier? He does, he says. So my Hugh, he presents a request for a grant to this governor. And my Hugh—he gets it! So, my friends, on behalf of all our failing businesses here in Hemlock Falls, I say: *Hola!*'' She grabbed her large leather purse and pulled out a number ten envelope. She turned it outward, so that all at the table could see the gubernatorial seal on the upper left-hand corner. ''This letter? It promises the funds. Through this county program to which my Hugh has made application. Friends! We are in business. I thank you.''

This time, with Selena safely seated, the applause was long, loud, and even rowdy. Quill herself began to cheer.

''Mrs. Summerhill? Mrs. Summerhill.'' Mayor Henry lumbered to his feet. ''Thank you all, thank you. Mrs. Summerhill gave a very nice report. But I think you should all understand just what this money's for. You may have noticed in the newspaper'' (Quill hadn't. She hadn't had time to read the newspaper or watch the news since their financial crises began.) ''that the governor's office announced the passage of Senate Bill 172, which establishes a fund to promote tourism in Upstate New York. This fund is on account of we're in a depression, and the rest of the durn country's in hog heaven. What Hugh Summerhill did was hook up with some folks he knows in Albany and get them to cut us a pretty big piece of that pie. The State's sending some fella from the budget office down to speak to us tomorrow. He's going to explain how much money there is, and how we can get it. It appears that this money is just for businesses that will he'p promote tourism, folks. So, of course, we hope that you, Quill and Meg, will be right there along with everyone else. Because,'' he said with the ingenuousness that helped him get reelected every four years, ''the Inn's the biggest tourist attraction around here.''

''State money, huh,'' Meg said. It was late at night, well after eleven. They were in Quill's suite. Quill had lit sandalwood incense against the sour smell of smoke that still hung in the air. Although the actual damage from the fire had been contained to the room where Ellen Dunbarton died, the smoke odor permeated everything. They'd opened every single window in the building during the day, and it had helped some but not much. ''So that's why Marge is being so friendly. And it's why she wants to buy us out, of course. We're saved, Quill!''

''Yes.'' She nursed her glass of wine. If John was right—and she'd never known John to be wrong about financial matters—it didn't matter how many tourists showed up to celebrate the grape. They still wouldn't be able to make the mortgage payment. ''You can't just meet payroll and pay the bills every month,'' he'd explained over and over. ''You have to anticipate that money buys less and less as the years go on, and that your assets are costing you *more* to keep as the years go by. You're not listening, are you, Quill?''

She hadn't listened.

Quill and Meg sat on the pale leather couch facing the French doors. They were closed against the chilly night air, but she'd left the drapes wide open, and they had a fine view of the stars. ''State money,'' Quill said aloud. ''The meeting's at Summerhill tomorrow at noon. In the tasting room.''

''How much money is there?''

''It's a matching fund. I suppose we'll find out how much is allocated to our county tomorrow, when the man from Albany fills us in. You get fifty thousand dollars in grant money for every employee attached to a new business. Hugh's idea, apparently, is to form an Upstate Winegrowers' consortium and have each of the village businesses belong. We're ideally suited, of course, since we're the largest place available for dinners and wine tastings and the like. Esther West, on the other hand, is opening a side business specializing in wine thingies, so that she can be eligible for funds, too.''

''Wine thingies?''

''Wine-related products. Glasses with the Hemlock Falls logo on it—did I tell you the Chamber is holding a referendum to change our town symbol to something grapey?'' .

"We have a town symbol?"

"I think it's a cow at the moment. Because of all the dairy business. Anyway, Esther wants to sell souvenirs and momentos. The kinds of touristy things people can take away with them after a festival."

"So why am I dubious? For that matter, why are you dubious?"

"It's the loss of control. If we join this consortium, who's going to be dictating the way we do business, Meg? And you won't let a New York State red in our cellar, and neither will John. Well, neither *did* John. They just aren't good enough yet for a first-class restaurant. And the tourists are coming in to drink New York product. In something like this, there are going to be a whole lot more people calling the shots. It's an awful lot like a business merger, Meg. Which means that we're going to lose some independence."

"Better than our shirts."

"Are you sure about that? You're the first one to scream bloody murder when somebody tries to tell you how to cook."

Meg looked startled. "Who's going to tell me how to cook?'

"I don't know. But I've got a pop quiz for you. Who calls the shots in the village now?"

"Marge." Meg sat bolt upright as this sank in. "Marge Schmidt!"

"You get an 'A.' Who offered to buy the Inn last night, before news of this fund got out? Who was as sweet as rhubarb today, organizing the volunteer cleanup of poor Ellen's room?"

"Rhubarb's not sweet."

"No, but it's as sweet as Marge gets."

"Point taken."

"What I do know is that this winegrowers' union will radically change the way we do business. So I don't

know if we should leap at it. And I certainly don't see
it as our salvation. Not yet. And there's something else.''

"Ah.''

"What do you mean, ah?'' Quill said crossly.

"I mean all of these objections have sounded vague.
No facts. Just feelings.''

"You should have heard Selena's speech. The facts
were there, all right, but no one knew what she meant
until Elmer got up and explained. She said she doesn't
have the kind of brain that retains them. Her brain is
more feminine, she said.''

"Oh, baloney! It's work to pin things down, Quill.
And just like somebody else I know, Selena's a leetle
lazy intellectually.''

"Are you accusing *me* of being intellectually lazy?''

"Heavens, no.''

Quill, who was tired, chose to let this pass. It was too
late (and Meg was probably too right) to go into her
character deficits.

Meg stretched her legs onto the oak chest Quill used
as a coffee table. "Anyway. It sounds like an incredible
opportunity to me. Just when we're really down on our
uppers, along comes this fabulous idea to get tourist
trade into a sinking economy. I mean, face it, Quill. Upstate New York probably wasn't the best choice to open
a business. The taxes are intolerable. John's been telling
us for a year that we simply can't afford to operate. Do
you realize that if we were running this business in a
state without a state income tax that we would have
enough cash to keep John on at a livable salary? That if
we didn't have to pay almost twenty thousand a YEAR
in worker's compensation taxes we could keep Dina on
full-time and she could finish her dissertation?!''

Quill gazed at her, openmouthed. "When did you re-
tain all this? Business never interested you?!''

"I haven't been completely deaf to John's warnings.

Look, all I'm saying is that your life's work is in this place. I don't want to see it go down the tubes any more than you do.''

"You'll put Summerhill port in the cellar? Their table red on the wine list?''

Meg was pale, but her voice was steady. "I don't think it will come to that. I think it's negotiable. A lot depends on how this meeting goes tomorrow. If it looks like we're going to be railroaded into compromises we can't make in good conscience, then we'll just kiss that grant money good-bye and find our way out of this mess some other way. But we can do it, Quill. *We can do it!!*''

Quill tried not to look as sour as she felt. "You're right.''

"Right? I'm inspired. You call Selena right now and set up a meeting for us tomorrow, before that person from Albany talks to the town. We want to have our ideas about the Summerhill–Inn at Hemlock Falls Axis lined up and ready to roll when the politico asks his questions.''

"What axis are you talking about?''

"Gourmet dinners and winery tours? Are you kidding? It's political power, Quill. It's that axis.''

"The Axis powers lost the war.''

"Pooh! If we work together, I can plan menus that'll draw the gods from Olympus. I can cook dinners that will make almost anyone forget about the taste of New York reds. Go on, Quill. Call Selena now. Take her up on her offer to work together. It doesn't have to be formal—tell her we'll meet her just before the noon meeting for the public.''

Quill hesitated. "Are you sure?''

"Positive. Come on, sweetie. This whole week has been a big depressing mess for you. I mean, you're so bummed you even adopted an ugly dog. You have to cheer up before we end up with a menagerie. Call Selena, Quill. It's going to be fun.''

Not certain as to how much of this enthusiasm was forced, and how much was genuine, Quill gave up. She looked up Summerhill Winery's number, talked to Hugh, and arranged a "preliminary discussion of possible joint plans" for eleven the next morning.

Quill hung up and chuckled. "He may be 'her Hugh,' Meg, but boy is he stuffy.''

"Are we on?"

"We're on." She looked at Meg intently. "Meggie. Tell me something. How come you've got all this information about taxes and worker's comp on the brain anyway?"

"Because I've been listening to John for the past six months even if you think I haven't. I know what's going on, Quill, even if you think I don't.''

"You do, huh?"

Meg sprang to her feet. "Forget it. All I want to know before I go to bed is why you aren't jumping for joy that the cavalry's coming over the hill with reinforcements.''

"Because," Quill said slowly.

"Because? That's it? Because?"

"It's too pat. You realize that everyone in town knows we've been in trouble?"

"I suppose."

"The insurance policy business . . ."

"Where you 'forgot' to tell John you'd written those checks on the business account, and the premium check bounced? Yeah.''

"I did forget," Quill said weakly. "And if I have to say I'm sorry one more time I'm going to throw a fit of hysterics you wouldn't believe.''

"Okay, okay, okay. I'm sorry. So, everyone in town knows that we were about to be uninsured . . .''

"I mean, we bank here, and the insurance policy that was canceled was from the Peterson Agency, which is right on Main Street next to—" Quill stopped.

"Next to what?"

"Marge's diner," Quill said slowly. "Don't you think it's just a little bit coincidental that the fire occurred the day the policy lapsed?" she asked, after a moment.

"Ol' Sock-it-to-me Burke certainly seems to think so," Meg said.

"Well, I think so, too. I think someone is trying to put us out of business."

"You inhaled too much smoke last night."

"Think about it, Meg. Everyone knew we were in the middle of turning that suite into two rooms so we could get a little more income. The remodeling hadn't started, but we weren't booking anyone into that room. Until I took Ellen Dunbarton and her friends on that tour, and she loved the view, and asked to sleep in it at the very last minute, and if I hadn't said fine, she'd still be alive." Quill put her hand to her eyes for a moment. Meg patted her knee. "Anyhow. For all the world knew, that suite was empty. I tell you what I think, Meg. I think that somebody torched that room on purpose. Without knowing anyone was in it, to be perfectly fair. But I think someone wants to buy us out. Force us to the wall. Get us to the point where we can't afford to go on anymore."

"And who is this mysterious someone?"

Quill couldn't say it. Not even to her sister. But she thought it. Unworthy, nasty, spiteful, unjustified as it was, she thought it.

Marge Schmidt.

CHAPTER 4

Quill woke early to sunlight flooding her bedroom and a deadweight at her feet. She lay motionless for a moment, then wiggled her toes under the blanket. The weight shifted, rolled, then thumped to the floor. "You," she said to the dog.

He approached the bed cautiously, head down, tail waving frantically. He nudged her hand with his head, then leaped away. He smelled awful, a combination of smoke, mud, and unwashed dog.

Quill sat up. "How are you getting in?"

He went to the bedroom door, barked once, then looked appealingly over his shoulder.

"I take it there were no alarms in the night, or you would have licked my face off."

He sat down with a sudden, exhausted movement and put his head between his paws. His days in the wilds of Hemlock Falls were doing nothing for his looks. He was dirtier than ever, and there were bare spots on his sides. She looked at the bedside clock: six o'clock, and the sun was already well over the horizon. Hooray for May. She loved it when the days got longer. She supposed she could sneak into the kitchen and get the dog something to eat. Unless she had something appropriate in her little refrigerator. She mentally reviewed the contents: white wine, some cheese, eggs, and skim milk. And a loaf of Meg's rye bread.

"Bread and milk, boy?" She supposed she'd have to think of a name. With his pendulous lower lip, grizzled whiskers, and slyly mischievous expression, he looked a little like a sketch of Max Beerbohm she'd seen in the Oak Room at the Algonquin. "Max?" she said.

"Woof."

"Come on, Max. Food, and then maybe a bath."

She threw on her oldest pair of jeans, a T-shirt she used to paint in, and pulled an old pair of tennis shoes over her bare feet. Max followed her downstairs. When she reached the foyer, he turned left, to go down the hall to the Tavern Bar. Curious, she went after him.

The Tavern was quiet, deserted, smelling faintly of smoke—the cigarette kind rather than the fire. The only places that had been affected by the conflagration of two nights ago were the second and third floors. Max headed directly for the long bank of windows facing the vegetable gardens. He crawled under the small round table set into the corner and disappeared from view. Quill crouched down and went after him. Max was a large dog. At his normal weight, he'd be close to her own of 120. Any hole he could go in and out of, she could, too.

Max had been getting in and out through a loose bottom windowpane. Quill poked experimentally at the crumbling wood and groaned. More repairs. More bills. And this expense could have been prevented. At some point in the Inn's history, this side of the building had housed a conservatory, and Quill had insisted that they leave the charming roof-to-foundation windows in place when she and Meg had done renovations eight years ago. The contractor had warned her the frames would rot out, and he'd been right.

She crawled out the opening and into the damp morning air. Max barked happily at her. "You didn't pull this away by yourself, did you, Max?" She took a close look at the wood. Someone—and she didn't believe it was Max, had pushed the frame in from the outside; the newly splintered wood around the frame pointed into the room, not out. And the damage was recent.

Quill stood up. This entire side of the building would be in full view of anyone walking the grounds or working among the raised beds. She could see the garden shed from here, and the whole length of the path winding around this side of the house. No trees, no high shrubs. And no floodlights. The outside lighting was all at the front of the Inn, not back here where there was nothing in particular to see. So whoever had broken in had done it at night. And within the last forty-eight hours. The floor beneath the table had been dry; there had been no rain yesterday. Quill got down on her hands and knees and examined the frame closely again. She found a scrap of reddish-gold hair (her own), tufts of dirty brown fur (which explained the bare spots on Max's side), and a bottle cap, pierced through the middle. She'd seen that bottle cap before. "Ellen Dunbarton," she said to Max. "Now why in the heck would Ellen Dunbarton be crawling into the Inn at night? Why didn't she just ring? Because whoever let her in would know she'd been out, that's why. But who would care? Unless somebody here was suspicious of her already? Because she didn't want anyone to know she'd been out?"

Max, who had been following this monologue with upright ears and a puzzled expression, barked loudly. "Shh, Max. You'll wake everyone up. Whisper, Max, whisper."

"Woof," Max said in a very small voice.

Quill was absurdly delighted with her first foray into

dog training. She crouched and ruffled his ears. "C'mon, Max. Let's go get you some food. Breakfast, Max, breakfast."

Since the Inn was still locked for the night, she crawled back in the way she'd come out. Max wriggled through behind her, and together they went to the kitchen. Quill rummaged through the Zero King, giving Max a running commentary of the contents. "Well, there's some leftover chicken liver pâté, but not much. Meg uses one part butter to one part chicken liver, did you know that, Max? Guaranteed to give you a major heart attack. And the cognac in it will make you sneeze. Let's see. Well, there's rice, Max. Which is supposed to be good for a dog in your condition, which, if you'll pardon me, is perfectly awful. How would you like it if I beat up a couple of eggs in the rice, and later we go down to Nicholson's and pick up some real dog food. Something healthy."

"So you've named him," John said. "I told you that was the beginning of the end."

Quill whirled, startled. He was dressed in a three-piece suit, and he was freshly shaved. She caught the faint drift of shampoo. "I hardly recognized you."

He spread his hands in a deprecatory way. "I've got a meeting at ten."

"In Syracuse?"

"Long Island."

Dismayed, Quill said, "So soon?"

"Waiting isn't going to help, Quill."

"But we haven't even had time to say good-bye. Oh, my, that sounds like a bad Country Western ballad, doesn't it? What I meant is that I haven't had time to adjust to this, John. You're part of the Inn for me."

"Like the furniture?"

She was taken aback at the bitterness in his voice. "Like the furniture?!"

He took a step nearer. Max growled. Quill took a deep breath, then another. "I was just about to make some breakfast. And coffee. We need coffee."

"Coffee? You mean you'd like to sit down and talk?"

"I think that's a good idea, don't you?" Quill was proud that her voice was steady. The set of John's shoulders relaxed, and he settled onto a stool at Meg's worktable. The moment—whatever it was, and Quill knew she was afraid to guess—seemed to have passed. Quill poured them both some orange juice, started the coffee, then dumped leftover rice, two eggs, and some beef broth into a bowl for Max. "I'm not a bad hand at an omelet, you know."

"Sounds good."

She turned up the Aga, broke four eggs into a copper bowl and whipped them briskly to a froth. "I'm not used to being uncomfortable with you, John." She got out the omelet pan, poured a little olive oil in it, and set it on the burner.

"You're not used to talking about feelings, Quill." He smiled a little. "Unless it's squabbling with Meg."

"I think I'm more used to putting feelings on canvas." She poured the eggs into the pan with extraordinary care. She didn't want to look at him.

"You put your political views on canvas. Not emotions."

This made her indignant. "That's a rotten thing to say. And I'm not particularly political. If I were a political sort of person, I'd throw out half the people who show up at this Inn."

"Then I should have said observations, not political views. You observe life, Quill. You don't really live it. It's one of the reasons—" He stopped, perhaps, Quill thought, because the coffee he was drinking was too hot.

"One of the reasons what?"

"One of the reasons why you won't marry Myles."

Quill flipped the omelet with a quick twist of her wrist and set it back on the burner with a sharp bang. Her immediate response to this was four letters, seven if you counted the pronoun ''you,'' and she'd never spoken it aloud in her life. Instead she said tightly, ''Back off. Just back off.''

''I've backed off for seven years. That's enough time served, I think.'' He stood up. Quill forced herself to stand still, chin up. ''So all I'll say is this. I've loved you all that time. Your hair never stays up. Half the time you run around in a droopy skirt with your shirttail hanging out. You can't drive, you won't add up the checking account, and the rest of the time you spend avoiding doing real work, real painting. And—'' He checked himself. ''You're beautiful. I've loved you from the moment I saw you. And I'm never coming back here again.''

He turned on his heel and walked out.

Max whined.

Quill let the omelet burn and cried until she couldn't stand the smoke anymore. She dumped the pan in the sink.

''Jeez-Louise, what the heck did you do in here this morning?'' Meg banged into the kitchen dressed, Quill saw, to go out. She wore her best black chinos, a lichee-green vest, and a white cotton shirt. She'd tied a little enameled butterfly on a rawhide string around her throat. ''Aaagh! The dog!'' She eyed Max, who'd taken a position on the rag hearth rug in front of the cobblestone fireplace. ''He needs a bath.''

''It's not 'the Dog.' His name is Max. And I'll give him a bath later. When it gets really warm outside.''

''Uh-oh. So you named him. John said once you name an animal, you're doomed to own it for life. Looks like he's right. Doreen's going to have seven fits and a temper tantrum. That coffee?'' She grabbed a cup, then sat in the rocking chair next to Max. She nudged him amiably with her toe. Max growled and bared his teeth. She tucked both feet under the chair. ''Jeez. Where is he?''

''Right there.'' Quill got up from the stool where she'd been sitting, head in hands, and went to the sink. She began to scrub the omelet pan with a wire brush.

''Not the dog. John. His car was out front when I got up this morning, and when I came down, it was gone.''

''So's John.''

''Gone?''

''To Long Island.''

''Already?'' Quill could feel Meg's gaze on her back. She refused to turn around. After a moment, Meg added, ''I was right, wasn't I?''

''You were right.''

Meg sighed happily. ''I love it when you say I'm right.''

''It's not funny, Meg.''

''No. It's not. I'm sorry.''

Quill scrubbed at the last of the burned egg, rinsed the pan, and set it in the drainer. She turned around.

''Oh, Quill,'' Meg said. ''I'm so sorry. You look like you've been crying for weeks.''

''Just cool it, will you?''

''Well, you do.''

Quill felt the tears start again and she waved her hands helplessly in the air. ''Say something.''

''What?''

''Anything.'' Quill gulped. ''If you don't I swear I'll keep this up all day.''

''Might be good for you,'' Meg said quietly.

''I don't want to talk about it.''

''You never want to talk about it.''

''Whose business is it if I DON'T WANT TO TALK ABOUT IT!?''

''Yours, of course. I just want to say one thing, and then will never ever mention John again, all right? We've lost a valuable friend. We've lost a terrifically shrewd and capable business partner. If you'd talked about it, worked through it, addressed it, years ago, he might still be here. And happily married to somebody else. Okay?''

''What do you mean, happily married to someone else?''

''What? You want him to pine away for you forever? Come on, Quill. And you accuse *me* of being the romantic. People get over things. It isn't easy. I should know. And you should know that I know. When Simon died, you know what happened to me. I wanted to die, too. And look. Eight years later I'm just as in love with Andrew Bishop, the best-looking—and only—internist in Hemlock Falls. Don't be so afraid of pain, Quill. It can't kill you. Not unless you let it.''

''Lecture over?''

''For the moment.''

''Good. Because I've had it with your blithe assumption that everyone can be as open and confrontational as you can without risk. Okay?''

''Okay.''

''So we're going to talk about something else. Right?''

''Whatever you want. How come you're not dressed?''

Quill looked at her T-shirt and jeans. ''I'm dressed.''

''I mean to go to the winegrowers' meeting. Didn't I sit in your room last night while you called a meeting with Selena and Hugh Summerhill to see about scheduling romantic wine weekends for any hapless tourists that may come our way? Wasn't this the first strike in the war against high taxes, insupportable business conditions, and the generally lethargic condition of the Upstate New York economy?''

''Oh, my gosh.'' Quill ran her hands through her hair. She'd washed it twice since the fire and it still smelled of smoke. ''And the guy from Albany's going to give a speech about the fund. What time was it? Noon, right? At Summerhill. And the discussion with Selena and Hugh was at eleven . . .''

''Yep. Now look, it's six-fifteen. The dining room opens at seven. I've got Kathleen coming in and one *sous*-chef, Bjarne, but breakfast is going to be heavier than lunch today. So you've got your choice, you can waitress in the dining room and let Kathleen help me in here in the kitchen or you can help me in the kitchen, and let Kathleen do the waitressing. Which?'' She cast a significant look in the direction of the scoured omelet pan.

''I'll help out in the dining room. It'll be just like old times, when we were starting out.''

''Great. But it'd be better for people's appetites if you changed those clothes. And Quill, your hair still smells like you had a close encounter with Smoky the Bear. Did you try the tomato juice?''

''I'm not going to wash my hair in tomato juice.''

''Sure you are.'' Meg held up a ''wait a minute'' finger, disappeared into the pantry, and reemerged with a forty-ounce bottle of Campbell's Tomato Juice (Not from Concentrate!).

Quill regarded the bottle dubiously, took it, splashed her face with cold water to erase the tearstains, then headed for the dining room doors. She was accompanied by the patter of untrimmed feet. She stopped, the juice bottle under one arm. ''Dang,'' she said. ''What about Max?''

''Can he wait tables?''

''I'm serious, Meg. What do I do with this darn dog?''

''Beats me. He's your dog, you figure it out. All I

know is that I don't want him in my kitchen, I don't want him in my rooms, and I'm pretty sure he'll bite the guests. So as long as he isn't on the grounds or in the building, or near me at *any* time, I don't mind him at all.''

"The garden shed?" Quill said to the dog. "No, you'd hate being locked up all day. What if you just go OUT, Max. And come back when you're hungry again. Got that? Go OUT. Keep away from people, other dogs, and Selena Summerhill, the dogcatcher." Max cocked his head, got up, turned and nosed his way through the dining room doors. They heard the click of his feet on the hardwood floor, and then nothing.

"Where's he going? Don't tell me, I can guess. He's going to sit in Doreen's mop closet and delight her with a savage attack when she gets her bucket."

"He's a very smart dog, Meg. I'll show you where he gets in and out later. Which reminds me, Meg. I have a clue."

"Yeah?"

Quill told her about the hole in the wall, and added, "Ellen didn't want anyone to know she'd been out. Do you find that strange?"

"That's supposition, Quill. Who's to say that Max didn't push himself in? What proof do you have that it was Ellen?"

"The bottle cap."

"Phut! She could have dropped that anytime. You'd better tell Mike to fix it, or we'll get wood rot or something."

"Don't you think I ought to let Davy Kiddermeister know?"

"Know what!? That you've got a burrowing dog? Your detective instincts are getting the better of you."

"There's a mystery here, Meg. I'm sure of it."

"The only mystery is how we're going to survive the

next couple of weeks,'' Meg said irritably. ''This was a terrible accident, Quill. Let's not borrow trouble.''

''I'm not so sure.''

Meg muttered something rude and busied herself with her pots.

Quill went up to her room to shower and change. It was without surprise that she discovered tomato juice didn't lather. It also made her feel sticky. By the time she was (relatively) tomato juice-free, it was after seven and the dining room would be open and the Crafty Ladies (who rose early) banging their forks and knives on the table like Jimmy Cagney in *White Heat.*

The Crafty Ladies were seated and waiting for service, but they were in no mood to be assertive. ''We called Ellen's family this morning,'' Robin said in a subdued voice. ''It was horrible. Horrible.''

''I'm very sorry.'' Quill hesitated. ''It's a cliché, of course, but if there's anything I can do, I wish you'd let me know.''

''Seems to me you did quite a lot already.'' Mary Lennox, in a yellow twinset this morning, gave her a short, approving nod. ''Not everyone would have dragged Ellen from that room.''

''I didn't stop to think,'' Quill said truthfully. ''If I had, I probably wouldn't have done it.''

''We talked to that young sheriff,'' Fran Grimsby said. ''About releasing the body.''

''Davy Kiddermeister. He's the brother of our waitress here, Kathleen.''

''If you ask me, I don't know if that young man knows whether he's coming or going,'' Fran said tartly. She was wearing the same hand-painted muumuu she'd had on the day before. The yoke had a bright orange sun which warred with pink surfers under a bright blue sky. The skirt was splashed with red hibiscus. ''Do you know he actually warned us not to leave town before the inquest?'' She snorted. ''Can you believe it?! What do you think the chances of that boy finding out what caused that fire are, anyway? Sounds to me like he's learned all his investigative techniques from the television. That's all young people today know about anything. From television.''

''Do any of you know . . .'' Quill began, then stopped. ''That is. Is there any reason Ellen would have wanted to meet someone here at the Inn secretly?''

The Crafty Ladies looked at her, clearly at sea.

''I *beg* your pardon?'' said Mary faintly. ''Secretly? What in the world are you talking about?''

''There's this dog,'' Quill began again.

''I told you,'' Fran said to the others. ''Small towns. Small towns. This is terrible. Terrible. Poor Ellen's horribly dead and look. People are talking already. And it's not even true!''

Tears filled Mary's eyes. She blinked them back. ''I can assure you that we never met anyone before in this horrible place. Any of us!''

Quill began to feel like a rat. ''I'm sorry. Truly. It's just that when something like this happens, your imagination begins to run riot.''

''Small towns,'' Fran said darkly. ''It goes to show.''

''Maybe we need a lawyer.'' Mary nervously fingered the pearls at her neck. They were genuine, at least eight millimeter. Quill was glad to see her surmise about the profitability of the craft business had been correct. ''Don't you think we need a lawyer?''

''A lawyer?'' Quill said, startled. ''Whatever for?''

''Shipping the body,'' Mary said simply. ''All that sort of thing.'' The tears brimming in her eyes spilled over. Quill felt awful. ''A man is so useful at times, don't you think? I mean, it's not very nice to say so these days, but there's a time when a girl just needs some protection. At our age, I guess you just have to buy it.''

"I see," Quill said, who did, in a way. "There's a very good one in town. Howie Murchison. Would you like me to give him a call for you?''

. The four women exchanged glances. "We'll see how it goes," Fran said. She seemed to have been elected spokesperson since Ellen's death. "We haven't had too much experience with lawyers.''

"I want to go home," Freddie Patch said. "This has been too awful to even think about. I want to see my grandchildren. There's nothing that'll cheer a person up more than grandchildren.''

Robin Robinson, who'd replaced her sequined sweat-shirt for a more seemly hand-crocheted sweater, patted Freddie's hand comfortingly. "We can't leave yet, any-way.'' She turned to Quill, her eyes gray and watery behind her spectacles. "Our president's been delayed again. We got a fax this morning. It'd be foolish to leave until we get our little business plans settled.''

"What about Ellen's funeral?" Freddie wailed. "We can't miss Ellen's funeral.''

"The sheriff won't release her—ah—the remains for a few more days yet. Not until the investigation's complete.'' Fran sat back in her chair with a "that's that" sigh, and picked up the menu. "Now. Who's for break-fast?''

Freddie, who couldn't have been more than four feet eleven standing, and seemed even smaller in the dining room chair, beckoned Quill to come closer. She bent down, and Freddie whispered, "We did want you to know that we don't believe for a moment you or your sister set that fire.''

"Of course we didn't!" Quill said.

"And that insurance money? There wouldn't have

been enough to cover your losses at the Inn—so that's not a motive.''

Quill straightened up and looked at her, astonished. "Who told you that?"

"That nice Marge Schmidt," Robin said. "We ran into her after that informal meeting the Chamber had here yesterday. She came into the Tavern Bar where we were all having our little—you know—drinkies before dinner, and she was asking us all kinds of questions."

"Questions like what?" Quill asked grimly.

"You know, were the rooms comfortable? Did we like the highfalutin food, or did we prefer plain old American cooking? That kind of thing."

"We told her we liked the food," Mary volunteered. "That World's Biggest Cream Puff was just delicious. Except there was some liquor in it."

"Brandy," Quill said.

"Right. Brandy! In a dessert! Anywise, I liked it a lot." This was said with a small air of defiance, as though there were those at the table who clearly had not. "Not every day, of course. I mean, gourmet (she pronounced it goremate) is so *rich*, don't you think?"

"I like a nice Jell-O ring for dessert myself," Fran said. "I've got a recipe with Cool Whip, cottage cheese, and pistachios if you'd like to pass it along to the cook."

"What else did Mrs. Schmidt want to know?"

Mary thought for a moment. "How comfy the beds were. Whether we missed not having a TV in the rooms. Whether maybe it'd be better to have, like, video games and an arcade out on the flagstone terrace for the kiddies. I told her it would be nice to bring my grandchildren to someplace like this, but I didn't much like arcade games. You get too many young people that way. You know, the kinds with tattoos and rings on their bodies."

"*My* grandson Jeffrey has a ring in his ear and it's perfectly acceptable!" Fran said with a huffy glare.

Mary twinkled. "Of course, dear. But Quill knows what I mean. Some of those nice brightly colored plastic swing sets for the kiddies. That'd be the thing. Out by the gazebo."

"We'll think about it," Quill said, forcing a big smile. "Have you decided what to have for breakfast?"

"Marge Schmidt was talking about her Breakfast Bake. Do you have a Breakfast Bake?" Freddie asked. "Ever since she gave me the recipe, I've been dying to try it."

"I'm not sure. Maybe Meg would like to try to make it. What's in it?"

"Condensed milk. Three cups shredded wheat. Eggs. That Kraft cheese, you know . . ."

"Velveteen?" Quill said.

"Velveeta. And you mix it all up and bake it for thirty minutes in a 350 oven."

"It sounds . . ." Gruesome. Repellant. Disgusting. Quill pinched her knee hard and said smoothly, ". . . as though it would take too long to bake today. But we'll see. In the interim, is there anything on the menu you would like?"

"The Omelet Suzette," Fran said. "With none of the sauce on it, please. Just plain. And a side of bacon. And toast. And some hash browns."

"That sounds good, Fran." Mary smiled at Quill. "I'll have that, too."

"I'll have the omelet, except I don't want the eggs beaten up and I want them over easy. And the rest of the sides Fran ordered," Freddie said. "Do you have wheat toast?"

Robin, on discovering that the Crepes a la Quilliam were flamed in cognac, shuddered, and asked for plain crepes, with syrup: Mrs. Butterworth's, if that was okay.

"I don't even know how to price this stuff," Meg

complained when Quill handed the breakfast orders over.

"Call up Marge," Quill said. "I told you, didn't I? Can you believe it? She went to the Tavern yesterday after all that support she offered us and tried to snatch our customers right under our noses! They were happy enough with our menu yesterday. They were perfectly willing to try new stuff. Now look at this: It's diner food. We can't charge gourmet prices for diner food!"

"Well, charge diner food prices."

"Great, then we'll be broker than we already are. Where are you going?"

Meg took off her apron, removed her chef's toque, and beckoned to Bjarne, the Finnish *sous*-chef. "Two on a shingle, a stack of cakes, a side of the hog, and three hashed." She raised her eyebrows at Quill and said loftily, "I don't mind having this cooked in my kitchen. I don't mind my *sous*-chef cooking this in my kitchen. The one thing I am not going to do is *cook it myself*!"

"This is delicious!" Freddie Patch said. "I've never had hash browns like this before. There's just a little bit of—um—what is there just a little bit of?"

"Garlic, parsley, a pinch of onion, paprika," Quill said. "The secret's in the potato. You need a firm white potato, shredded fine and chilled in ice water. Not a baking potato, not a red, and for goodness' sake, not a Yukon Gold."

The Crafty Ladies blinked at her. Now, Quill thought, that they are relatively settled and eating good food, is the time to do a little investigation. There had to be a really good reason why Ellen Dunbarton was crawling into the Inn two nights ago. And despite what Meg said, she knew Ellen had been crawling into the Inn two nights ago. "Would you mind if I sat with you a little bit? As you can see, we don't have anyone else in the dining room at the moment.''

"Make yourself at home," Mary said. She frowned to conceal her pleasure. "We've been wanting to have a little talk with you ever since we arrived."

"You have just a beautiful place," Freddie said.

Robin nodded vigorous agreement. "Ideal. Just ideal. The flowers. The waterfall. The decorations! You know that Mrs. Stoker?"

"Doreen, yes. Our head housekeeper."

"She said you're more famous than we thought. As a painter."

"I suppose so," Quill said cautiously.

"So you're the perfect person to talk to," Freddie said. "Just perfect. As an artist yourself, you'd be the first to sympathize."

"It's our crafts," Robin said. "That Mrs. Schmidt . . ."

"Um," said Quill darkly.

"She said that there's going to be big changes around here. Really big."

"What did she mean, big?" Quill asked, alarmed.

Robin blinked at her. "Why, the winegrowers' association. And the plans for a huge summerlong festival."

"Oh, yes. That."

Robin beamed. "It sounds wonderful, doesn't it?"

"It sounds like an opportunity," Fran broke in bluntly, "and we thought we'd see about getting a piece of the action ourselves."

"Fran," Freddie said gently, "don't be quite so aggressive, dear. It's hardly feminine."

"It's hard to be feminine these days and make a buck," Fran said. "It's hard to be feminine anytime and make a buck."

There was a soft murmur of agreement from the other ladies.

"Anyways, Marge told us about this Esther West and how she's thinking about importing some nice things for tourists."

"What? Oh. Yes. Esther runs a retail store in Hemlock Falls. West's Best Dress it's called. She's the logical choice to order tourist items; she's had a lot of experience with clothing and I shouldn't think it'd be too much of a stretch to order wine goblets and whatever."

"We're the logical choice to do it," Fran said with belligerent firmness. "Talk about experience. Ellen here worked at Tracey's in Housewares for thirty years. I saw all kinds of stuff as a customs agent in New York City. I remember where to get it, too. Those cute little telephone dolls, for instance, come right from Korea, eight cents a piece, F.O.B."

"Freight on Board," Mary explained kindly.

"All kinds of stuff." Fran took a breath. "Robin was in the law."

"Really?" Quill asked.

"Just a paralegal, but I learned a lot about contracts," Robin said modestly. "It was a real estate lawyer's office, actually."

"And there you are. She can look at the contracts and read them if anyone tries to cheat us. We've got talent coming out of our ears, haven't we, girls?"

Modest giggles greeted this sally.

"What was Ellen Dunbarton's husband like? What did he do?"

"Ellen? She was married to a travel agent. Darn good one, too. He got us some great deals on trips, let me tell you. We've seen some terrific places." Mary was animated in her excitement. "Hong Kong, Mexico."

"That's enough, Mary. Quill here doesn't want to hear all about our trips. Next thing, you'll be hauling out those danged slides and we'll all need a nap *before* lunch." Chuckles, this time, from the group. Fran turned earnestly and said, "Quill, if you've got some time today, we'd like to show you what we can do. And you'll want to see the whole magilla, all the products we got. What we can't get, we can make."

"Whoa, whoa, whoa." Quill held up her hands. "I'm sure that all this is true. But I'm not the person to talk to. Hugh and Selena Summerhill are the chief organizers behind the wine festival, and Selena mentioned yesterday that the State is sending an advisor in to talk with us about the restrictions that come with this grant money."

"Money," said Fran. "That's it. Show me the money."

A louder burst of laughter greeted this daring foray into current movie slang.

"Did you talk with Ellen about this—um—before she . . . well . . .''

"Passed on?" Freddie suggested. "How could we? We didn't know about it ourselves until yesterday afternoon."

"Oh. That's right, isn't it?" Quill bit her lip. Now what? "I meant to ask, before, when you mentioned you talked to her family this morning. Are they coming to get her? Her husband or someone else?"

"Richard's in the hospital," Mary said. "Bad arteries, they say. Hasn't been good for a long time."

"No, he hasn't been good," Freddie agreed sadly.

"Her daughter, maybe. But she's a no-good."

"Mary!" said Robin. "It's not right to speak ill of the dead."

"That daughter's not dead. She's just a waste of time. Big fancy lawyer in Detroit." Mary sniffed. "Hasn't spoken to her ma in five years," she explained. "Ellen worked herself to the bone all those years to support Richard's travel agency, and Richard being so sick all the while, and what does she get for it? Kid that won't even send her a Mother's Day card."

Quill, suddenly, felt the fool. The idea that this wholly normal lady with a normal set of problems would be crawling in and out of the Inn in the middle of the night was suddenly ridiculous.

"It's kids today," Freddie said with regret, jerking Quill back to the moment. "Poor Ellen wasn't the only one to have problems. We've all had them one way or another. Your boy, Fran . . ."

"That's enough about Jeffrey," Fran said curtly. "There's nothing wrong with my Jeffrey."

Drugs, Freddie mouthed silently. Then chirpily, "Let's not talk about that now. Let's talk about the happy things. What do you think, Quill? Would you introduce us to Mr. Summerhill, did you say? Is that the man in charge?"

"He and his wife Selena, yes. You met her day before yesterday, when we were out by the garden shed trying to catch the dog."

"That Mexican?" Fran said doubtfully.

"Fran! Move into the nineties." Freddie rapped Fran's arm with her table knife. "Honestly, you'd think that one of her closest friends wasn't a perfectly nice Mexican, Rosa Marguiles. Would you want Rosa to hear you say 'that Mexican' like that, Fran?"

"Besides, she's Spanish," Quill said.

"That's what they all say," Fran said.

Freddie shook her head. "She doesn't mean those things, Quill." She sighed. "So what do you think, Quill? Will you help us?"

"I'd love to help you, yes. I mean, not only do I think

I owe you something to make up for this terrible fire and Mrs. Dunbarton's ... um ...''

"Passage," Freddie said helpfully.

"Yes, passage. But I think you guys have a great idea and a lot of talent, and of course you can do well. But you don't need me to talk to Selena and Hugh. You can drop by the Summerhill Winery anytime and talk to them yourselves. You wanted a wine tour, too, didn't you? That might be a perfect time to sit down and talk about your proposal."

"Without an introduction?" Mary said. "I don't know. I'd be embarrassed, I think. I mean, she's a big shot, obviously, owning a whole winery and whatever. We can't just walk up and introduce ourselves."

"Sure you can," Quill said cheerfully.

Rocky Burke, looking the better for a solid night's sleep, came into the dining room from the foyer. He looked around, and seeing no one to seat him, sat himself at table seven—the one overlooking the Falls.

Quill nodded at him and got to her feet. "I see I have another customer. So, if you'll excuse me, I'll leave you now. I'll be back to check on you in a few minutes."

"Now see that, Fran," Quill heard Freddie say in an undertone as she approached Mr. Burke with a menu. "That's class. If we're going to do this as a real business, and do it right, that's what we'll need. A little class."

"Mr. Burke," Quill said. She laid the breakfast menu in front of him. "Would you like coffee or orange juice?"

"Sure," he said gloomily. "Both. And both fresh, if you don't mind. Can't stand coffee that's been stewing on a hot plate for hours."

"Our coffee's brewed at the table, and the orange juice is freshly squeezed," Quill said. She would keep her temper with this guy, just as she'd kept her temper with the unpleasant Fran Grimsby.

"Fine. And the eggs Benedict. Bring some coffee for yourself, why don't you? I've got a couple more questions for you."

"Sure." Quill went back into the kitchen. Meg was nowhere in sight, so she gave Bjarne the order for the eggs, and squeezed the orange juice herself. Just before the painful budget crunch, she'd talked John into buying individual Melitta coffee carafes for each table. The coffee could be ground at the table, and made in front of the guest. It worked out well for those guests who had a real appreciation of good coffee. And Rocky Burke, for all his boorish behavior, seemed to like good coffee. She loaded a tray with two glasses of orange juice, and two small drip pots, then asked Bjarne to serve the eggs himself when they were finished. "Table seven," she added.

"Ya. This is good to do. To have the chef appear. The hashes? Did they like that?"

"They loved it. And they'll love it if you stop by and ask them if they loved it. Table five. Well, you'll see. There's only two tables out there, and I'll be at the other."

"Business is picking up," he said gloomily, then winked. Bjarne was tall, pale, with eyes the color of a glass of plain water. He had, she realized, made a Finnish joke.

"Business is picking up," she agreed.

Rocky Burke swallowed the orange juice with an appreciative grunt.

"How's the investigation going?" Quill asked sympathetically.

"All right. I've been all over the place." He eyed her. "You're not going to believe it, but this place exceeds the New York State fire code."

"It does?" Quill said, pleased.

"Yeah. You two spent a ton. Didn't need to, but it's nice to see from my perspective. Codes here are stiffer than any other place in the U.S."

"They are?"

"Yeah. Lotta stupid requirements, if you ask me, but then, nobody did, did they? It's the city."

"New York City?"

He pointed a forefinger at her. "R-i-ight. Lot of slumlords that just as soon you burned up as pay the rent. Lot of these requirements are defensive, if you get my drift. But no, except for the fact that you had a fire that killed Ellen Dunbarton, aged sixty-two, married with three kids, you're in fine shape."

"Are you being sarcastic?"

"Nope. Just a little disappointed that it looks as though I'm going to have to pay that claim."

"So you don't think that my sister and I set that fire."

"Hell." He shrugged. "There's a certain profile to an arsonist, you know what I mean? Neither of you fit, and you haven't got anyone that works for you that fits either. Besides, whoever set that fire was a pro."

"A pro?"

"Big-time. He, she it, whoever used phosphorous. Hard to get. Used it right. Which is even harder. More than one arsonist's been blown up with his, her, its phosphorous bomb. Small loss. So. If I hadn't had my hackles raised, I never would have found it. Somebody climbed up your balcony and tucked the phosphorous bomb with a remote switch behind the bed curtains. They backed down, got away as far as a mile, maybe, and set the damn thing off. It ignited like that"—he snapped his fingers—"and what's more, consumed most of the evidence along with it. You can stick that sucker in your pocket—the whole thing's the size of a thick wallet. Thing is, our friend trimmed the fuse before he, she, it left. Must have fallen out of the perp's pocket, because I found it on the stone floor of the balcony.'' He reached into his breast pocket and showed Quill a plastic bag. A short piece of insulated wire was inside. ''There are scorch marks very typical of a phosphorus fire on the wall behind the drapes, near the phone stand. I understand that you put that fire out with your handy dandy extinguisher, or that evidence would have gone up with poor Mrs. Dunbarton, too. That was another thing that convinced me you didn't have a part in this, Cookie. Why would you have preserved evidence of the crime? Unless you were stupid.'' He looked at her, head cocked on one side. ''And you don't look stupid. Pretty, a little scatterbrained. But not dumb. Nossir.''

''Thanks, I think. I preferred your politically correct 'he, she, it,' frankly.''

''Your type would.''

Quill showed her teeth in a tight smile. ''Do you have any theories as to why the fire was set?''

''Got a preliminary autopsy report from the village doc. This guy's no slouch either. Wouldn't think an out-of-the-way b—''

''DON'T say 'burg,' '' Quill snapped. ''You're being too tough-guy to be believable.''

He shrugged, finally abashed.

''Your eggs,'' Bjarne announced, and set the plate of eggs Benedict down with a flourish. ''And yours, as well, madam.'' He set a second, smaller portion in front of Quill.

''Why thanks, Bjarne. I'm starved as a matter of fact.''

''So,'' Bjarne said glumly, ''how do you like it?''

''You the chef?''

Bjarne nodded.

''Wait a minute.'' Mr. Burke cut the eggs Benedict with care, making sure to include the crumpet, back bacon, eggs, and sauce. He ate it. He chewed thoughtfully. "Lime instead of lemon in the hollandaise," he said.

Bjarne nodded, sad as a hound dog.

"And this bacon's home-cured."

"It is. Our master chef, who has left the kitchen to me, takes great care with the bacon."

"Left the kitchen to you?" Quill said.

"For the time being," Bjarne admitted. "I am looking forward to this happening more often. If the eggs are good."

"The eggs are very good."

"Um, Bjarne . . ." Quill stood up. She had a sudden vision of Meg stamping down the driveway, her knapsack on her back, running away from home. "Maybe I'd better . . ."

"No, no, Quill. I will just stop and see if the Crafty Ladies require something different." He sighed. "You just do not know, with food. They may have hated it."

"This food's terrific, pal," Mr. Burke said. "Hope you get to do more in the kitchen."

"It is up to her." Bjarne shook his head, a Finnish Eeyore. "Yes, it is all up to her." He shuffled to table five, to address the Crafty Ladies.

"Guy needs Prozac," Mr. Burke said.

"He's a Finn," Quill said, with the feeling that this should explain it, but didn't. "Now, about the autopsy."

"You're not going to like it. I suggest you finish your Finnish eggs. I'm going to, before I give you the details."

They ate in silence for a while. Quill, who was very hungry, wondered why she didn't feel more optimistic. Fifty thousand dollars would go a long way toward payroll and the overdue grocery bill. If they could hold off until the winegrowers' association had the grant money coming in, there might be a way out of this after all.

If Rocky Burke really intended to settle the claim.

That was it. She didn't trust his confiding, open air. She didn't believe that she and Meg "didn't fit the profile of an arsonist." He thought he was being clever.

"Excellent!" Mr. Burke said. He breathed out in a satisfied way. "You ready?"

Quill nodded.

"You already knew the sprinkler system for that room was turned off."

"Yes. I tried to figure out why that happened, what the arsonist could have been thinking of."

"You don't have to be a rocket scientist to figure that one out, Cookie. So as much damage as possible would be done."

"Oh, I see."

"We didn't get any fingerprints from the shutoff valve, of course." His eyes slid sideways, met hers, then slid away again. She was right. He did still suspect them. "As for the deceased—the doc thinks it was duct tape, but he won't be sure until he gets the results from the forensics lab in Buffalo."

"Duct tape? What do you mean, duct tape?"

"Ellen Dunbarton's hands were strapped behind her back, and her mouth was taped shut. He stared at her openly now. "No doubt about it. She was murdered."

Quill, who had been rather wildly thinking of someone, anyone, who would want to put them out of business, sat up with a jerk. "You mean—the fire wasn't arson? It was homicide?"

"Exactly what I mean, Miss Quilliam." He stretched. "So that check? It'll have to wait till the perp's arrested and very probably convicted." He grinned. The smile didn't reach his eyes. "Takes a long time in this country."

"Tell me something. Why would I want to murder a guest? Why would my sister want to murder a guest?

And for God's sake, why would I choose such an ugly way to do it?''

"Lot of crazies in the world. How should I know why people do what they do?''

Quill looked over at Freddie, Mary Lennox, and Robin. She even felt awful for the horrible Fran. "Has anyone told them?''

"Not my job, Cookie.'' He got up and flung his napkin on the table. "Be seeing you.'' His glance was speculative. "One way or the other.''

CHAPTER 5

Hugh Summerhill looked all that his name implied: tall, erect, with thick dark hair silvered at the temples. He was very good-looking in a Louis Auchincloss sort of way. He was some years older than Selena; Quill had heard there had been a first marriage, with children, that had dissolved in divorce several years before he'd purchased his twenty-six acres of farmland in Hemlock Falls. He sat at ease in the Summerhill living room, legs crossed, with a detached, pleasant expression.

Quill sat across from Hugh and Selena, deep in a comfortable leather chair. She'd been in many rooms like this one as a girl in Connecticut, including her own family's. The floor was polished oak. The couches were soft, well worn, and plushy to sit in. They were covered in a subtly elegant floral pattern—almost chintz, but not quite. Books were scattered around the room. They spilled over the cherry end tables and on the floor near Hugh's recliner. More volumes were stored haphazardly in the floor-to-ceiling bookshelves dominating the north wall.

The south wall looked out over Cayuga Lake, blue-gray under the spring sun. There were spring flowers everywhere: lilacs, apple blossom, a few branches of flowering plum.

Selena bloomed like a hothouse lily in the middle of this shabbily comfortable restraint. She wore a bright orange T-shirt, white trousers, and sandals on her slender feet.

"May we have some coffee, Selena?" Hugh's voice was cultivated, assured, resonant. "Meg and Quill should undoubtedly shore up their defenses against the assault from the man from Albany."

"But of course!" Selena unfolded herself from the couch. "You take a bit of cream, Quill. And, Meg? Black, as I recall." She disappeared into the kitchen, the heavy scent of gardenia in her wake. Hugh wrinkled his nose slightly; it was, Quill admitted, a little over-powering this early in the day.

"You've met him?" Meg asked. "The bozo from the State office?"

"No." His tone was amused. "Not this particular bozo. But I agree with you." He dropped his left eyelid in a wink. "Most politicians are bozos."

"What sort of approach to the—ah—bozo did you have in mind?" Quill asked.

"I take it there's some interest, on your part, in presenting a joint effort between Summerhill and the Inn to encourage oenoephiles to come to this area?"

"We're not sure," Meg said candidly. "A great deal would depend on the parameters we set up. Yesterday at the Chamber meeting, Selena said . . ."

He waved one hand in a dismissive gesture that was at once paternal and affectionate. "I drilled Selena on her delivery to the Chamber at the meeting yesterday, but I didn't have to check with Harvey to know how it went. She was scatterbrained, ineffectual, and utterly charming."

Meg coughed.

Quill pulled on her lower lip. "I thought she made a very knowledgeable speech."

"Selena doesn't have the presence to make a knowledgeable speech, much less a coherent one, do you, my darling?"

Selena, carrying a loaded tray in from the kitchen, set it down on the coffee table and threw her arms around Hugh's neck. "I do not, *cariño*. But you love me anyway, do you not?"

"Indeed I do." Rather awkwardly, he slipped his arm around her waist and squeezed.

Quill pulled harder on her lip. She didn't dare look at Meg.

"Sit and pour out for us, my darling."

"With pleasure, *cariño*." She sat close to him, and served him first. He refused the cup, and nodded toward Quill. "Ah. Of course!" She poured a small dollop of cream into the cup, presented it to Quill, and then served Meg. She poured out for Hugh, then herself, and settled happily back into the circle of his arm.

Meg, who was sitting at right angles to Quill, bent over and stared intently at the tip of her shoe. Quill glanced at her, curious; Meg turned her head away from the Summerhills and mouthed, Oh, *thank* you, my darling! then straightened up.

"Are you too warm, poor Quill?" Selena said with concern. "Hugh. Perhaps we should put the air-conditioning on. Quill's face is quite flushed."

"Oh, no! I'm fine. The coffee was a little warmer than I expected." She coughed hard, then assured Selena that no, no, she didn't want an ice cube for her cup and said, "Meg and I discussed the possibility that we might design a series of gourmet dinners in conjunction with the presentation of the Summerhill Chardonnays, Hugh."

The discussion was leisurely but productive. They agreed to each establish a tentative joint agreement, and reconvene the discussion later in the week. At that point, Quill suggested, they should bounce the idea off the Chamber of Commerce, to see how the town reacted to it. "It is public money," she said, "and we'll need to find some way to benefit everyone."

Hugh glanced at his watch. "The public meeting is due to start in fifteen minutes. If I know the villagers, they'll be arriving right about now. I asked Pfieffer to stop by a little early, so I could take the measure of the man. Selena, how are the preparations for lunch?"

"Very good. You will be pleased."

"Go into the kitchen and make certain everything is in order, will you please? And then meet us in the tasting room. The only place," he added, turning to Quill, "where there is enough room to accommodate the *hoi polloi*." The doorbell rang. Hugh rose. "That will be Pfieffer. Will you think me rude if I don't accompany you to the tasting room? I'd like a few moments alone with this man. You know your way."

Heigh-ho, dismissed, Quill thought. "Of cour—I mean, yes, we do. We'll see you there, Hugh." She raised her voice. "Selena? Thank you for the coffee!"

"*De nada.*"

"Oh, thank you, thank you, *thank you*, my darling!" Meg cooed as they made their way down the drive to the winery building. She stopped in the middle of the pavement, put both hands on her hips, and deepened her voice. "Sit, Selena, my darling." Then in falsetto, "Thank you, thank you, thank you, my Hugh!"

"Meg, shut up!"

" 'Are the villagers assembled with the properly humble subservient attitude before I come in?' " Meg growled. She stuck her stomach out and swaggered. " 'Are they ready for my magnifi—' "

"Meg, darn it! They'll see you." Quill grabbed her

elbow and jerked her forward. "So he's a little pompous."

"So the Pope's a little Catholic. Darn, I wish Doreen had seen that."

"Zowie." Quill shuddered. "Just behave yourself in the meeting, okay? He's a dork, but he's a dork with good ideas."

"So you *are* listening for the call of the bugle, the thunder of the horses' hooves, the shouts of gleeful—" She broke off at Quill's bewildered expression. "The cavalry. You're a believer. Finally."

"Oh, that." She smiled. "Maybe I am."

Meg shrieked and clutched her. "Quill. Look at the cars! The place is jammed already!"

Quill sat squashed in the tasting room of the Summerhill Winery. Most of the area wineries built tasting rooms, and the Summerhill room was one of the most pleasant she'd seen. The floors were new oak, stained clear and highly polished. The north and south ends of the room had large windows overlooking the vineyards. The east wall held hundreds of bottles of the Summerhill wines: Chardonnays, Chablis, white table wines, and some of the new ice wines that an inventive vintner created after an early frost destroyed his harvest. The fourth wall was the tasting area: a long thin counter with stools conveniently placed for the tipsy or tired.

The area was good-sized, approximately thirty by forty, but the Summerhills hadn't anticipated village interest in the availability of state money to bolster faltering tourism, and it was very crowded. Meg and Quill had walked in to discover it was S.R.O., and not much of that available either. Selena, entering the room in a gardenia-scented whirl, behaved with an unexpectedly decisive charm. She moved Mr. and Mrs. Freddie Bellini (Bellini's Funeral Home) out of their seats and to the back of the room with the tactful reminder that tourists who died were generally shipped home for burial. Both Bellinis were mollified by a large glass of Summerhill Chablis. She seated Meg and Quill in their former seats. She whispered, "A dreadful year, that Chablis, if I do say so myself, but the Bellinis? They will not know the difference. Sit, sit! There will be lunch after, of course. For you and some others. Not the car dealers, of course, or the pet store. *Madre de Dios!* But, when I give the sign to empty the room, do not go!"

The Chamber was out in force. Marge settled herself squarely in the front row and gave Quill a toothy grin that she didn't believe for a minute. Betty wasn't there—Quill devoutly hoped she wasn't back at the Inn weaseling cooking secrets out of Bjarne, who'd been left in charge of the kitchen. Elmer and Adela Henry had dressed for the occasion, Adela in a large hat that clipped Dookie Shuttleworth under the eye every time she made a vehement comment to her husband. Since Adela was famed throughout Hemlock Falls for both vehemence and volubility, Dookie was in significant danger of a scratched cornea. Quill winced, watching them.

"There's Stoke," Meg said. "I don't see Doreen with him."

"I asked her to sift through that room before it got cleaned up," Quill said.

"Three-ten? Why?"

"In part, because Marge Schmidt volunteered to head the cleanup crew."

"Quill, you can't think that Marge had anything to do with Ellen Dunbarton's murder!"

"I don't know what to think," Quill said frankly. "Of course I don't see Marge as a murderer. But she's one heck of a business competitor. Maybe she set that fire not knowing anyone was in there."

"Bull," Meg said rudely. "Then who tied up Ellen Dunbarton, and why?"

"What if the two incidents aren't connected?"

Meg shook her head decisively. "No way. It makes no sense whatsoever."

"Actually, I agree. And actually, I don't think Marge set that fire. It seems to me that Burke was partly right; there are types of people that commit certain types of crimes. If Marge were going to murder anyone, she'd hit him over the head with a baseball bat on Main Street at twelve noon. And if Marge wants our Inn so she can cut a larger swathe in town when all this grant money comes flooding in, she wouldn't set a fire to force us out; she'd do something legal and sneaky, like buying out our mortgage. But you know what? Marge may know something about who did kill Ellen Dunbarton. I wouldn't put it past her to search that room herself, thinking she'll find some evidence overlooked by the police."

"We've done that in the past. And if you asked Doreen to search that room, we're doing it now."

"So?"

Meg laughed. "So? Nothing like consistency, sis. Glad to see you're in better spirits, anyway."

"I think," Quill acknowledged, "that I was more depressed by John's departure than I cared to admit."

"No kidding. You know what I think? I think you should write to John. Just a chatty little note at first, followed by increasingly expansive letters. I think it'd be good for both of you. I think—"

"I think you should be quiet," Quill said firmly. "There's Hugh. We must be about to start."

He walked to the front of the room and waited for the babble of voices to die down. "I'd like to welcome you all to this first meeting of the Hemlock Falls Winegrowers' and Tourism Association. As you may know, we have designed this group to be a subsidiary of our parent organization, the Winegrowers' Association of the State of New York. I see most of our fellow growers here—the Blacks from Grape Noir, the Hutchinsons from Verdant Valley, and I see a lot of our Hemlock Falls business people, as well. The agenda for this meeting today is short; we are going to hear from Paul Pfieffer, the governor's representative. Mr. Pfieffer is director of this county's fund for the Revitalization of Tourism.''

"R.O.T.?" said Meg. "It's called R.O.T.?"

"Musta bin named by a Republican," Marge said.

Hugh was unruffled. "Ladies and gentlemen? Mr. Pfieffer."

Paul Pfieffer was thin, gray, acidic, and very, very dull. He began by thanking the governor (who wasn't, as far as Quill could tell, within one hundred miles of the Summerhill Winery), the Democrats in the State Legislature who had approved the appropriation of funds (Marge had been right—R.O.T. was courtesy of the Republicans, who lost the vote on how much to appropriate but got to name the fund), and for all she knew, since the room was warm and she slipped into a doze, he thanked his sisters and his cousins and his aunts as well. She drifted sleepily through the reading of the bill itself, and came to attention when Mr. Pfieffer finally cut to the chase.

"In short," he said, "there is a total of four million, six hundred and fifty thousand dollars available to those businesses of Hemlock Falls who wish to support, or are in any way connected to, the growth of tourism in our area. Twenty percent of this money is available as an outright grant to candidate businesses; the remaining eighty percent is available as a fifteen-year loan available at two percent."

"Two percent!" Meg said.

Quill looked at Marge. She was absolutely expressionless, but her eyes were glittering like the night lights on a gun turret. She thrust her fist in the air.

Paul Pfieffer twitched. "Yes, Miss . . . um . . ."

"Schmidt. Marge Schmidt. What kinda contingencies are attached to this loan?"

"Contingencies? I don't understand."

"A politician that don't understand contingencies?" Marge said, not at all pleasantly. "Don't make me laugh. Contingencies. No-no's. How can I use the money and how can't I use the money?"

"It can be used for expansion," Pfieffer said primly, "or for payroll. For remodeling. For business-related expenses such as advertising . . ."

Harvey Bozzel's hand immediately went up. He waved frantically for attention.

"Cool it, Harve," Marge said, without looking back. "Can you use it for acquisitions, Pfieffer?"

"It may be used for acquisitions if the acquirer is already in a tourist-related business and if the acquiree is engaged in a tourist-related business *at that time.*"

Quill, who had no idea why Pfieffer needed to invest the final prepositional phrase with such verbal significance, poked Meg in the side.

"Does that mean what I think it means?" Meg whispered.

"That Marge can use this money to buy us out? Yes." Quill twisted her hair around her forefinger. "Bloody hell, I knew she was up to something. I knew it."

The meeting broke up. Pfieffer made a quick and well-timed exit, before anyone realized he was gone. Selena surveyed the disappointed members of the newly formed Hemlock Falls Winegrowers' and Tourism Association, and with a perspicacity Quill hadn't expected, shouted, "He's in the parking lot!" This left eleven people in the room. Quill, Meg, Marge, the mayor and Mrs. Mayor,

Hugh and Selena, Esther West, Harvey Bozzel, and the Reverend and Mrs. Dookie Shuttleworth.

"*Bueno*," Selena said. "My ploy worked. I told Mr. Pfieffer to leave by the crushing room. He is not in the parking lot at all! He is waiting for his lunch. So, all those people, with their hands outstretched and their earnest pleas for the cash, will be able to go home. Now, I think, Hugh, we should have some lunch and discuss what is to be done. Come with me to the house, please."

Selena's Spanish heritage was evident in the kitchen, which Quill hadn't seen on her first visit to the house. The floor tiles were warm bronze. The kitchen cabinets were a dark teak in the Mediterranean style. Quill exclaimed aloud when she saw the tiled countertops. Each had been hand-painted in blues and yellows. "Very Portuguese," she said. "Where did you get them?"

"Selena hand-painted them herself," Hugh said. He slid his arm around her shoulders and gave her a dignified kiss. "Won't you come into the dining room and sit down?"

Paul Pfieffer, a glass of wine in his hand, was peering nervously out the window when they walked into the dining room. He jumped when Selena swept the party into the room, and mumbled hellos. He was clearly uncomfortable.

The dining room table was refectory-style, and had been set with a Portuguese pottery that matched the kitchen countertops. Thin crystal wineglasses were in front of each place setting. Hugh pulled the corks on two unlabeled wine bottles, and began to pour. "This is a red we bottled six years ago, after we harvested the first of our Pinot Noir grapes. I think you'll like it." He raised a forefinger in Selena's direction.

Selena struck a small bell by her glass, and a young girl brought salads in from the kitchen. "Our daughter, whom you have not met," Selena said. "Victoria, this is Miss Sarah Quilliam, whom you so much admire. She has seen your paintings, Quill, in her art class at school.''

Quill blushed and looked at her plate.

Selena finished introducing the others, commanded that no business should be talked at the table, and asked Dookie to extend God's grace over the table.

Quill found herself eating an excellent lunch, finishing with a creamy cheese she had never tasted before.

''My family sends it to us each year for Christmas,'' Selena said. ''And the Pinot Noir? What do you think? We have not retailed it, as yet. You are the first to try it.''

The wine had been drunk to general approbation. But, as the Reverend Shuttleworth freely admitted, none of them except Quill and Meg knew anything at all about wine, except that the Lord approved, thank heaven, and for that he was grateful. Quill knew a fair amount—Meg a great deal. She glanced at her sister, who shook her head slightly.

''Delicious,'' Quill said. ''We'd love to buy a few cases for our own use.''

''We were hoping, perhaps, that you would agree to stock your cellar at the Inn with this,'' Selena said somewhat ingenuously. ''It is not selling as well as we hoped. The brokers who buy in bulk, they tell us there is a prejudice against New York reds.''

''This mean we can talk bizness?'' Marge demanded. ''Is the lunch over? It was good, by the way.''

''For business?'' Selena said. ''We defer to my Hugh.''

''Good.'' Marge smacked her hand on the table. ''What I say is this, Hugh. We make a run at that money, and we get it.''

''That's an . . .'' Hugh paused, searching for the most tactful word, ''an admirable, if somewhat belligerently stated, sentiment, Marge. But to think of it, it's the truth, so why try to dress it up in tact? I agree, I think those of us here at this table should make a run at that money and get it. We have here all of the movers and shakers in Hemlock Falls. And I think we can be counted upon to use the money for the good of the town.''

"So that's why we're here? To make decisions for the village?'' Meg's voice was calm and reasonable, but her left foot was jiggling up and down. It was, Quill knew, a bad sign.

"What Meg means is that this isn't really a public forum,'' Quill intervened. "And we haven't been elected to make decisions, have we?''

"Some of us have,'' Adela Henry said majestically.

"There will be no decisions made here. None,'' Mr. Pfieffer said crossly. "I was told this was to be an informational meeting only.''

Meg bit her thumb and stared past Adela Henry's left ear. "I'd just like to point out that none of the other growers are here. And Howie Murchison, the town attorney, isn't here. Nor are Ben Croh from the Croh Bar, or Tilly Angstrum from the village Bed and Breakfast. These are all movers and shakers in Hemlock Falls, too.''

"Quite minor ones,'' Hugh said mildly. "With no influence whatsoever.''

Meg's gaze dropped directly to Adela's. "And voters, of course. They're all voters.''

Adela shot a glance at her husband and looked thoughtful.

Harvey Bozzel smoothed his hair with a careful hand. "The Reverend Shuttleworth's here at our specific request.''

"*Our*, Harvey?'' Meg's tone was dangerously sweet. "And it's just like you to drag the minister into this.''

"And the world knows how honest the Reverend is.''

The world also knew how frequently the input vanished from Dookie's hard drive. Even with the best will in the world (and by far the most Christian spirit of any other Hemlockian) Dookie had a difficult time navigating the harsh realities of life. Most eyes at the lunch table were on him now. Dookie smiled benignly and said, "The wine was quite good, Selena."

"And what, Harvey?" Meg drummed her thumb on the table. It sounded far more ominous than it should. "Because you've talked the Reverend Mr. Shuttleworth here into coming for lunch, you think the rest of the town is going to be happy about all of the money going just to us?"

Paul Pfeiffer threw his napkin on the table. "I knew this was a bad idea. You'll have to excuse me. Ladies?" He nodded to Quill and Meg. "You have clarified a situation that required clarity. Señora Summerhill? Thank you for the lunch. Good day to you all. My office may be reached through the regular channels. We will be delighted to review any written application for the disbursement of these funds." He burped. "Excuse me. The official review, of course, shall be conducted at the R.O.T. offices in Albany. And not at lunch. I may as well inform you now that I have taken rooms in the village and you will see me on the streets of Hemlock Falls. Do not speak to me unless I speak to you."

He left silence behind him.

"We don't need Mr. Pfeiffer's direct input to formulate a plan," Harvey said at his most mellifluous. "We can review it all here, together. Now, if you'll just let me duck out and get my briefcase . . ."

Meg twisted her face into a ferocious scowl. "Harvey! No dice, Harvey. We do this in a public forum, or we don't do it. Get it?"

"Now, Meg, far be it from me—"

"Oh, pooh on far be it from you." Her eyes slid sideways and rested for a moment on Marge Schmidt. "I just want to know one thing, Harve, and then Quill and I are leaving. When did you know about this money?"

Harvey giggled. "I don't know why you're asking me, Meg. I'm sure I heard it when the rest of you did. Yesterday, when the governor's office announced it to the press."

"And I'm just as sure that you and a few others knew about it long before this."

"It's not important, Meg, really," Quill said. "Why don't we go?"

"Marge?" Meg faced her directly. "You've always been straight with us. When did you know about the amount of money that had been allocated to Hemlock Falls?"

"Coupla weeks ago. A month, maybe. I got a friend on the Ways and Means Committee."

"Why do you need to know this, Meg?" Quill asked in an undertone.

"Because if we'd known a month ago, John would have stayed, that's why. A month ago, with this in our future, we wouldn't have had to be thinking about filing for Chapter Eleven. That's the problem with secret meetings. If we'd known about the availability of these funds when you all did, our reputation would have been intact; I wouldn't be cooking hash browns for ladies who make money belts out of Kleenex boxes!" Furious, she turned to the mayor. "You knew, too, dammit. If you'd shared the information with us, a lot of things would have been different. Don't you think you owed us that much?"

"I do not think," Dookie said gently, "that raised voices will solve the problem here. Meg, it appears to me that apologies should be freely given and freely accepted. Shall we have a moment of reflection?"

"No, sir, we will not. We will have a moment of leave-taking, which my sister and I will take right this minute.'' Meg slapped her napkin onto the table, then stood up. In the middle of this tension, the phone rang.

"No, no!" Selena cried in distress. "Please, Meg, you mistake the matter." She ignored the insistent ring from the kitchen. "All of us know how public-spirited you and Quill are. We would not have invited you here if we had intended any—what is the expression, Hugh, more than one dealing?"

"Double-dealing, my darling. And please answer the phone."

She fluttered up from the table and grabbed Quill by the arm. "Do not let this end in bad feelings, Quill. I will be right back."

Quill spoke diffidently into the stiff silence. "Um. I don't know just how public-spirited we are at the Inn, but there's no doubt that we have an obligation to do the best for the village we live in. Laws," Quill said, "are for all of us. This notion that only the privileged few should benefit from monies gathered from the citizens of this state is a bad notion."

Meg rolled her eyes and drew her finger across her throat. *Cut!*

Quill ignored her. She was on a roll. "I support my government," she said earnestly, "and I support the freedoms of our country, but I also support the laws . . . yes, Selena?"

"It is that dog," Selena said apologetically. "There is no license, but it is yours, yes? I am afraid I must go catch it, Quill. It is chasing the chickens of Mr. Peterson's farm."

"Oh," said Quill. "I'll be happy to go—"

"Oh, I don't think that would be appropriate, do you, Quill?" Hugh smiled at her, his teeth white and perfect in the middle of his grin. "Selena's just upholding the law. Selena's the dog warden, and you'll have to follow the rules and pick it up at the pound."

"Hugh, darling. That would be cruel! I will bring the dog back to you, Quill. But it must have the license and soon. It is the la—" She stopped and clapped her hand over her mouth.

Meg threw her hands in the air. "That's it. Come on, Quill." She turned for a parting shot as they left the dining room. "Anybody wants us, come by the Inn. We're the two bag ladies on the driveway with the tin cups and the unlicensed dog. Thanks again for the open discussion, guys."

"Wow," Quill said, when they were in her battered Oldsmobile on their way back to the Inn. "You blew."

"Just call me Krakatoa." Meg stared out the open window. "You, on the other hand, started tap-dancing with all the righteous aplomb of Newt Gingrich. Did you lose your mind?!"

"I was just trying to salvage the situation for us. You were a little hard on them, Meggie."

"I was not. I wasn't hard enough!"

Quill drove quietly for a moment. Summerhill was only a few miles off Route 15, no more than twenty minutes from the Inn. The day was fine. Quill loved the light that came in spring: she always thought of it as slender, yet voluptuous, like the statue of Niobe in Paris. Perhaps she should start a series of Water Studies, and paint the pool beneath the Falls in each season. "You know," she said, after the angry red left Meg's cheeks, "there's a terrific imbalance in this family. You have too much of the in-your-face spirit, and I appear to have too little."

"Do you think it would have been right to stay there at that secret little grabbers meeting?"

"No, I don't. But I also think that Dookie would have pointed out, in his nonconfrontational, abstract, totally inoffensive way, that perhaps we should bring this to the attention of the rest of the town.''

''Since nobody listens to Dookie, nobody would know it was his idea.''

''But that's how it works, Meg. Haven't you noticed? Maybe the mayor would say, 'Might better get so-and-so's idea about that,' and then Esther might say she'd feel more comfortable if the whole Chamber were involved, and bingo! They'd end up doing the right thing. I suppose everyone's greedy in one way or another . . . What's that?'' She braked hard.

Meg, used to her sister's erratic driving, hung on to the dashboard and said merely, ''What's what?''

''That sign.''

''It says, CRAFT SHOW, BARGAINS GALORE. You see those signs all over this part of the country this time of year. What's so unusual . . . oh.''

''Yeah. That's what's so unusual. It's us.''

''Room 314, The Inn at Hemlock Falls. Wine tourists welcome. Oh, dear. The Crafty Ladies.'' There was a second sign on the turn from Route 15 to Hemlock Drive, and a third at the foot of the driveway to the Inn itself. ''Lot of cars parked at the top of the hill,'' Meg observed. ''My goodness, there's one of those Blue Bird Tour buses. Golden Age Golden Tours, it says.''

Quill pulled the Olds into the garage. ''You want to come up with me?''

''I think I'd better check on Bjarne in the kitchen. There may have been a lot more people for lunch than I'd expected. He's probably sunk in gloom. I should have hidden the boning knife; it's the sharpest I've got. Or he may be cheerful in the face of disaster. You never know with a Finn. But let me know if there are any real bargains.''

''Ha.''

Quill walked the long way round to the front door. The foyer was filled with middle-aged ladies in pant-suits, ladies in cotton twill shorts and bright shirts, and elderly gentlemen wearing patient expressions. All of them wore hats. Quill wondered about retired people in hats. In the short (and disastrous) time she and Meg had spent in Florida last year, she'd noticed that everyone over fifty-five seemed to wear hats on vacation.

Doreen was standing behind the counter with a smug expression. "Hey," she said as Quill came in that door.

"Hey, yourself. What's all this?"

"Good idea, innit? That Fran had it. You know all that luggage the Crafty Ladies brung with them?"

"Filled with product, I expect."

"You betcha. You know what? Got a couple of book-ings for tonight, too."

"From this crowd?"

"Not exactly. Although one couple woulda stayed, 'cept the fire in 310 made the lady real nervous. Tolt her the fire was set, so she wouldn't think it was the wiring or nuthin', but it didn't seem to help. Place was too nice to leave, they said, and who wants to go see the hog farm tomorra anyways? That's what's next on this here Golden Age tour. So if we get that room fixed, we'll get guests like you wouldn't believe, as long as the craft show goes on."

"You said we had two bookings, though."

"Ayuh. Some fella named Smith called, gonna check in tonight. So him, and some fella name of Pfieffer . . ."

"Paul Pfieffer?"

"Yeah. Booked him into 212."

"Mr. Burke is in 212."

"Mr. Burke's gonna check out, soon as he's finished his lunch."

"Did he leave a check?" Quill asked without hope.

Doreen looked dark. "He did NOT. That bozo. I held

on to his luggage for a bit, but he started hollerin' for the sheriff so I had to give it up.''

"Doreen!"

She snorted. Doreen was a master of the scornful snort. "Like that squirt Davy Kiddermeister could find his a—''

"Stop. Davy Kiddermeister may be young, but he *is* the sheriff and he *is* empowered by the state of New York to arrest you for theft, or kidnapping, or whatever keeping a person's lugg—'' She grabbed her hair with both hands and tugged it. "Why do I even bother?!''

"You might better leave things to me.''

"Right. You said Mr. Burke's in the dining room?'' She allowed herself some hope. "Did we have a lot of people for lunch?''

"Nope.''

"We didn't?'' Quill surveyed the lobby. "There's a lot of people here. Some of them must be hungry.''

"They was.''

"Didn't Bjarne want to feed them?''

Doreen pointed. Quill looked in the direction of her finger. She hadn't noticed the sign before; it was at the side of the entrance to the dining room, concealed by the rush of people up and down the stairs. "DINING ROOM CLOSED FOR REPAIRS. What repairs?''

"To that Bjarne's nerves,'' Doreen said simply. "People started orderin' and he started runnin' around the kitchen, gigglin', like, and said there wasn't enough herring.''

"Was anyone ordering herr—?'' Quill interrupted herself. "Never mind. I have to say that was quick thinking, Doreen.''

"Mr. Burke got fed before Bjarne went nuts, so I didn't think quick enough.''

"I'll talk to him about that insurance check right now.''

• • •

Rocky Burke sat at table seven, contemplating the view of the Falls. His feet were propped on the chair adjacent to his. He was sipping coffee. He sat up as Quill approached and waved at her to sit down. "Great lunch," he said. "Great view. Great place."

"Thanks." Quill regarded him steadily. "Doreen said that you were checking out."

"*My* work's done." There was the slightest stress on the pronoun.

"So you're headed back to—where is it?"

"Syracuse." He shot a glance at her, then looked away.

"And you've decided that my sister and I are innocent of arson?"

"Seems that way."

"But you aren't going to give us that check."

"Nope. Well. If it hadn't been for the fire, it would have been a nice little vacation. By the way, I didn't mention this, did I? You know that Signor what's-his-name."

"Bellasario?"

"The old guy. Great. Just great. The boys and I had a great time."

"That's just. . . . great," Quill said dryly. "Does this mean you're leaving a check for us?"

"Persistent, aren't you? Tell you what, Cookie. We'll be in touch."

"I thought that one of the selling points of Burke's Insurance was the quick way you paid claims."

"Um. Yeah. There's quick and there's quick, Cookie. What may seem slow to you is real quick to us." He punched her lightly in the arm, in a fraternal way.

"Mr. Burke, I know that the circumstances of our policy were unusual. But we do have a policy, and we do have a claim. We have to get that room repaired."

"I heard that the folks in town were going to give you a hand with that."

Quill flushed. "They offered, yes. But does that change the circumstances of what you owe?"

"Can't say that it does. You don't," he murmured to himself "see a lot of the good side of people in insurance."

"Mr. Burke, an offer is not a performance. Now I don't want to have to drag Howie Murchison into this—"

"Who?"

"Our lawyer. Are you refusing to pay us?"

"Oh, no, not at all. You have a legitimate claim, you get a legitimate check. Burke's Insurance guarantees that."

Quill chewed her lower lip. Mr. Burke got up and retrieved his briefcase from under the table. "I'll see you around, Cookie."

"What happened to make you change your mind?"

"Hah?"

"I asked you why you think my sister and I set that fire."

"Did I say that?"

"You didn't say a word. And you haven't left a check either. So something's happened to affect the way you look at us. We didn't fit the profile of arsonists, you said."

Burke shrugged and walked away. He reached the archway that led to the foyer, and Quill called after him. "Who told you the Chamber was going to help us fix that room?"

"Some skinny short broad, Cookie. Looked a bit like a short-order cook."

Betty Hall. Marge's partner. Marge would have told him herself if she hadn't thrown him out of her restaurant. Which was not a bad idea. The last she saw of Mr.

Burke was the backside of his well-pressed suit. Quill sat at the table for a long moment, thinking hard. Meg poked her head out of the swinging doors to the kitchen and whistled, jerking her from her abstraction. "He's gone," Quill said.

"What?!"

Quill got up and walked across the room. "Gone. Checked out. *Hasta la* bye-bye."

"No check?"

"No check." She peered past Meg's shoulder. "How's Bjarne?"

"Okay. I gave him a shot of vodka. He'll be fine. Question is, will we be fine? If we don't have that check, how can we get the room fixed?"

"The Chamber volunteers?" Quill said doubtfully.

"Sure. After I teed everyone off this morning. Aaagh." She rested her head against the door and rubbed it back and forth.

"There's one way we can get that check."

"Find out who set the fire," Meg said. "Easier said than done. I mean, *why?* You can suspect Marge Schmidt all you want, but I don't really think—"

"I don't think so either. I mean, she's taking advantage of the situation, that's for sure. No, she'd be the first to tell you that all's fair in war and business. But hurt somebody? Not Marge. She's a shark, but a sand shark."

"A sand shark?"

"Sand sharks are very nice, as sharks go. They don't eat people. No, this is a murder with a motive. A personal motive. Who here knew Ellen Dunbarton?"

"Just the Crafty Ladies," Meg said. "You don't think . . .? Of course you do. One of them!? Jeez!" She straightened up. "You want to go up and take a look at the scene?"

"I sure do. And I wouldn't mind seeing how all this craft stuff is doing either."

The foyer had cleared of people, not, as Meg and Quill discovered when they went upstairs, because of lack of interest, but because the Crafty Ladies were out of crafts.

"Sold the lot!" Freddie Patch said in soft delight. "Can you believe it?"

Quill surveyed the room. The ladies had been inventive. Several long planks had been brought in from the garden shed. They lay between two chairs and were covered with a bedsheet. The carpet in the room had the messy, after-the-ball look that comes from a lot of people tramping through a confined area. A few sequins glittered on the improvised counter, several petals from silk flowers were scattered near the door, but it was clear the sale had been a success. Robin and Mary bustled about the room clearing away tissue paper and folding bags.

"We sent Fran to take down the signs," Freddie said. "And none too soon! There's not a thing left! Not a thing. Oh, I *wish* I had my workshop here! I don't think we've ever had as successful a sale, do you, girls?"

"There's something so satisfying about someone paying actual cash money for something you've put your heart and soul into," Robin said. Her face was suffused with contentment. She looked exactly like the pre-1970 Betty Crocker, when the consumer market expected their mothers and grandmothers to be plump, rosy, and comfortable.

Robin patted Quill's arm. "You let us tidy up in here, Quill. We don't want to put the housemaid out. But, boy, could we use some tea."

"In the gazebo," Meg said suddenly. "We'll meet you out there. It overlooks the Falls. Would you like a full English tea? Scones? Devonshire cream? Strawberries? On the house, of course.''

The three women exchanged guilty looks.

"Do we dare?" Robin asked.

"Try and stop me!" Mary said. "We'd love to."

"But only if you two join us," Freddie said. "And of course we'll pay. We know how tough things are for your little Inn at the moment." She patted Quill in a kindly way. "But you know, dear, everyone goes through tough times. We wanted to tell you that. The only thing about getting older is that you realize things get better, then things get worse. It's the way life is."

"Give us fifteen minutes," Meg said. "We'll meet you there." She tugged Quill out of the room and into the hall. Once outside the room, and away from the Crafty Ladies, they stared at each other.

"I don't believe it," Quill said.

"Neither do I." Meg rolled her eyes. "It's like accusing your mother."

"There have been some pretty rotten mothers," Quill said. "Still . . ."

"I wish I hadn't offered them a free tea," Meg said gloomily. "We can't afford to give people free teas. Especially innocent people. Do you really think we're going to find out anything incriminating about Ellen Dunbarton? All the former female guards in World War Two concentration camps are dead by now. They didn't have women combat troops in Vietnam, so no one could be wreaking revenge for a long-ago massacre. What in the heck could have motivated Ellen Dunbarton's murder? And in such an awful way?"

"We have to try to find out. And your cream teas, Meg, would soften up Attila the Hun."

• • •

Quill was as baffled at the conclusion of the cream tea as she had been at the beginning. Spring was softening into summer, and the afternoon air was a gentle bath of warm gold light. The gardeners would be out in full force all over the village, Quill thought. She caught a scent of burning in the air, one of the Petersons in the Gorge, getting rid of the dead wood. The Falls were in full flood and the water sprayed high; for a short time, the sun was at just the right angle, and a rainbow arced over the Gorge.

"This is one of the most beautiful places we've ever been," Freddie said. She set her teacup down on the little table inside the gazebo. The five of them just fit around it. "And that was one of the most delicious teas I've ever had."

"Fran is going to be so sorry she missed it," Mary said regretfully. "She left to get those signs down almost two hours ago. I wonder where she got to."

"There were a couple of wonderful shops in the village," Freddie said practically. "I'm sure she got caught up in those. She'll be here. Quill, are those sweet peas planted around the base of this little hut?"

"Yes." Quill finished the last sip of her tea and absently picked up another scone. "They'll be out in July."

"I don't think so," Mary said. "Not if you don't stop that dog from peeing on them. Dog pee simply wrecks shrubbery." She leaned over the railing and said, "Shoo! Go away!"

"Max!" said Quill. "What color is it?"

"What color?! It's a sort of a grayish-brown dog."

"No, the—um—dog pee."

"Why, yellow, of course."

"Good," said Quill. John had been right. His injury was healing itself. "Hey, Max!"

"Woof!" Max said.

"That is the ugliest dog I've ever seen," Meg said.

"Whose dog is it?" Freddie looked disapproving. "It's very dirty."

"I've been meaning to give him a bath." Quill got up and looked down at her dog. "Hey, Max. What have you been up to? Don't tell me, Mr. Peterson's chickens. Did you thank Selena for dropping you off?"

"Woof," Max said again, more urgently. "Woof!" He ran backwards, toward the Gorge, and looked over his shoulder at Quill.

"Did you find something cool?" Quill asked in a voice even she felt to be too syrupy.

"Is that the dog that saved your life?" Freddie asked in a hushed voice.

"Yes."

Max began to bark in a "come here right *now*" sort of way. He ran to the edge of the lawn, and disappeared over the lip of the Gorge.

"Max!" Quill went down the steps and across to the edge of the lawn. The Gorge plunged steeply down to the river here. Quill saw the gray-brown flash of Max's back plunging through the brush. A thin spiral of smoke drifted over the river. Max's barks scaled into hysteria. Quill took a deep breath and started to go after him. She inhaled again. Her head swam. She forced herself to stand still. She breathed shallowly, but the terrible odor carried on the smoke seemed to cling to her like grasping hands.

It was familiar, that smell, and she trembled. She'd washed herself again and again, scouring it away the night before.

"Meg," she said quietly. "Give the sheriff a call, will you?"

CHAPTER 6

"We can't leave," Robin sobbed. "Our president's due any day now."

"Can't you call her?" Quill asked gently. "You must tell her what's happening here."

"We've sent her a fax. If it is a her. We think it's a him."

"You think it's a him?"

"We're going to meet him for the very first time!" Robin made a determined effort to keep her tears at bay. Quill felt her own eyes fill in a sympathetic response. "He's so proud of what we've accomplished. Fran thought he might look like Richard Gere." She lost the battle. Tears rolled down her face. "Now she'll never see him."

They were in the foyer. The carpet and floor were still littered with the debris generated by the traffic from the impromptu craft fair. Quill, Mary, Freddie, and Robin were squashed uncomfortably on the leather couch in front of the cobblestone fireplace. The surviving Crafty Ladies had insisted on sticking together, in full view of the sheriff, the state troopers, and the inevitable rubber-neckers who had arrived at the site of yet another murder. Quill sat back. There was some insanity at work here, and it wasn't limited to the murders. Now was not the time to probe.

The volunteer firemen had put out the flames before Fran's body had been totally consumed. Quill had spoken quickly to Andy Bishop, who had told her that, just like Ellen Dunbarton, Fran's mouth had been taped shut with duct tape, her arms bound behind her. There were a few differences, he said. He'd get back to her.

Quill got up. Freddie clutched at her. Her face was rubbed pink with tears. "Where are you going?!"

"Just upstairs for a moment. You know what? Why don't you go into the Tavern and sit down. Quite a few people are in there already. You'll be safe there. Ask Nate—" Not Nate; he'd started his job at the Croh Bar yesterday. "Tell Kathleen I said to give you some sweet sherry."

"Would there be any martinis?" Robin asked timidly. "I do like a vodka martini."

"Enough to sink a battleship. Why don't you go on, now." They walked together down the hall, fear in the set of their shoulders. Quill began to make her way up the staircase, and almost collided with Paul Pfieffer coming down.

"I understand a body has been discovered here on the premises," he said with disapproval.

Quill bit back the retort that it wasn't *her* fault. "In the Gorge. Which is actually village property." She eyed him with a bit of disapproval herself. This gray, prim man had his hand firmly on the checking account that could save their Inn. And he would check in in the middle of the worst brouhaha they'd had for months. "We open our doors to the volunteers when anything like this occurs. If it does." Since murders had, in the past, occurred quite frequently at the Inn, she abandoned this attempt at lobbying.

"Community spirit is quite important."

"We do our best. Have you come down for dinner? You'll notice the sign that the dining room's closed. That doesn't apply to the guests. We have quite a bit of trade, despite what you may have heard to the contrary, and we didn't feel it was right to continue to entertain while all this was going on. We don't want anything to get in the way of the investigation. If you'd like to eat, just tap on the doors to the kitchen. The chef's in there."

"That's your sister, isn't it? The one who spoke up at lunch today."

"Meg."

"Humph."

"If you'll excuse me . . ." She edged her way past him, and up the two flights to the third floor. The yellow tape reading POLICE LINE DO NOT CROSS was still in place at the door to 310. Quill ducked under it. Doreen was on her knees, sifting through the pile of debris around the bed. "Find anything yet? I thought you were going to do this while Meg and I were at the Summerhill meeting."

"I woulda missed the craft show."

Quill looked, but there wasn't any place to sit down. She leaned against the wall instead. "We won't find anything of use anyhow."

"Might. Give me a sec." She gave Quill a sharp look, filled with affection. "How you holding up?"

"Oh, fine," Quill said bitterly. "Just fine. I'm becoming as oily a manipulator as Harvey, as good a liar as a used car salesman, and as greedy as Marge the Barge herself. My character's in *good* shape."

Doreen chuckled. "You'll be all right. Big difference between lyin' for a livin' and fibbin' a little to live."

"There is, huh?"

"Don't be too hard on yourself, missy. You're just tryin' to keep body and soul together. You might recall that all you have to do is give the sher'f a call . . .''

''If you mean Myles, I keep telling you, he's not sheriff anymore.''

''More's the pity. Anyhow, he'll come right home and take you away from all this. All you gotta do is call.''

''And what about Kathleen, and Mike the groundskeeper, and—''

''Me? I can take care of myself. Kathleen'll find something to do. And Meg's got the doc.''

''What we have is ourselves,'' Quill said crossly. ''You really want me to give up and let some guy pull us out of our troubles?''

''Sher'f ain't 'some guy.' ''

''We are capable of handling all of this ourselves.''

''You know what I think?''

''I'm about to find out, aren't I?''

''You watch your tongue, missy. I think you feel so bad about John, that you're proving we don't need him. And we do.''

''I do feel badly about John. I feel awful about John.''

''Guilty, too, from the look of you.''

''I do?''

''Look, Quill, thing about men is, they haven't a notion. They're simple, like. They know sisters, they know their mas, they know bossy, like their fourth grade teachers, and of course, they know girlfriends and spouses, like. What they don't know is friends. You ast me, John got friendship all mixed up with the spouses and girlfriends. What I think is, you should, you know, write up a few letters, friendly, like. Then write longer ones, and longer ones, and pret' soon . . .''

''Was it Meg's idea or yours?'' Quill asked testily.

''We kinda cooked it up together. Seein' as how it knocked you for such a loop.''

''It didn't knock me for a loop. I'm handling it.''

''Ahuh.''

"And I don't want to talk about it."

"That sounds familiar. Far as I see it, you don't talk, you might as well be dead and buried. What else is there but talk? You stop talking and look what happens. War, pestilence, plague, and goodness knows what all. Now, if people just talked—"

"Doreen!"

"Ahuh. I ain't done yet. But we can talk about it later. Look here." Doreen sat back on her heels. "Whad'ya think of that?" She extended her palm.

"It looks like a triangle. The orchestra kind."

Doreen snapped her fingernail against the blackened metal. A crystalline *ping* filled the air. "Where d'ya suppose it come from?"

"I don't know. Was it used as some sort of craft thing? The Ladies turn all sorts of articles into things they weren't supposed to be in the first place."

"I took me a good look at that table. They had Sandy Clauses made out of old panty hose, them little fans out of plastic spoons, coffee cans made into bird feeders. But no triangles."

"Maybe Ellen kept it because she liked the noise?"

"S'odd, is all. Sher'f tolt me one thing about investigating, the odd thing might be the important thing." She rose to her feet with a grunt. In the devastation of the room, and the half-light from the shattered windows, she looked gaunt and tired. Quill looked at her with a flash of remorse. Doreen had never told them how old she was. She'd never filled out an employment application. She'd just appeared at the back door one day, her appearance roosterish, her attitude prickly, taken up her mop and bucket and that was that. Quill knew that Axminster was her third husband, and at one time or another, younger, miniature versions of Doreen had shown up at the back door and proved to be offspring. She knew Doreen's life had been hard, physical work from the time she was thirteen. But Doreen had never volunteered much, and Quill respected her reticence.

"Doreen, when's your birthday?"

"August twelfth. I'm a Leo. You know that."

"I meant the first one," Quill said softly.

"Oh." She scratched her chin. "You won't tell Stoke?"

"No."

"He's sixty-four, ya know. Might make a difference. Does with some men. Did with my second, as a matter of fact. Thing is, we go gray late in my fambly."

"And?"

"And I'm seventy-two."

"Seventy-two?" Quill kept her voice well under control. "Wow. You'd hardly know it."

"Always been that way with the Muxworthys. Gramma Muxworthy died at a hungry and six, and Ma still raises and cans her own beans. What do you think of that?"

That instead of scrubbing floors and toilets, you should be sitting in the sun among flowers, Quill thought. That I should be making your bed, and ironing your skirts. That, dammit, a younger, stronger person should be on her—or his—knees, getting wine stains out of the dining room carpet. She wouldn't say it now; Doreen was shrewder than a banker and sharper than an L.A. divorce lawyer. But there would have to be more changes at the Inn.

"You think this might be important?" Doreen turned the triangle over curiously.

"Possibly. Let's take it down to Meg and see."

"A triangle?" Meg dropped the cloth she was polishing the counter with and turned the instrument over in her hand. "Did she like to listen to it before she went to sleep?" She dropped it with a clatter, and again the chime filled the air. "Beats me. You guys want some dinner?"

"Wouldn't mind." Doreen eased herself onto the kitchen stool. "Stoke's out interviewin' the town on this four million bucks the government's got to give away. I remember when Roosevelt was elected all the hoo-ha from the rich folks about the government giving away money for food. Now the government's giving away money for folks on vacation, and you don't hear a word about it."

"You remember *Roosevelt*?" Meg demanded. She looked at Quill. "Franklin·Delano?"

"Sure do." Doreen grinned at Meg. "You don't tell Stoke, neither."

"Okay," said Meg, stunned. Her lips moved. "Over seventy?" she said finally. "You're over seventy?! What the heck are you do—"

"Meg!" Quill cut in sharply. "I'm starved. What do you have to eat?"

"Cold cucumber soup. Fresh bread. Some roasted lamb and new potatoes. I decided," she added, "to serve one entrée tonight, and tough bounce to anyone who won't eat lamb. There's strawberries and cream for dessert."

They ate in silence. Quill turned the events of the past two days over and over in her mind. "Here's the deal," she said aloud. She waved her fork in the air, making her point. "First of all, five ladies checked in here two days ago for a week. Right? They said they were here to plan their new line of craft kits for two years from now."

"How'd they sell 'em?" Doreen asked.

"Mail order. Ellen Dunbarton explained it to me. All they did was buy a 1-800 line, which is really cheap, and print up a catalogue. They contacted a whole bunch of suppliers of the components of the kits—safety pins, beads, artificial flowers—and had them on standby for order.''

''So they never had to buy an inventory,'' Meg said.

''Not a penny went to inventory. They get a call, they tell the customer it's a week's guaranteed delivery, then call their suppliers. The suppliers drop-ship the order, and they all get together and assemble it, then mail it. They bought a mailing list from one of those craft companies, I believe. Ellen said it cost them a dime a name. She said it's how Spiegal's does business.''

''Pretty clever,'' Meg said.

''It's very clever. The thing is, what kind of trouble could five churchgoing type ladies have possibly gotten into with a backyard mail-order business?''

There was an angry knock on the swinging doors. Meg rolled her eyes. Doreen muttered, ''Now what?!'' Quill pushed the doors open gently.

Paul Pfeiffer said angrily, ''There is a large, ugly dog in your dining room. This is a violation of the New York State health codes.''

Max shoved his way without ceremony into the kitchen.

''YOU!'' Doreen said in a voice of loathing. ''GIT!''

Max whined and wriggled. Meg bounced off her stool and said, ''Come in, Mr. Pfeiffer. We were just about to have some dessert. And my sister was just about to take the dog outside. After that, she plans to call the dog-catcher who, instead of surreptitiously returning the dog to her, will take it to the pound. Weren't you, Quill?''

''Selena?'' Quill said feebly. ''I hate to disturb her now, Meg. It's after eight o'clock and you know how hard she works. Why don't I just take Max to the garden shed?''

Max whined loudly at the words ''garden shed.''

''There is also a lost-looking gentleman in the foyer,'' Mr. Pfeiffer said icily. ''He is looking for the receptionist.'' He craned his neck to look over Quill's shoulder.

"You said something about dessert, Mâitre d' Quilliam?"

"Coming right up. And some freshly ground coffee,
perhaps with a bit of cognac on the side?"

"The meal was delicious," Mr. Pfieffer said grudg-
ingly. He edged past Quill and the dog. "You'll do
something about that animal before morning? I have
friends in the health department."

I have friends in the health department, Quill mouthed
silently at his back.

"About that guest in the foyer?" Meg said in a mean-
ingful way.

"It's Mr. Smith, I think, waiting to check in. I'll take
care of it. Come along, Max."

"And I'll be getttin' on home to Stoke," Doreen said.
"Night, Quill. Night, Meg." She gave Pfieffer a look so
malign, he jumped. "Don't you keep this kitchen open
too late, you hear?"

"Mr. Smith?" Quill asked as she walked into the
foyer.

"I am at that." The pronoun was soft and long, an
"aah" rather than an "eye." Mr. Smith didn't look lost.
He looked confident, clever, and rich. He was also
blond, Southern, and buff—he reminded Quill of the
current President. A person, she told herself, whom you
might expect to use charm over substance. But likable.
Very likable.

"Miss Quilliam." He was dressed in a summer
weight navy sports coat. The buttons were from a well-
known yacht club in Connecticut. He had on well-
pressed gray trousers, Oxford blood loafers, and a white
cotton shirt, open at the collar. Quill suppressed the impulse to call Harvey Bozzel. "Harvey?" she would say.
"I want you to take a peek at your dream man. Your
role model. The advertising man's advertising man."

"Miss Quilliam?" he repeated. His voice was louder, firmer, than it had been at first, with empathetically kind overtones; the sort of voice, Quill was sure, he would use as he opened the door for a little old lady on crutches.

"Miss—"

"Yes, yes, yes. I'm Sarah Quilliam. Please call me Quill. You're here to check in?"

He nodded at a black leather suitcase near the door. From the discreet line of Vuitton. At least he wasn't a reporter. She'd been afraid of reporters since the discovery of poor Fran's body. Quill moved behind the registration desk and took up the pen. He gave his name as Thorne Smith, with an "e" (now why did that seem familiar?); address Boston, (by way of Atlanta—she was certain from his accent); car, Mercedes, Massachusetts plates; occupation. . . .

"Marketing," he said easily.

There really wasn't any way, Quill thought, to inquire about what kind of marketing. Black marketing? Industrial marketing? Grocery marketing? At the rate bodies were piling up, she was suspicious of anyone checking into her inn.

"It's okay, isn't it?"

"Hm?"

"That I'm in marketing. Investments, to be precise. An advisor in real estate, to be more precise yet."

Quill opened her mouth, then closed it. Four million was a decent sum, even these days. The government's fund had been announced in the paper; the total sum available to outlying counties all over New York State was close to one hundred million. It wasn't reporters she had to be worried about: murder was becoming far too commonplace to bring the media out unless the victim was famous, or the crime so brutal it would give pause to millions of Americans eating breakfast (and ratings to

the lucky station). She thought of Fran's frank and exuberant shout of the day before: SHOW ME THE
MONEY. Well, the governor had. And look what the
dog had brought in.

"Nice dog," said Mr. Smith dubiously. Max sniffed
thoroughly around his feet. He bent and patted him.

"That's odd," Quill said.

Mr. Smith's expression clearly said he thought Quill
was odd but was far too sophisticated to say so. "An
odd dog?"

"It's just that he's quite people-shy. Or he has been.
Maybe because he's feeling better. He peed yellow today, you know."

"*Did* he?"

Quill shook herself. "I'm sorry. It's been a tough couple of days, a tough couple of weeks, as a matter of fact,
and you must think I'm completely crazy."

"Not at all."

"Well. I'd better get you checked in before you flee
to the Marriott."

"I've been at the Marriott for the past few days. I'd
be happy to go back."

"Full up, I believe," Quill lied cheerfully. "Now.
Would you like a view of the waterfall? No, maybe
you'd better wait until tomorrow. I don't think the
body's up yet. What about a nice view of the rose gardens?"

"The body."

"Accident," Quill said briskly. "Here you are, room
200. Top of the stairs, then take a left. Will you need
help with your luggage?"

"No. No."

"And have you eaten?"

"Ah, no. I passed a diner on the way in. As a matter
of fact, our company's received some very good press
about the diner. It looked interesting. Hemlock Home

Diner? Fine Food and Fast? I make sort of a hobby of diners. You must know all about it.''

So Marge was, as usual, two steps ahead of her. A representative for wealthy investors in town, and she'd already conned him, somehow. Her dander up, Quill further perjured her soul. ''The food there? Grease up to here.'' She tapped her chin. ''The specialty in our dining room tonight is roast leg of lamb, a fresh mint sauce, the British way, with vinegar, new potatoes, and fresh parsley. You've heard of our chef, of course. Rated three stars by *L'Aperitif*.''

''Really?''

''And our wine list is very complete. What do you think?''

''As a matter of fact, the local wines are of equal interest to my company. Do you carry local wines?''

''We have a wonderful Chardonnay from Summerhill Winery. A marvelous varietal from Noir Hill, and some very decent red from Arcadia Vineyards.'' That, at least, was the absolute truth. ''Now, the diner?'' She shook her head gravely. ''The diner dinners are alcohol free. The owner,'' Quill added darkly, ''has a thing about liquor. Don't even think of going in there with yeast on your breath.'' Marge *did* have a thing about liquor; she drank her whiskey neat, and more than once had offered the opinion that wine was for weenies.

''Can I reserve a table for you for dinner?''

''I need a reservation?''

''Yes,'' Quill said diffidently. So he would see the room was empty when he sat down. So what?

''Fine. In about—'' He checked his watch. It was a Rolex. Not even gold. The platinum version. That watch would pay Doreen's salary for a year. ''Twenty minutes?''

''Hmm?''

"Twenty minutes?!" The idiot-child kindliness was back in his voice.

"That'll be 8:33, sir. We will seat you then."

Quill hurried into the dining room. Kathleen was still busy in the Tavern Bar, apparently; Mr. Pfieffer's table hadn't been cleared. She piled the dirty dishes on one arm and swept back into the kitchen. Meg was wiping down the sink. "Hey," she said.

"Hey, yourself."

"We've got one more for dinner."

"Send him to Marge's, Quill. She may be a sneaky son of a gun, but she's a terrific cook. I'm pooped. I'm beat. I'm so tired I could scream. Do you realize I've taken care of this whole kitchen by myself since this afternoon? That means dishes and cooking and cleaning up and more dishes and more cooking and MORE cleaning up in case that little weasel Pfieffer decides to call his buddies at the D.O.H. That damn dog, by the way, *is still here!*"

Quill reached down and absently scratched Max's ears. "Good boy. Mr. Smith will have the lamb."

"There isn't any lamb. You ate it all."

"You had some, too!"

"We ate it all, then. It's finished. Kaput. Gone."

"Can you make some more?"

"I cannot."

"Isn't there anything for dinner?"

Meg muttered under her breath and flung open the freezer door. "There's pizza," she said after a long moment.

"Pizza? Frozen pizza? In your kitchen?"

"It's Bjarne's pizza. He has a thing for American junk food. He doesn't think I know it's there, but I do." She took it out and weighed it in one hand. "Feels like the tasty five toppings variety."

"The package says 'herring.' "

"Bjarne's little joke. Or maybe it's herring pizza? What do I know?" She flung it back into the freezer and slammed the door shut.

"We have to feed this guy something, Meg."

"Why?"

"Because he's a rich investment counselor from Boston."

"Last time I looked, we had zero to invest."

"You're not getting the point," Quill said patiently. "He's here because of all that state money. He's an advisor, Meg. That means he advises people to invest in guess what . . ."

"Bankrupt inns?"

"Inns that need a little infusion of cash to be wildly successful. Meg, don't you see? This must be part of the governor's plan! When you put a lot of public money into a place, the private money is sure to follow. Mr. Smith is the thin edge of the wedge . . . no . . . no . . . you know what he is?"

Meg heaved a huge sigh.

"He's the advance man for the cavalry!"

"The cavalry being the hordes of the wealthy about to descend upon us? Sure."

"He *was* going to Marge's for dinner. Heard good things about the diner, he said. He hadn't, by the way, heard a word about you."

"Oh?" Meg scowled, and for a moment Quill thought the competitive spirit had won out over fatigue and despair. "Screw it. I'll feed him pizza."

"Meg!"

"Don't worry. I'll fix it up."

"What will I call it?"

"*Fou de suer* pizza."

"Fou de what?"

"I forgot. Your French sucks. Foo-duh-sur."

Quill went into the dining room. The influx of visitors

had spread detritus here, too. She pulled the carpet sweeper out from its place behind the maître d's podium. She swept the more visible parts of the carpet. Max, at first convinced the sweeper was a threat, bit it, sneezed, then retired to the maître d's podium to sit and wait. She filled Thorne Smith's water glass. She was waiting in the empty room when he came down the stairs.

"Reservation for one?" she asked. "For 8:33?"

"Yup."

"We can seat you now."

He looked at Max, who wagged his tail with a helpful expression.

Quill seated him, unfolded the napkin with a professional snap, and spread it on his lap. "Would you care to see a menu?"

"I thought there was only lamb."

"Well, I was wrong about the lamb. The chef and I haven't been communicating well lately. I thought you might like to see a menu to discover what we can offer when we aren't . . . um . . ."

"Aren't?" he said helpfully.

"So busy."

He was, Quill decided, a very nice man. He didn't look around the room with a pointed expression. The only other person she knew who would have done that was Myles McHale.

"Maybe I'll take a look at the menu tomorrow."

"I can offer you the wine list."

"That depends on what's for dinner, doesn't it?"

"Foo-de-sur pizza," Quill said.

"What?"

"Foo—"

"I heard you." He started to laugh. "Jee-sus! Okay, I'll have the pizza. And a good strong red to go with it."

"Great!" Quill smiled at him.

"And, Quill?"

"Yes?"

"Tell your sister I think you're crazy, too."

Meg looked at her face when she banged into the kitchen and started to giggle. The kitchen smelled delicious. Whatever Meg was making, Mr. Smith was going to like it a great deal. "You jerk," Quill said without heat. "*Fou de suer* indeed. Look, you serve the poor guy, will you? Sit down with him, too. What does Harvey say? Schmooze him a little."

"Oh, *gag*, Quill! I can't believe you said that!"

"Well, you know what I mean. Just be pleasant, okay?"

"And what are you going to do?"

"A little follow-up with the Crafty Ladies."

Freddie, Mary, and Robin were seated in the middle of the Tavern Bar. A few of the tables around them were filled, mostly with volunteer firemen and a state trooper or two. Quill passed Davy Kiddermeister, nursing a beer and in close colloquy with Denny Webster.

"Yo, Quill." Davy got to his feet. "I've been wondering where you were. How you holding up?"

"All right, I suppose. This is terrible, Davy. Do you have any leads yet at all?"

Davy was as fair as his sister Kathleen was dark; this was a disadvantage in a young sheriff who blushed easily. His ears and cheeks turned bright pink, but he said steadily, "I'm afraid we don't know much at all yet. Doc Bishop's got this body at the Bellinis', too. And the fellas from forensics in Syracuse are back. They might turn something up."

"Same M.O. as the other, looks like," Denny said. "It's a terrible thing. We were just talking that maybe we should get the mayor to declare a curfew."

Davy nodded agreement. "Thing is, with this killer running around loose, we don't know if anyone's safe. You be sure and lock your doors tonight, Quill."

"You think it's just a series of random killings, then?" Quill shook her head. "I can't believe that. I mean, the killer climbed up the balcony to get into Ellen Dunbarton's room and deliberately set that fire. Not only that," she added, hoping the sarcasm didn't show up in her voice, "he gagged her with duct tape and taped her arms behind her back. Doesn't that seem as though the murderer targeted her particularly?"

"Maybe the fire and the murder were separate, like," Denny said.

"Separate?!"

Davy's face burned an even brighter red. "It's just a theory, Quill. See, Ellen Dunbarton wasn't burned to death. And Fran Grimsby wasn't either. Both of them were strangled."

Quill breathed out, slowly. "Before the fire?"

"Looks like."

"So they didn't . . ." Burning to death had always seemed so horrible. Then she thought, strangled first?

"Probably didn't feel much at all," Davy said. "Anyway, this makes us think the first fire may have been a different thing altogether." His eyes shifted away from hers.

"You mean that Meg and I did it."

"Yuh."

"You know me, Davy. And you know Meg. Neither one of us would have done such a thing. Under any circumstances. No matter how broke we were."

"You see all kinds of things in the insurance business," Denny said helpfully.

"Now where have I heard *that* before?" Quill snapped. "Mr. Burke is feeling somewhat abused, I admit, but that does not mean that his suspicions are justified.''

''Whatever you say, Quill. So . . .''

''And,'' Quill went on, her temper up, ''you ought to consider that an attempt was made to burn the second body, too.''

''Copycat,'' Denny said wisely.

''Oh, pooh!'' She cast an expert glance at the table. ''Do either of you need another beer? Or more peanuts? If not, I've a few things to do before the night's out.''

''Just one thing.'' Davy turned his beer can in his hand. ''You haven't heard from the sheriff, by any chance?''

''You're the sheriff, David Lincoln Kiddermeister. And no, I haven't heard from Myles today. Excuse me, will you?'' Exasperated, she wound her way through the rest of the room to the bar. Kathleen greeted her with a tired smile. ''How are you holding up?''

''Not bad. The tips are pretty good.'' Kathleen brushed her hair back from her forehead. ''Who's been taking care of the tables in the dining room?''

''Me. We'll close at nine-thirty tonight, Kath. Oh, and don't forget that the beer's free to the volunteers.''

''Got it.''

Quill chatted with a few more customers, then went to the Crafty Ladies' table and sat down.

''You must be run off your feet,'' Freddie said sympathetically.

''I'm used to it. Have the three of you eaten anything tonight?''

''Oh, yes. Kathleen brought us some delicious soup from the kitchen, and very good bread. Cucumber, the soup was.''

''Cold,'' Robin offered. ''But we didn't mind. With everything that's happened, it's a wonder the kitchen got anything out at all. We're sitting here feeling so useless!

We're not used to just sitting, you know.''

"Well, you should be,'' Quill said warmly. "Think of all the times in the past when you've been run off your feet between kids and jobs and husbands. I think you deserve to sit. I hope Kathleen remembered to bring you the sherry?''

"She brought us a drink in a little teeny glass, but we think she just may have gotten mixed up,'' Freddie confided. "But, as Robin says, with all that's been happening, it's no wonder. The stuff in it tasted like furniture polish. Just a little bit.''

"So we told her how to make a Fuzzy Navel,'' Mary said. "*That* hit the spot.''

"I'm glad. You know that Doreen and I have moved you to the second floor. You'll be right near my suite, and my sister's. And you're all in the same room. We'll leave the lights on in the hall, if you're at all nervous about staying on.'' She cocked her head, puzzled. "I'm not sure why you just don't go home.''

"The president's coming,'' Mary said simply. "We've never met the president.''

"I don't understand.''

"It's like this. We're all retired, you know. I'm sixty-three.'' She paused.

"No!'' Quill said.

"And Freddie here's sixty-eight, if you can believe it.''

"I can't,'' said Quill. At the moment, they all looked considerably older than their actual ages.

"And I'm the oldest of the bunch. Just seventy,'' Robin said. "Might as well confess it now, before the girls here turn me in.''

"I wouldn't believe it of any of you.''

Mary adjusted the lace collar of her twinset. This one was a pale violet. "Well, as I was saying, we were all retired, and we kind of had been in business together all those years anyway.''

"What she means is, we were all in the same business," Robin said, a little sharply. "Babies, husbands, and boring jobs. Don't boast so, Freddie. It'll always catch you out."

"I'm sorry, dear. You're right. Well, we all get together for coffee Monday mornings."

"We can't do that anymore, can we?" Mary's eyes clouded with tears.

"Hang on, puss." Robin grasped Mary's hand and squeezed it tightly. "Hang on."

"For a few years, we'd been talking for weeks about how useless we felt." Freddie sat back with the air of having unburdened herself. "That was it. After years of being on our feet, and busy, well—the kids were grown . . ." She interrupted herself. "Do you call your mother once a week, Quill?"

"My parents died in a boating accident nine years ago."

"Well, you should call once a week. And you would, I'm sure, if your mother were alive. But children these days . . ." She shook her head. "So there we were. Beached."

"And the package came," Robin said. "You know, it was one of those 'earn thousands of dollars at home in your spare time' sort of things." She turned to the others. "I still think Ellen sent in an ad and just didn't tell us. She never wanted to admit how lonely we were, or how desperate . . ."

"Now *you* hang on," Mary said. She put an arm around her friend. "But we had fun, didn't we?"

"We surely did. And if you ask me, we *improved* that darn business plan. You see, Quill, the way it was set up, you were supposed to send money to the president of the Crafty Ladies Kit service and get instructions on how to run home parties. But home parties—ha! What woman these days has time to give parties?"

"We did," Freddie said. "But then, we're retired. And we weren't as in need of money as some poor housewife is."

"We improved the plan," Mary interrupted. "We wrote to the president, Mr. Vinge, or maybe it's Mrs. Vinge, we never did find out."

Freddie had lost her sad, depressed look and was animated. "We wrote with all our suggestions for improvement. Just-in-time inventory, will-call supply chain, toll free 1-800 number. And the president wrote back! He said—I feel sure it's a man—that our suggestions were excellent. He suggested that we try them for a year, and if we were showing a profit—and we are, Quill dear—that he'd buy our ideas and franchise them."

"Franchise them?"

"Like Burger King," Robin explained. "For a down payment, you get the whole business idea, and the Crafty Ladies logo and a start-up plan. You even get financing, if you need it. Mr. Vinge said we would get ten percent of everything if we went national. Do you know how much money would be in that?"

"Sometimes," Freddie confided in a hushed voice, "we all get together and try to figure it out. How much we might have, I mean."

"I see." Quill got up. She wanted to put her arms around them all and keep them safe. She'd found the motive. Or at least she was pretty sure she'd found the motive. "By the way—do any of you play the triangle?"

"The triangle?" Mary said. "You mean the little bell chime thingie in orchestras?"

"Yes. Or does the triangle have any significance for you? Any at all?"

Three bewildered faces stared at her.

"Never mind. You three take care of yourselves, okay? Meg and I will be right down the hall from you, and if you need anything, anything at all, don't even stop to think. Just come and get me."

"We promise," Freddie said with a twinkle. "Thanks, Mom!"

Quill exited to a chorus of delighted giggles.

"It could possibly be a great deal of money," Howie Murchison said. He yawned into the phone. "Hard to say. But businesses like Tupperware, and those Copper Craft things are worth quite a bit. Can't this keep, Quill? It's not all that late, I grant you, but I'm an early-to-bed kind of guy. Besides, I'm a lawyer, not a businessman. Why don't you ask Jo—sorry, I forgot. Why don't you call Mark Jefferson at the bank . . . sorry, I forgot that, too. What about Marge?" He stopped. Quill could hear him breathing into the phone. "Nope. I can see why you called me."

"And just what have the gossip mills been saying?" she asked sweetly.

"Ah. Well."

"Who was it?" Quill demanded. "You know me, Howie. When my dander's up, I don't quit."

"Dander," Howie mused. "Now there's a word from my grandmother's days."

"I've been talking all night to women who might well be your grandmother, Howie Murchison. So. Was it Esther at one of her shrimp and mayonnaise lunches you don't think anyone knows about? Or was it Miriam Doncaster, at an *intime* little dinner in Syracuse? Who's been talking about us?"

"Does everybody in town know about my dates?"

"That," said Quill ruthlessly, "is the price you pay for being an eligible bachelor. About the gossip: You tell me what you've heard, and I'll tell you if it's true.''

"That your mortgage's a month overdue.''

"Blabbermouth Jefferson. And he's right. And?''

"That you're furious with Marge because she made an offer to buy out the Inn and you think she's trying to drive you out of business.''

"Esther," said Quill. "And John?''

"That you rejected John for Myles, and he's run off to nurse a broken heart in Grand Rapids. No, call me a liar. Long Island, that was it.''

"That either came from my very own dear sister or Miriam Doncaster. Probably Miriam. Trust the town librarian for the romantic view.''

"Are you in trouble, Quill?''

She closed her eyes. She could see Howie sitting in his leather armchair, gray, balding, slightly paunchy. He'd have on his disgraceful loafers and be drinking one more glass of wine than he should. "I'll manage, Howie.''

"You call me if you need me. My pension's secure. I don't need the fee.''

"You're a sweetie. Now. Just let me be sure I understand this. One, under the circumstances I described to you, this Mr. Vinge would definitely owe the Crafty Ladies a substantial sum of money if he took their ideas and used them to change his business procedures. Oh, and if he profited by the ideas.''

"That's not exactly what I said, but it'll do.''

"Two. If there are no Crafty Ladies around to make the claim, he's home free.''

"That's an assumption you made, Quill, not I.''

"Hey, it gives me enough to start on. I've got to solve this case, Howie. I know what you didn't tell me about town gossip. That Meg and I set that fire for the insurance money. We didn't.''

"I take it you two are planning on solving this case?''

"We don't get that money unless I clear our name. We need it. But there's worse, Howie. I'm afraid there are going to be more murders. What do you think of that?"

He sighed. "You have any idea when Myles will be back?"

"Nope. I can handle this on my own. Thanks, Howie. You can go to bed now."

"I'm going to. Take care of yourself."

It was late, after eleven. Quill prowled the Inn, making sure the doors were locked and the windows shut and bolted from the inside. Max had disappeared again, sometime earlier. Quill hoped he wasn't after more chickens. Farmers in Hemlock Falls shot dogs who chased their chickens. She wondered who had let him out, and then recalled the door. His makeshift dog door; damn it all. She got a hammer from the kitchen tool kit, went into the Tavern Bar and crawled under the table concealing the hole. She'd have to ask Mike to take care of it in the morning. In the meantime, she whacked a few fourpenny nails in place and tested the frame by pushing hard against it. It held.

She went to her room, suddenly exhausted. She forced herself to brush her teeth, shower, then fell into bed. She looked at the clock: 12:30, and Meg would need help in the kitchen at six.

She slept.

"Dammit, Max!" she said. She pushed at the source of the warm breath on her cheek and rolled over. She pulled the covers over her head. Something pulled them down. Furious, she sat up and turned on the bedside lamp.

"Who the hell is Max?"

"Myles!" She held out her arms. "Oh, thank goodness. Myles!"

CHAPTER 7

The thin spring moon spread a fan of pale light across the floor. Quill lay with her head against Myles' shoulder. She rubbed her cheek across his bare chest.

"Max snores," Myles said.

Quill propped herself on her elbow and looked over her side of the bed. Max lay tucked in a ball on the floor. His forepaws jerked. He was dreaming. She really did have to get the window under the table in the Tavern Bar fixed; maybe Myles could fit it with a spring hinge. She turned to look at Myles, a broad-shouldered shape in the dark. He hadn't really taken to Max yet. As a matter of fact, nobody had. Maybe she'd try again to fix the dog door herself. "I've been meaning to give him a bath." She yawned. "What time is it?" She felt him move and stretch an arm out to the bedside table.

"Two o'clock."

She rolled over and ran her hands down each side of his neck, then rested her palms on the heavy muscles there. "Men are denser than women."

"That may be very true." He tightened his arms around her. She could feel him laughing.

"I meant muscle-wise. Flesh-wise." She reached

down and touched the length of him. "Soft-tissue-wise."

"You feel lighter. Have you lost weight?"

"I don't think so. Although it'd be the only good thing to come out of this sorry mess."

"You get any thinner and I'll have a talk with Andy Bishop. Why don't you tell me about the sorry mess."

"You need to sleep, my dearest dear. How long was the flight from Frankfurt?"

"Seven hours. Another two at Kennedy, and then an hour to Syracuse. Not bad."

She didn't want to ask the question, but she did. "When do you have to go back? Let me rephrase that." She sat up and put on a streetwise accent. "So, sailor. How long ya in town for?"

"A week or two. Maybe more. A lot depends on the situation in Bonn."

He wouldn't tell her more than that. He never did. "You didn't come back because you thought I was in trouble, did you?"

His hands were rough, large, callused. She loved his hands. He picked up the hair from the back of her neck, kissed her there, then ran one hand down her back in a long gentle stroke. "I told Carter I had a family emergency."

She turned and glared at him in the dark.

"But there's a great deal for me to do in Washington. I switched assignments with Moorhouse in D.C. So I'm back in the States for the duration of the assignment. How long I'm in Hemlock Falls depends on how much I can get accomplished on-line."

She didn't say anything, thinking this over.

He made a movement, oddly tentative for a man of his size and assurance. "You might consider, Quill, that I'm a part of your life. Of all your life. There isn't one category just for lovers, and a separate category for inn-keeper, and a third for artist. They're all integrated. Or they should be. And don't confuse my presence with interference. When have I ever made a decision for you?''

She sighed.

''So I'll be here, but just at the times when it's right.''

''Right,'' she said reflectively.

''Right. As in appropriate, fitting, usual. For example: 'Myles, I need to talk to you about this,' or 'Myles, this was not a good day. Do you want to hear why?' or, better yet—'Myles, I had a great day. How was yours?' '' He stopped stroking her back and gave her a light, affectionate slap. ''It's easy. Now get me something to eat, woman.''

She threw on a robe, switched on the lights, and went to her refrigerator. Max followed, delighted to have human company at this hour, and peered in the opened door with her. ''Cheese omelet with toast?''

''Sounds fine.''

Myles kept very few clothes in her suite: some shaving gear, a few shirts. He pulled on the robe she kept for him and sat at her small kitchen table, long legs stretched out, his gray eyes narrowed. She gave him a succinct account of the past week's events while she cooked.

Quill poured them both some orange juice, divided the omelet neatly in half, and put the plates on the table. ''That's it.'' She rubbed her face with both hands. ''Between the financial mess and those poor women, it's been quite a week.'' She felt her face grow warm with indignation. ''Dookie Shuttleworth is right, you know. The love of money is the root of all evil. This Vinge finds a few women in the way of his profits and phhht!'' She snapped her fingers. ''Get them out of the way. Marge Schmidt sees a chance to pick off eight years of Meg's hard work and bloody! Friendship goes out the window.''

"What is the financial situation exactly? John told me it's fairly serious."

Quill closed her eyes. "It's two o'clock in the morning, Myles. It's the wrong time to talk about the financials."

He laughed a little. "Not if the State's going to nail the doors shut tomorrow morning. Can you make payroll this week?"

"John made arrangements with that computer service in town to issue paychecks to Doreen, Kathleen, and Bjarne. Meg and I are on very short rations. I'm sure the company will call me if that changes. He did say he'd set aside a minimum payroll until the end of the summer. Then, I don't know."

"And the other bills? You've missed one mortgage payment. Mark Jefferson isn't going to start pressuring you until you're three or four months in arrears."

"I know we'd be fine for the summer if Burke would just issue that check. And, Myles, by then we'd have a much better handle on the grant from the governor's office. And I know Marge wouldn't be so interested in buying us out if she didn't count on a lot of money coming in from private investors after the grant money's in circulation. I didn't tell you about Thorne Smith, did I?"

"Thorne Smith?" He drew his eyebrows together. "Why does that name sound familiar?"

"Beats me. He's an investment advisor from a big Boston firm. He seems to be here because of the Winegrowers' Association."

"What's the name of the firm?"

Quill told him, then asked if he recognized it.

"No. But I'll check."

"He looks successful, behaves with confidence . . ." She rubbed her nose. "Gee, that name sounds familiar to me, too. Hang on a minute." Her kitchen was divided from her small living room by a breakfast counter. She stored her own laptop computer under one of the shelves. Myles watched as she dragged it out and logged on.

"I do have a question, however. What was the purpose of the meeting at Summerhill yesterday?"

"Why . . ." Quill hesitated, thinking while her modem connected with the Internet. "I don't know."

"Before Meg got edgy, Marge said what, exactly?"

"She wanted to plan how to use the four million dollars."

"She never got a chance to explain?"

"No. Come to think of it . . ."

He waited, drinking his orange juice. Quill stared at the computer screen, then absently keyed in the address of the New York City Public Library. "Who was the fellow who looked around in wild surmise upon a peak in Darien?"

"Stout Cortez. And I believe the poet was referring to his tenacity, not his girth. Why do you ask?"

"Because Meg and I engaged in some. Wild surmise, that is. When I think about it, neither Meg nor I have the least idea what Marge had in mind. For all I know, she and the Summerhills wanted to use the money to establish a charity for the restoration of impoverished inns. We just assumed that they wanted it all for themselves." She closed her eyes in chagrin. "Oh, dear. Oh, *dear*. Would you look at me? This financial crisis is uncovering some very unpleasant parts of my character."

"Financial distress can twist the best of us."

"I'm embarrassed."

He smiled. "Why don't you sit down with Marge and Hugh and ask them what they have in mind?"

"I'll go out to the winery today."

"I love it when you're humble, Quill. While you're in this unusually abashed and vulnerable state, why

don't you let me loan you the fifty thousand that's due
from Burke?''

''No.''

This didn't seem to surprise him. He finished his omelet, then said, ''The bank won't loan you the money on
it unless Burke is willing to guarantee payment. Since
the arson investigation is still open, that guarantee isn't
going to happen. One way or another, the check will
eventually come in. You need it. You know what can
happen if you don't make payroll, Quill. The State can—
and will—put a lock on your front door. John would
advise you to take this loan. My interest rates,'' he said
with a grin, ''are pretty low.''

''I don't like it.''

''It's a good idea for a lot of reasons. It'll take the
money pressure off temporarily. You're going to have
to make some changes at the Inn, that's clear. But you
want a clear head and a rational state of mind to do that.
Hard to sustain if you're fending off creditors.''

Quill rubbed her face with both hands. ''One of the
many many reasons I love you, Myles, is that you always make sense. I'll talk to Meg.''

''Good. Let's take a look at the other problem. Do
you want some advice on how to look at these crimes?''

Quill eyed him a little warily. She gave herself a few
moments and queried the Reference Library about
Thorne Smith. Then she said, ''Yes. I think I do.''

''Talk to Andy directly about the autopsy results. Go
over the evidence bags Davy's collected yourself. Don't
take his word for it, or let him give you a list. You said
Doreen went through the room where Ellen Dunbarton
was murdered?''

''She found a few things. Nothing that seemed important.''

''Every anomaly, no matter how small, is vital in an
investigation. What about your suspect?''

The screen blinked invitingly at her. She ignored it. "Paul Pfieffer, Myles. It has to be. He's got the business background. If his second career as a direct market salesman came out, it would jeopardize his job with the state. And he's got that jumpy, anal retentive attitude a lot of state employees seem to have.

"Then there's Thorne Smith. He's been at the Marriott during the entire time the Crafty Ladies have been here. He's slick, smooth, and you only have to look at him to realize how much he likes money.

"The other alternative is just plain Mr. X. There's no reason for this murderer to show himself. Quite the reverse. But if it is Mr. X, I have no idea where to begin looking for him. It's probably that X lives in Hemlock Falls, don't you think? Why else have the Crafty Ladies check in here? We have how many people living in the village? Three thousand and some odd. I don't know how to begin The murders Meg and I have solved in the past have risen out of personal motives. The players have always been onstage before. This could be a Patricia Cornwell situation, don't you think? By that I mean forensics are going to solve this case, not intuition and deduction. Oh, I considered the fact that it's someone we've known for years, like Marge. But come on! Or the Summerhills, or one of the Petersons—*anyone* could be involved. But it doesn't add up."

"If it doesn't add up, it's because we don't have enough facts in place." She was pleased by his use of the pronoun. Myles had always resisted her involvement in his cases in the past. On the other hand, he wasn't the sheriff now, he was a private investigator himself. He drummed his fingers on the table. "Do you mind if I poke around a bit myself? This case is interesting."

"Davy and the fire chief would love to have you poke around a bit. They keep asking me when you're coming home."

"I'll see what I can do."

"You'll tell me everything, Myles, won't you?" she said anxiously. "I mean, I feel that all of this is my responsibility. I worry that—" She felt tears behind her eyes. "Oh, nuts. It's nuts. What's the matter with me? You're much better at everything than I am." She frowned fiercely at Max, who had curled up at her feet. "The cavalry's come over the hill, Max, and the white wimmin have been saved from a fate worse than death." She switched the frown to Myles. "I'm so *glad* I amuse you."

He rubbed his chin, partly, Quill suspected, to conceal the grin on his face. "Listen to me, Quill. That somewhat incoherent metaphor implies that either I or you or perhaps both of us want the kind of marriage where there's a general and a private. I'm speaking of a marriage in principle, you understand, since you're so skittish about the fact. We aren't a paramilitary organization, my darling. We're two overlapping circles, right?" He made a circle out of the thumbs and forefingers of both hands and held them up. "We, Myles and Quill, are in the center. Quill *qua* Quill is to the left. Myles *qua* Myles is to the right. Together, but separate." His glance fell on Max, whose tail thumped approval at the tone of voice, if not the sentiment. "I suppose we've got to include that damn dog, too."

Quill, the query about Thorne Smith forgotten, shut down the computer, and turned off the light. "Myles," she said into the dark. "Have I told you lately that I love you?"

Quill came downstairs at seven o'clock the next morning, feeling guilty. She'd had every intention of getting up at six to help Meg in the kitchen, but the alarm had wakened Myles, of course, and there you were, she thought. She felt wonderful. Three cheers for the snake in the apple tree.

"Quill!" Freddie Patch's worried voice stopped her headlong rush to the kitchen. The three remaining Crafty Ladies were seated at their regular table. "Could we talk to you for a minute?"

They all had coffee and orange juice at least, Quill noticed. Poor Meg. If she accepted that loan from Myles, they could afford help, at least until this was all over. "Of course. I just want to check on Meg, then I'll be right back."

Quill pushed open one of the double doors to the kitchen and peeked in. Doreen was standing at the work-table, hulling strawberries. Meg was at the oven with a pan of uncooked muffins. "Hi, guys!" She walked in. Doreen sniffed. Meg slapped the muffins on the oven rack and slammed the door shut. "Sorry I'm late."

"Everything's under control," Meg said. "Except my normally excellent temper. We can't close the kitchen because we need the income, as pitiful as it is, from the two and one half guests that are staying here. We can't get help because we're broke—" She stopped herself, and looked closely at her sister "Is Myles home?"

"Did you hear him come in last night?"

"Nope. Slept like a log. An overworked, underpaid— make that no-paid—log. Andy wanted to take my blood pressure three times last evening because he thought I was dead. I have none. Because I am dead. On the other hand, you're blooming. I'll bet your blood pressure is just fine. You worked as hard as I did yesterday, and you had about the same amount of sleep, and goodness knows you are even more worried than I am about the lack of money, but you don't look dead. Since I am a part-time and, if I do say so myself, highly qualified amateur detective, I deduced, cleverly, that Myles came home."

"I'm impressed," Quill said. "I really am."

"Also, he come by for coffee a few minutes ago." Doreen dumped the hulled strawberries into a colander and began trimming a new pint. "He left that"—she nodded toward a white envelope on the counter—"in case you and Miss Hissy here wanted to take that loan."

Quill picked up the envelope and opened it. The check for fifty thousand was inside.

"I'm goin' to the bank this morning," Doreen offered. "To deposit my paycheck. If I got one. I can take that there with me."

Quill looked a question at Meg.

"Are you out of your mind? Of course we should take it!"

"What if we can't pay it back?" Quill asked quietly.

"You remember those 401k's John set up for us."

"He said never never never touch them."

"When needs must, or whatever that expression is. I'll guarantee my twenty-five thousand from my 401k, Quill. You do what you want."

"It's all we've got left."

Meg shrugged. "So? I can always get a job as a chef. You can teach art to the artless."

"And I'll take in laundry," Doreen said. "You laugh, Meg. I done it before."

"I'm not laughing."

"You want I should deposit that there?"

"Yes," said Quill. "Go ahead. And the paychecks should be in the morning's mail, Doreen. That payroll service on Main Street is doing them."

"I don't need mine for a while yet. But I'll see Kathleen gets hers. And Mike."

Quill didn't know what to say, so she didn't say anything. But she gave Doreen a kiss, and made a face at her sister.

"This here order's ready for table five," Doreen scolded. "You get it right on out."

Quill took the three bowls of strawberries, brioche, and a jug of cream to the ladies at table five. "I'd like to sit with you for a while," Quill said. "But if we get guests in for breakfast, I'm going to have to wait on them. Our waitress—um—called in sick."

"The financial situation hasn't improved any?" Freddie said, with unexpected shrewdness. "You can always tell when you have to lay off the help. I'm so sorry. And I'm afraid we're going to add to your troubles. We're leaving."

Quill had been too busy to notice before, but none of the three women at the table looked at all well. Freddie's soft white hair hadn't been combed. Mary's eyes were deeply shadowed. Robin's hands trembled as she ate her toast. Quill sat in the vacant fourth chair and looked at them with concern. "Did anything happen last night?"

"Noises in the corridor." Robin shuddered. "We didn't sleep at all."

"I'm afraid that must have been a friend of mine. It was very late when he got in."

"Terrible sighs and moans."

Quill kept her composure. "Max the dog, I should think. He went out early this morning."

"We don't feel safe here," Freddie said softly. "We just don't feel safe."

"I don't blame you at all. But do you think moving is going to help?"

"We can't leave Hemlock Falls until Mr. Vinge comes, we just can't!" Mary cried. "There's all this money at stake."

More than they've seen in their whole lives, Quill thought, and sighed. "I understand. But I want to ask you something. What if Mr. Vinge killed Fran and Ellen?"

Freddie's soft mouth formed an astonished "O."

"Mr. Vinge?" Robin said. "Mr. Vinge? But he's going to pay us! Why would he want to hurt us?"

"I see what you're saying," Mary said slowly. "It's because he owes us, isn't it? It's because we've come up with all these good ideas. He wants to keep them for himself."

"I'm afraid so. At least, that's my theory." They looked, if it were possible, even more frightened than before. Quill made her voice as reassuring as she could. "You know what? You all need some food. Have your breakfast, and then we'll talk about it. I," said Quill, "have a plan."

"To help us? We can eat and talk at the same time," Freddie said eagerly. "We do it all the time at canasta club. What's your plan, Quill? Here. See? I'm eating my strawberries." She placed a spoonful of them in her mouth and chewed energetically.

"Are we going to be decoys?" Freddie asked. "Like on the cop shows?"

"The decoys always get into trouble on the cop shows on TV, Freddie," Mary said. "I'm sure Quill has a better plan than that."

Actually, Quill didn't have a better plan than that. "I wasn't thinking of using you as decoys, exactly. More along the lines of getting Mr. Vinge to show himself. Without danger to any of you. But first, I need to know where he is, and how to reach him."

"Good morning," said a dry voice in Quill's ear. "I assume, since these people are having breakfast, that food is available."

"Mr. Pfieffer!" Quill jumped, recovered herself, and got to her feet reluctantly. "I'll be right with you. Please have a seat where you would like. Freddie? Mary? Robin? I'll see you all for tea? As usual?" She invested her voice with heavy significance.

"Tea? Our usual tea?" Freddie blinked in confusion. Mary poked her sharply. "You know!" She hissed loudly, "The Plan!"

"Oh, of course." She dimpled. "You know," she confided, "this is quite exciting."

"At three, then" Quill said loudly. "In the gazebo."

"Three, at the gazebo." Robin dug into her capacious purse and withdrew a little pen and a cloth covered notebook. "Recycled detergent carton," she explained proudly, displaying the notebook. White powder showered onto her strawberries. "You just find a few scraps of cloth, trim the cardboard with a pair of pinking shears, and staple the unused backs of Christmas cards together for the paper. Very sturdy, and of course it doesn't cost a dime. You have to buy the pen, though." She put on her reading glasses, squinted at the opened pages, and said as she wrote, "Th-re-ee oo'-clock. Gazebo. There! We'll see you then!"

Paul Pfieffer cleared his throat in a pay-some-attention-to me! way, and Quill nodded hastily. "You all stay right around here, today, please. I don't want to lose anyone else."

Quill was rushed off her feet in the next hour, and the kitchen crew was put under a severe strain. It hadn't taken the village gossip mill long to discover Mr. Pfieffer's whereabouts or to catch wind of the presence of the rich investment counselor from Boston. Nineteen of the twenty-four members of the Chamber of Commerce showed up, "just for coffee and a little something," as well as the Kiwanis, the Lions Club, the Ladies Auxiliary, and what seemed like an entire busload of the Hemlock Falls Future Farmers of America. As far as Quill was concerned, the absentees were more important than those present. "Marge and Betty haven't poked their heads in all morning," she said hurriedly to Meg, "and neither have Selena and Hugh Summerhill. Worse yet,

Harvey isn't here. Harvey's always where the real action is. And everyone manages to drop casually into the conversation: 'Seen that Mr. Pfieffer around?' or 'Heard some fella from Boston was here,' and there'll be a significant pause. Well, tough. Pfieffer ate and went, and I haven't seen Mr. Smith at all.''

"Who cares?" Meg filled four plates of scrambled eggs with bacon, added a sprig of mint and a whole strawberry to each serving, and slid the plates onto a tray. "Table six. The mayor and his banker pals. You know, I could have made it as a short-order cook."

"You may end up as a short-order cook if the Summerhills and Marge are plotting a way to keep all that government money themselves." She stopped herself and said conscientiously, "Although we don't know that, do we? They may be planning to use it for the good of the town. If they can get their hands on it. Anyway, after the rush is over, I'm going to take a little trip out to the winery. I'll bet you fifty cents that's where our conspirators are." She picked up the tray and braced it on one hip.

"If you're abandoning me, then get me some more staff!" Meg shouted after her.

The dining room cleared out at eleven. Quill resisted the temptation to sit and put her feet up. Instead, she went into her office. She left the phone on automatic answer. She entered the fifty-thousand-dollar deposit in the computer, then picked up the phone and called Kathleen, Nate, and Dina Muir, in quick succession. Fulltime, she said to each of them, at least until the end of June. She took the list John had left and wrote out checks for the most pressing of the bills. Two estimates for rebuilding the burned-out suite lay in her ''In'' basket. She reviewed them, dismayed. Labor rates had gone up since she and Meg had last remodeled. And the price of lumber was extortionate. They could talk about Hurricane Hugo all they wanted, she thought darkly, somebody was making a pile of money off wood. She placed a call to Peterson's Hardware and asked that the most pressing work be done right away. "The wiring, the Sheetrock, and the windows on the balcony," she said. "That's all I can afford for the time being, Petey. The flooring and the rest of it is just going to have to wait." He told her he'd be there that afternoon, and Quill rang off with a sense of having accomplished a great deal. There was just one more thing to check. She dialed 597-FOOD. Betty Hall answered the phone. Quill pinched her nose closed with one hand. "Marge Schmidt? This is the state insurance commission calling."

"Ain't here."

"It's quite important to reach her. Tell her we called."

"Wait!" Betty's voice was anxious. "This about her application to be a broker?"

"I'm sorry, I cannot discuss applications for broker's licenses over the phone." This was true. Quill didn't know a thing about applying for a broker's license.

"She's at a meeting. I'll give you the number."

"Sorry."

"Summerhill Vineyards," Betty said desperately. "The number is . . ."

Quill smacked the phone into the cradle with all the rudeness of a state employee on her way to lunch. She'd been right.

The door to her office opened. "Hi!" Dina said. "I'm back. You look happy. Did we win the lottery?"

"Just a reprieve. We aren't out of the woods yet. I've got to go out. Could you handle all the phone messages? I haven't gone through them yet."

"No problem."

"And bookings?"

"We've got bookings?"

"We just might. You never know. And if Meg needs you in the kitchen you'll give her a hand, won't you? And if Myles should call—did I tell you he came home last night?—tell him I've gone to the Summerhills for a meeting. You've got that number in the Rolodex."

"Things are sure hopping," Dina said, pleased. "Are you solving the murders?"

"At the moment, I'm saving the Inn. This afternoon at three, I'm solving the murders."

"Cool. Anything else?"

"I can't handle anything else! Mail these bills, if you would. And if Max comes in, give him chopped up rice, a couple of raw eggs, and some bouillon. His digestion can't handle anything else."

"Sounds gross. Bouillon, rice, and eggs. Got it."

"He'll want something else, but he can't have it. Keep an eye on the Crafty Ladies, Dina. And make a note each time Paul Pfieffer leaves and comes back."

"Paul Pfieffer?"

"Paul Pfieffer."

"Got it."

"One last thing. Would you see if Doc Bishop and Davy Kiddermeister can come over here about eight this evening for dinner? Tell both of them they can have whatever they want from Meg's kitchen."

"Got it." Dina flipped her long brown hair and sighed happily. "Nice to be busy again, you know? Makes a person feel more useful."

"It certainly does. Do you have any questions?"

"Yah. Just a couple. Who's Paul Pfieffer, which one is Max, how long is Sheriff McHale—"

"He's not sheriff anymore, Dina."

"—going to be in town, and what if David doesn't want to come to dinner?"

"Why shouldn't Davy want to come to dinner?"

Dina's clear brown eyes were as sorrowful as Max's. "We had a fight. He might not want to be in the same county as me."

"You're dating Davy Kiddermeister?"

"Just for laughs, you know? It's not, like, serious. But," she said with unexpected gravity, "it's like, don't call him Davy, okay? His name's David. It's more— responsible. He needs, like, more respect."

"How does David feel about you getting your doctorate?" Quill asked dryly. "You know, Dina, he's a nice, good-looking guy, but as far as I know, he's not much interested in a life outside Hemlock Falls."

"Quill! You have, like, these old fogy notions! If I have the bigger paycheck, does he, like, *care*? I don't *think* so." She rolled her eyes. "I think I got it all, okay? I mean, your instructions. So I know where you are; I'll call you if I have to." She fluttered her fingers. "I'll catch the phones. And I'll catch you later." She banged out the door to her workstation behind the reception desk.

Old fogy? Quill looked in the mirror hung on the back of her office door. Were those lines on her upper lip? Was she getting gray? She unwound her hair from the top of her head and examined her widow's peak. No gray. Just the usual red, darker than it generally was at this time of year, because she hadn't anytime to spend outside. And old fogies didn't single-handedly save their family business while simultaneously solving the biggest crime of the year in Hemlock Falls.

"Maybe Miss Marple did," she said to her reflection. She sighed heavily. "Except that she had a private income, so she didn't worry about the business side of life." She checked the time: noon. With any luck, she'd catch Marge and the Summerhills right in the middle of planning to appropriate all that cash for themselves.

* * *

Yesterday's clouds were cleared, and the sun was shining. Driving the Oldsmobile to the vineyard, Quill's spirits rose. She hummed that she loved Paris in the winter, she loved Paris in the fall, then sang, full-throated, "*I love Paris in the springtime!*" and ignored the speed limit. She turned left at the gold-lettered sign that said SUMMERHILL WINERY. The sign giving the hours for the tasting room had a placard over it: CLOSED FOR TODAY ONLY. Quill followed the arrows up the hill.

Most of the boutique wineries in the area were built on the slopes of hills surrounding the lakes. Summerhill Winery was no exception. Lake Cayuga glittered in the sunshine below the fields. The air was scented with apple blossoms and flowering plum. The grapevines were just coming into leaf. The rows between the long vines had been neatly raked. The fields themselves were deserted. The vines were trimmed and culled in early winter, after the harvest, Quill knew, so maybe there wasn't a great deal to do in the spring. Either that, or the Summerhills couldn't afford the labor. But the whole property looked trim and well cared for. It was hard to believe that the Summerhills were in financial trouble. Selena and Hugh had twenty of their twenty-five acres under cultivation, slightly more than the average winery here. Selena had told her once they pressed more than sixty thousand gallons a year.

They should have been profitable. But for the taxes, Quill thought. I'll bet the taxes are eating them alive, too. I'm facing two certainties of life right here, right now: Death and Taxes.

Five acres at Summerhill were allocated to the winery itself, the house, and two barns that had been part of the farm when Hugh had purchased it several years before. Quill pulled into the blacktopped driveway, braked, and muttered, "Aha."

Four cars sat in the parking spaces in front of the

tasting room: Marge's Lincoln (brand-new), Harvey's Cadillac (old, but lovingly polished), a Mercedes with Boston plates, and a Ford Taurus with an Avis sticker on the license plate. Quill recalled reading that the state of New York had switched to Avis as its rental dealer of choice.

The parking lot was quiet. Anyone who was here was inside. Quill noticed that the windows on the south end of the building were open to the air and the view of the lake. They'd probably gathered at that end of the room.

She had options. She could march in, sit down, and discover what was going on through sheer force of personality. She could go home. Or she could reconnoiter. Quill was of the opinion that reconnoitering was a term Special Forces invented as a euphemism for eavesdropping. She'd often thought that very few of the fictional private eyes she liked to read for fun properly addressed the problem of the more character wrecking parts of being an investigator. Lew Archer never had to lie or eavesdrop. Easy Rawlins was as straight as they come.

But there were times when discretion was absolutely the better part of valor. If Quill marched into the tasting room and demanded to know what's what, Marge was fully capable of booting her out the door. There was also the distinct possibility that she'd hear more truth outside the window than inside the tasting room.

Besides, in one of Marge's more memorable phrases, "business was war." If she, Quill, really were in a war, and had to save the lives of her men, she'd reconnoiter away without a qualm. She straightened her shoulders and stuck out her chin: she wouldn't go so far as to imagine the sound of trumpets, but she did think of God, King Harry, and England.

The front door was on the south end of the building on the west wall. She'd have to pass it to get to the open windows. She walked by it on tiptoe, wishing she'd thought to wear her tennis shoes instead of her slappy Birkinstocks.

She stopped at the end of the west wall and heard the murmur of voices. She craned her neck around the corner and held her breath to hear better. The words were indistinguishable, the tone clipped, the voice masculine. Either Hugh or Thorne Smith.

"Haven't heard a thing yet worth a bucket of warm spit!" Marge's voice was very distinct. Bless that foghorn bellow.

Mutter mutter mutter, said the male voice in response.

". . . an infusion of cash, is all," Marge said. "Them two don't know shit from shinola when it comes to running a business! Raintree did all the financials. But you won't find a better cook than the brunette, and the redhead knows how to treat the guests."

Mut-ter mutt mutt mutter? This voice, also masculine, sounded like a horse clipper: thin, dry, and buzzy. Paul Pfieffer.

"Bullshit. He left because he was in love with the tall skinny one with red hair and she's been havin' it on with the sher'f . . . It's a good business, and they're pretty good folk."

Quill blushed. She could feel it. After all the suspicions she had had about Marge.

Mut-ter muttermutter?

"Not the current sher'f. The real one. Raintree's leaving wasn't a business issue at all. Woulda hired him myself if I needed a good business manager. But you'd have to go farther than some M.B.A. like Raintree to beat *me* at business." (This, Quill reflected, was true.) "Ask Jefferson down to the bank if you don't take my word for it. Snot-nosed bureaucrat who probably couldn't read a balance sheet anyways."

Wow. Quill flattened herself at the side of the building and reconsidered her decision to eavesdrop. Not only did

Marge appear to be on the side of the Inn, she didn't sound anything like a conspirator. She sounded just like she always did, ready to flatten anyone who challenged her (admittedly superior) business decisions. She could hear Marge's opinion of just about anybody anytime she wanted to go to the Hemlock Home Diner for Sunday breakfast. She didn't have to stand flattened against the side of a metal building in the hot sun. Besides, if there was any content to this meeting other than name-calling, it didn't appear to be imminent.

"You can shove that opinion right where the sun don't shine!"

Whack! That sounded like a chair going over. "Okay, boys," Quill murmured to her imaginary battalion. "We're going in."

SLAM! The front door banged open and Marge stumped into the parking lot, purse over one meaty shoulder, briefcase dangling from the other. "What are you doin' here?!"

Quill was ready for that one. She dangled her car keys. "Dropped my keys over here. I was just about to come in. How's the meeting going?"

"Thought you was too honorable to mix with pee-ons."

Marge's feelings were hurt! Well, well. Quill decided, magnanimously, to forgive her the "having it on" remark about her relationship with Myles. "Meg and I may have been a little hasty in our reading of the situation. May I join the meeting?"

"It's over." Marge eyed her up and down. " 'Cause I'm leavin' and they ain't gonna get a thing decided without me. Tell you what, though. I'll drop by the Inn tonight, about ten, we maybe can talk some."

"Okay."

She jerked her thumb backwards. "You gonna say anything to them four twits, you tell them this. Your inn's the on'y real attraction goin'. Wine drinkers? Puh! Ain't enough of them to count on, and besides, what ever all them boozers gonna do with their kids and families if they do come up to drink themselves silly? None of those wieners in there have a clue that they need to do more than package sales, and that's the plain truth.''

''We aren't set up for children either,'' Quill said doubtfully.

''Got a few ideas about that.'' She gave Quill a friendly blow to the arm. ''See ya tonight.''

Quill walked in on a clearly disgruntled group. Harvey was biting his nails. Paul Pfieffer looked as if he had indigestion. Hugh looked glum. Even Thorne Smith appeared slightly flapped. ''Hi, everyone. I just met Marge outside. Sorry I missed the meeting.''

''But we didn't invite you, Quill,'' Harvey said apologetically. ''Pfieffer said we'd pissed you off.''

''I did not use that phrase, Mr. Bozzel.''

''We all seem to have misread the situation,'' Quill said. ''But I'm certainly ready to listen now.''

''Please sit down, Miss Quilliam,'' Paul Pfieffer said, ''and we'll see if we can make some headway here.''

CHAPTER 8

It was almost a quarter after three when Quill got back to the Inn. She parked at the front entrance and hurried into the foyer. Dina broke into speech as soon as she came in the front door. "There's *tons* of messages. It is so cool."

"Really?" said Quill, pleased. "I'm running late for tea with Freddie Patch and her friends, but I'll come and get the messages after that. Unless there's a few that can't wait."

"You mean messages for you?"

"Yes, Dina. Messages for me."

"Most of them are for Sheriff McHale."

"He's not . . . never mind. Are there any at all for me?"

"Yeah. But you won't like it. At least you didn't last time and you wouldn't let them come."

"Let who come? What last time?"

"The *Geraldo* people. Please, please won't you let them do a story on the Murder Inn. It would be so—"

"If you say it, I'll scream. Are Freddie and her friends in the gazebo?"

"I guess."

"That's where I'll be until just after four o'clock. Will you please tell Meg I have very good news? I'll talk to her as soon as I can. And were any of those messages bookings?"

"The *Geraldo* people wanted to book a ton of rooms."

"They can't," Quill said flatly. "Anyone else?"

"Nope."

"I'll be back in an hour."

She was back in less than five minutes. "They aren't there. And don't say who or I'll throttle you."

"You mean Freddie Patch and those other old ladies."

"I thought I asked you to keep an eye on them, Dina. And don't call them old ladies."

"Sorry, sorry. I did watch them while they were here at the Inn! But I can't keep an eye on them if they're shopping. For that," Dina said with a rather malicious air, "I would have to quit my post. And I couldn't take all these messages for Sher—I mean, Myles. They went into the village just after you left. The tall one that wears those twinsets?"

"Mary Lennox."

"She said there were some really cute shops they should see, so they all went off."

Quill stared at her, unseeing. "They didn't receive any faxes, did they?"

"Faxes? No."

"Or any messages of any kind?"

"No. Honestly, Quill, I know you think that someone's knocking them off, but really, they just wanted to go shopping. And you know how some of these ladies are. Shop, shop, shop. Mall queens. It's easy to forget the time when you're hanging out shopping. I should know." Her face lit up. "See? I told you. Here they come."

Relief washed over Quill like a warm shower. Robin

and Freddie bustled in the door. They carried large tote bags (recycled boating cushions, Freddie had told her. And it's free!) decorated with glued-on seashells.

"Yoo-hooo!" Robin said. "Are we very late? You have such a wonderful village, Quill! And we had the best time at that Esther's shop. You told us about her, remember. You're doing so much for us, we thought we'd do something for you, so we went down and talked to Esther about setting up a gift shop here, at the Inn. She was thrilled, wasn't she, Freddie?"

"Thrilled isn't the word. My, I'm thirsty! Are we too late for our nice tea?"

"Let me take those bags for you," Quill said. "Dina? Would you run these up to room 210? Why don't you both come into the dining room and we'll ask Meg to make another cream tea." Good grief, she thought, as she ushered them to their regular table, I sound like a nanny. She made an effort to take the maternal note out of her tones and lower her voice. "Where's Mary?"

Robin smiled. "At that cute little garden shop near the post office. She'll be along directly."

Quill, unaware that she'd been tense, found herself relaxing. "The *Garden Gate*? That's new. The mayor's wife was the driving force behind that. It's staffed with the Ladies Auxiliary. Mary can't get into any trouble there."

Dismayed, Freddie cried, "I'd forgotten all about that! Do you think we should go back for her?"

"The path through the park is public. And I don't think Mr. . . . let's call him X . . ."

"Oh, do let's call him X," Freddie said. "It's much easier to handle this if we treat it as a game."

"Mr. X he shall be. It's unlikely he'd try to snatch a woman of Mary's age and station off the streets of Hemlock Falls. But just in case, let me give Davy Kiddermeister a call. I'll ask him to pick her up and bring her

home after she's through talking to Adela.'' She excused
herself to ask Dina to make the call, stopped to ask Kathleen to serve the tea in the dining room instead of the
gazebo, and returned to find Robin shrieking with laughter.

"Can you see it? Mary being stopped and carried
home by a policeman?"

"That young man needs something useful to occupy
him," Freddie said sternly. "What sort of progress has
he made on these killings? None as far as I can see.
Now, we . . ." She turned, beaming, to Quill. "We met
your friend. The one that came in late last night? My
land, what a gorgeous man. Now that's my idea of a
lawman."

"If we were only twenty years younger," Robin said,
"there'd be a fight over him. Freddie, do you remember
that darling Cuban man we met in Florida on that buying
trip?"

"You go to Florida on buying trips?" Quill said.

"The five of us had a little clothing business while
we lived in New York," Robin explained. "It did pretty
well, actually."

"It did? Good heavens," Quill said sympathetically.
"How did you all manage?"

"Oh, it did well enough for us to quit our day jobs,
as they say," Robin said. A little smile played around
her lips. "We did quite well, as a matter of fact."

"Let's not embarrass Quill with our reminiscences,"
Freddie said briskly. "And here's the tea. My." She bit
into a cream scone with a blissful sigh, then mumbled,
"I wish he were on this case."

"Myles? In a way we're both on this case, Freddie."

"Have you talked to Myles about the Plan?"

"Not yet." To her chagrin, Quill found herself saying, as though she were a TV cop, "We discuss our
cases frequently, of course."

"There were others?" Freddie said. "You've solved other murders?"

"Mary told us there were," Robin said. "Honestly, Freddie, your memory."

"If I lose it altogether, who cares? I sure won't know it." This sent both of them into gales of laughter.

Quill shouted, "I'd like all three of you to gather all the correspondence you've had with Mr. Vinge so we can go over it together." She bit her lip and lowered her voice. "There are a great many things we can learn from the letters. As I told Myles this morning, this is a case that's going to be solved through forensics, not guesswork. For a start, we'll track his address and find him. We'll see if he has alibis for the times of the two murders. We'll send the letters off for fingerprinting, and see if there's any cross match with known criminals."

"My goodness," Freddie said, impressed. "Do you charge for being a detective, Quill?"

Robin sighed and rolled her eyes. "Of course she doesn't! Whoever heard of an amateur detective charging a fee?"

"You should charge," Freddie said through a mouthful of Devonshire cream. "That is, if you solve the case. Anyhow, we don't have those letters with us. We'll have to call home and see if someone will put it in the mail for us."

"The sheriff's office here will call your local police—you're all from Trenton now, aren't you? If you can tell the police where to look, they'll collect the letters for you. They'll probably send the evidence by courier."

"We wouldn't want to put them to any trouble," Robin said doubtfully.

"Trouble? Robin, this is a murder case!"

"Oh, dear." Robin worked her lips. "I just hate the idea of having strange men go through my things."

Quill made a conscious effort to be calm and reassuring. "Then we'll have a policewoman do it."

"You know what, Freddie? We can call Mr. Kauffman. He lives just down the hall. He has keys."

"He waters your plants when you're gone, that sort of thing?"

"No live plants, dear. Plastic is much easier. It's just in case we forget something. Let's give Mr. Kauffman a call, Freddie."

"I think we should wait to see what Mary says. The letters are in her apartment." She worked her fingers nervously. "I wouldn't like to authorize anything like that without her consent."

"Where *is* she?" Robin added fretfully.

"Quill!" Dina appeared at the archway to the foyer, her face pale. "Could you come here a minute, please?"

"Sure. Will you two excuse me?"

Dina took her by the arm and pulled her out of earshot. "He says she's not there."

"Mary Lennox isn't at the Garden Gate?"

"Adela Henry said she took off for the Inn more than half an hour ago. She should have been right behind Freddie and Robin."

"Oh, no!"

"Davy's calling the firemen and state troopers. And Myles, of course. Should we help them search?"

"She can't have gotten far. She can't. Maybe she's just lost."

"I'd like to help," Dina said quietly.

"Put the answer phone on. And for God's sake, let me know as soon as you hear anything."

"I will."

"Dina, have you seen Paul Pfieffer? He was out at the winery with me this afternoon and I haven't seen him since."

"Paul Pfieffer? You think he's behind this?"

"Just tell Myles I haven't seen him since about a

quarter to three. I'd better get back to Robin and Freddie. This will be harder on them than it will on us.''

The evening dragged on with no word. Meg and Doreen joined them at dinner, leaving Bjarne in charge of the kitchen. They retired to the Tavern Bar and appropriated a large center table. Two events kept Freddie and Robin from sinking into tearful despair: Selena brought back a disgraced Max, who once again had been harassing Mr. Peterson's hens (''I take him home. I bathe him. He is a monster! Next time, I as dog warden tell you, it is the last!''). On hearing of Mary's disappearance, she cast a very worried look at Quill, accepted a glass of wine, and taught them curses in Spanish. Cursing in a language not your own, she'd explained, did not seem bad at all. She left, after she actually got Freddie to giggle. Marge stumped in at ten o'clock and kept them entertained with a series of disreputable stories about her rowdy girlhood.

But the periods in between were grim.

A small band of the searchers came in just after 12:30, Myles in the lead. His face was impassive. Davy Kiddermeister, Andy Bishop, and Dina hung back. All of them looked exhausted and dirty. Quill half-rose from her chair. Myles smelled of smoke. He nodded in response to her terrified look. ''We found her,'' he said.

Freddie started to shriek. Max sprang up from his place by Quill's chair and began to bark. Robin sat helplessly as tears ran down her face.

''The same as the others?'' Sympathetic tears choked Quill's throat. ''She's—you smell of smoke.''

Robin's nails sunk into Quill's arm. ''You said you'd save us! You said you'd save us!''

''Oh, Andy,'' Meg said, helplessly. ''Can't we do something?''

''I think it'd be a good idea to check them into the hospital for the next few days.'' Andy's face was sober.

"And then I think we should try and get hold of some relatives and send them home. This has gone way too far."

"What if Mr. Vinge calls, and we're not here?" Freddie sobbed. "After everything that's happened, we're going to lose this, too?"

"Mr. Vinge's already called," Andy said grimly. "Three times too often. What do you think, Myles? We've got plenty of space."

"You'll put a guard on the door," Myles said to Davy. "And, Andy, by all means, call the families. It will be easier on them if the families are here. But if they want to stay, I'd encourage it. Just for easier access to what they know."

"I'll call your daughter, Freddie." Quill clasped her hand. "Do you have her number? Her address?" Freddie sniffed hard, then wrote a Washington number on one of the napkins. The writing was shaky.

Andy shook his head. "What a night. All right, I've got room in the Jeep if I clear out the back. I'll drive them over myself." He left at a jog.

"Here," Marge said to Doreen. "I'll take young Freddie. You grab on to Robin, Doreen. Meg, you wanna pack up the stuff from their rooms? Quill? Do sumthin' about that damn dog, will ya?"

Quill curled her fingers in Max's fur. He licked her hand eagerly. He was trembling, but under her hand, he stopped his frantic barking. Marge hoisted Freddie out of her chair by the back of her neck and swiveled her head, her fierce gaze taking in the assembled group one by one. "I'm damn pooped, myself. Everybody go home and get some sleep. We're not goin' to solve anything tonight." Her sharp little eyes rested on Myles. "That right, Sher'f?"

Myles nodded.

"'Kay, then." Then, as pragmatic as ever, "Quill,

you got some time tomorrow, we still got business to talk over. No time to do it tonight, I guess.''

Quill held Max by the ruff. She was so tired, the room was a blur. A terrible vision was in her mind: Mary Lennox, bound and burning. Ironic that her way of death should recall her 16th-century namesake. ''Lunchtime,'' she found herself saying. ''But, Marge . . .''

''You wanna come to my place, I'll have Betty make something tasty.'' Marge's bellicose look softened. ''Sounds hard, but we gotta get movin' if we're gonna save your place.'' She jerked her chin at Doreen. ''Let's get rolling, folks.''

Meg silently led them out of the room. Dina sank into Meg's chair with a sigh and covered her face with her hands.

''You coming back to the scene, Myles?'' Davy's khaki shirt was grass-stained. Twigs snarled his fair hair.

''No. Just call me when you've confirmed the strangulation.''

''Yessir.'' He touched one finger to his hat. ''Quill? See you sometime tomorrow. Sorry we missed that dinner. I was looking forward to it. Dina, I'll have one of the boys drop you off at the dorm.''

''I brought my car, David. I can get myself home.'' Her bright brown eyes were dull; the circles under them were almost purple.

''Doreen has a few Stranded Traveler's kits in the housekeeping closet, Dina,'' Quill said. ''Why don't you pick one and use one of the rooms tonight. I've got clothes you can borrow in the morning.''

''Okay. Thanks, Quill.'' She took a deep breath. ''Anything I can do for you before I turn in?''

''Just get some sleep. I've got to call Freddie's daughter.''

''I'll walk you up,'' Davy said. ''I probably won't see you for a couple of days, Dee.''

She put her hand on his chest and looked up at him.
"Just catch this guy, David. I've never seen anything
more horrible in my life. She was *burned* to death. The
smell was awful. Awful. I'll never forget it, never." Her
voice rose, almost out of control. "He's a monster. Only
a monster could do that to that poor woman."

Quill watched them leave. Max squirmed impatiently
under her hand, and she let him go. He licked her hand,
then settled back onto the floor with a grunt. Myles sat
down next to her, and she put her hand over his.
"You're exhausted, poor darling. Did you get anything
to eat?"

"Marge sent Betty Hall out with sandwiches and coffee. Her turn, Betty said, since the Inn fed the volunteers
twice before."

"Where did you find her?"

"The overpass on 96 near the Syracuse exit. Motorist
used his cell phone and called to report a fire in the
ditch."

"It wasn't . . ." She shook her head with a rueful
sigh. "It seems stupid to call him X."

"No. The phone's registered to a restaurant supply
company in Rochester. Guy's a salesman for them. Just
passing through on his regular route."

"Not Jason Carmichael?"

"Yes. You know him?"

"He sold us the Aga. Nice guy."

Quill's head ached from too much wine that evening,
and too little sleep the night before. She rubbed her face
vigorously. It helped a little. "I asked Freddie and Robin
for the correspondence with Mr. Vinge. Mary's the secretary of their little company, so it's at her place. We
can get the police in Trenton to pick it up, can't we?
She was a little nervous about having strangers in her
home, so she was going to call a friend of theirs to
collect it. Neither of those poor women—I keep thinking

of them as the survivors, Myles!—is going to be in any shape to take care of that in the morning, so I'll do it. Do you know anyone in the Trenton P.D.?''

"Yes," he said after a moment, "I do. Or I did. I'll be damned."

"You seem surprised."

"Hadn't thought of him in years. I don't even know if he's still there."

"It might make Robin feel better if a friend of yours took care of it. You made quite an impression on them today."

He closed his eyes. "This shouldn't have happened."

"Freddie and Robin will be safe enough now at the hospital. How can you blame yourself? If anyone should feel responsible, I should. I left them alone all day. Dina's right. This murderer's a monster. Did she tell you, by the way, that I haven't seen Paul Pfieffer since the meeting at Summerhill this afternoon? Doreen checked his room three times this evening—he's disappeared."

"He bought a round-trip ticket to Albany by phone this morning." Myles looked at his watch. "I mean yesterday morning, departing at four and returning to the Syracuse airport about eleven. The Albany P.D. put a plainclothesman on him. He got into Albany at five, had dinner with a lobbyist and state senator for our district here, then he returned on his scheduled ticket. My guess is that he's upstairs and asleep right now."

"I left the Summerhills at quarter to three. He was still there."

"And it's an hour from the winery to the Syracuse airport. Pretty good alibi, Quill."

"No kidding. All right, what about—"

"Hey." His voice was gentle. "We're both all in. Let's go to sleep and we'll take this on in the morning."

"I need to call Freddie's daughter, first. You go ahead. I'll meet you upstairs."

They walked together to the foyer, and she left him to go to her office. Max walked toward Myles, looked back at Quill, sat down, scratched himself vigorously, then decided to accompany his mistress.

In her office, Quill sat down at her desk and smoothed the napkin on her desk. No names, just a phone number with the 301 area code. Maryland, then. She should be able to get here quickly, even if she had to drive.

Quill dialed the number. The phone rang for a long time, then a blurry female voice answered, "Yes!?"

Quill introduced herself, and asked if this was Freddie Patch's daughter.

The blurriness disappeared. "Yes. It is. Who is this again?"

"Sarah Quilliam. I'm afraid there's been another death. It's not Freddie," she said hastily. "But she's frightened. We checked her into our local hospital—she's not ill, it's just a lot more comfortable for them—and the local sheriff's department has put a guard on the room. And we're working on finding the man who's doing this. But she could really use your help."

"I'm sorry," said the voice distantly. "You said she's under police protection?"

"Yes. Twenty-four hours a day. And, of course, the hospital is a very secure place."

"Then she's fine, isn't she? Thank you for calling, Miss Quilliam."

The dial tone rang in Quill's ear. "I don't believe it," she said to the dog. "I do not believe this." Max whined. Quill sat back and stared at the ceiling. "Pfieffer's out of it, Max. But you know what? I never did follow up on Mr. Thorne Smith." She turned her computer on and went on-line.

· · ·

She banged into her rooms a few minutes later, her face pink with excitement. Myles was sitting on her couch, a drink in one hand, watching the spring moon. ''Thorne Smith,'' she said, ''is the name of some bone-head mystery writer who—''

''Wrote the Topper stories,'' Myles said. ''Yes. I should have remembered. My friend in the Trenton P.D.—''

''But, Myles! It's Mr. Vinge! It has to be!''

''The guy I knew at the Trenton P.D.? I don't think so.''

''What?! What are you talking about?! ''

''Name then was Henry T. Smith. My friend in Trenton.''

Quill's fatigue slowed her up. Once it hit her, she was wide awake. ''What? Oh, no, Myles. Not another undercover officer! I can't stand it!''

''What do you mean, not another? There was only one in all the years you've operated the Inn.''

''And you never said a word about it until I'd made a complete and utter fool of myself thinking the officer was a suspect in those murders.''

''The Hank Smith I knew favored blue jeans, tattoos, and souped up Chevys. Your description of this Thorne Smith didn't fit the Hank I knew.'' He smiled at a memory. ''I had Davy put a man on him today; didn't see him myself until he showed up to help with the search.''

''Did he recognize you, too?''

''Didn't see me. Didn't want him to.''

''And?''

Myles shrugged. ''If he'd discovered the body, I would have had my suspicions. Wouldn't be the first cop to go bad, won't be the last. But he didn't. We got that call from the helpful motorist, instead. So I'm not sure why Hank's here, or what he wants. It could be coincidence, but I don't like coincidence in murder cases.

I'll talk to him tomorrow. I want to call Trenton first. For all I know, he went to night school, shed the black leather jacket and the name Hank for good, and went into investment banking.''

''But you think we're back to X, Myles.''

''I do.''

''You never believed the killer is someone we've met.''

''Real-life cases don't work like that, Quill.''

''You just assume the killer's unknown and that the motive is established after hard evidence has led to an arrest.''

''Real police work is like that, Quill.''

''What do you mean, 'real' police work? I'd like to remind you that my so-called amateur methods have led to the successful conclusion of several cases in the past. Unless you think I was lucky.''

He rose and stretched. ''Let's get to bed. The jet lag's catching up with me.''

''You do think it was luck.''

''Not now, Quill. I want to sleep. I have to spend some time in D.C. tomorrow and the day after.''

''But you just—'' She gritted her teeth and made herself shut up. Who, she asked herself fiercely, demanded space to handle these crises herself? You did. Do not whine.

''You weren't,'' Myles said. ''You were about to, but you didn't say it.''

She raised her eyebrows innocently. He leaned over and embraced her, his chin in her hair. ''I'll call you with the answers from Trenton. Start a file on this case, Quill; it always helps to write things down. Davy's agreed to make all the reports available to us. I asked him to send them over tomorrow morning, as soon as the body's been taken to Syracuse. While I'm gone?'' He shook her gently. ''Do not go into dark warehouses, shut-down factories, or the east side of Syracuse looking for clues. Do not talk to anyone you suspect alone.'' He slid his hand firmly over her mouth, released it, and kissed the top of her head. ''Not for your personal safety, although of course I worry about that. But because a lone operator interferes with the evidence to such a degree that you'll never convict. How many cases can you think of in the past year where the evidence has been absolutely clear, and the killer's walking around free?''

Quill knew this was true.

''If you're going to do this, you're going to handle it like a real pro. It's not a jobette.''

''A jobette?''

''Work you do on a whim or caprice. A well-crafted investigation's crucial to conviction—and you don't do good work based on intuition and guesses. You do it through observation of detail. Examination of anomalies. Comparisons between behaviors. My advice? Wait for the file from Trenton. Collect the items of evidence from Davy. Wait until I get back, and we can establish a clear path to the solution.'' He yawned suddenly. ''Do you mind if I stay with you tonight?''

''I want you to stay with me. Tonight and always.'' She followed him out of the living room into the bedroom, Max at their heels. ''Luck!'' she muttered. ''Hah! It was brains, pure and simple.''

Myles kissed her and left early for Washington. Quill got up with him and settled herself into her office to work. She called the hospital and received the news that Freddie and Robin were playing canasta in the TV room. She recorded the cash the dining room had taken in from the day before, the receipts for the three of their twenty-seven rooms that actually held paying guests, and looked at the revenues for the month of May in dismay. At this rate, the loan from Myles would be eaten up far sooner than she'd planned. A quick review of the bookings for the next three months showed that the lottery angel hadn't recorded an influx of business overnight. She'd promised John she would pay attention to bookings, and she meant to fulfill that promise.

She called the Golden Pillar Travel Agency, an excellent client in the past. Would, she delicately inquired, an increase in the commission help at all? What would help, was the candid response, was more customers. No one wanted to travel this year. "And it doesn't make sense," Brian the office manager told her, "the economy's booming, or so the media says. It's just one of those cycles, Quill. We all have to live through it."

Triple A had a different take on the dearth of customers. "Credit card debt," Angela the domestic travel package rep said. "We're pretty tight with American Express. The great middle class has maxed itself out spending, and now they're paying down debt. Me included. Sorry."

Quill felt like the moose with the target birthmark in the Gary Larson cartoon. "What to do, what to do?" Stalled, balked, and stymied. An ad in the Travel section of the Sunday *Times* would cost more than their mortgage balance. John had placed ads in the travel and leisure magazines in February and March, when most people plan their summer vacations, and the only booking in response to that had been the Crafty Ladies. "Good result," she muttered aloud. She could see a new series of ads now: "Come to the Inn at Hemlock Falls for the Time of Your . . . Death!"

Her in-house phone buzzed and she picked it up. "It's just me," Dina said. "David's here with the reports for you. Shall I send him in? It'll be a few minutes. I gave him some coffee, if that's okay, and he's drinking it and eating some breakfast. He was up all night."

"Sure." Quill pulled open her bottom desk drawer and found a new manila folder. She printed "Dunbarton, Lennox, and Patch, et. al." on the edge. She took a clean sheet of typing paper and wrote:

1. observation of detail
2. comparasion of anomalies
3. compare with ordinary circumstances

She put this in the file. She'd accomplished this, at least.

Davy walked in. He was carrying a stack of papers. Dina edged in behind him. She whispered, "Okay if I sit in the corner and watch?"

Davy, puzzled, asked, "Why are you whispering?"

"Because I don't want to disturb you at work. I'll sit right here on the couch. I'll be very, very quiet. You won't even know I'm here."

"Fine." Quill stood up and reached for the papers in Davy's hand. He gave them to her.

"Sheriff said to leave the evidence locked up, but you should come down and take a look sometime today."

"Davy . . ." She stopped, caught Dina's eye, and corrected herself. "I mean, David. You're the sheriff."

"Nobody around here seems to think so. And I'm not doing a very good job."

"These are unusual circumstances. You recall that when Myles really was sheriff, he called on reinforcements all the time."

The pink in Davy's cheeks subsided a little. "That's true, isn't it?"

"The lone wolf investigator is much more liable to mess up the evidence," Quill said wisely. "An investigation should be solid, like a piece of furniture that's built to last."

"Beg pardon?" Davy said.

"Well crafted." She paused impressively. "Have a seat, David, and tell me what you think."

Davy was the sort of man who hitched up his trouser cuffs before he sat down. Quill wondered about this. Were his trousers too long? Too tight across the seat?

"... Quill."

"I'm sorry." She decided to title Myles' list of the three essentials of investigation Observations Related to the Case ONLY.

"I said that each of the ladies was killed the same way. Strangled, then the duct tape on their mouths and hands. Then they were burned up with the phosphorous bomb."

"Any ideas on why they were strangled first? Before they were burned?" She shivered, then forced herself into a more professional attitude. If she had to actually look at the bodies, it was going to be a lot tougher than hearing a mere description.

"I don't have any idea why anyone would do this in the first place," Davy said. "I know why people go over the speed limit. I like to speed myself. But I don't know why this guy does all this sh—I mean stuff to these poor women." His ears were red with indignation. "My mother's about the same age as these ladies."

"Mine would be, too," Quill said softly. "Now. What kind of physical evidence did you pick up at each scene?"

"The list is right there. The sheriff said to pay attention to any duplications. You know, something that showed up at all three scenes."

Quill scanned the list. Gum wrappers. A cigarette butt. Coke can. Scrapings from under the fingernails of one partially burned corpse. "Triangular piece of metal," she read aloud. "What's that?"

"I found it," Davy said proudly. "At the scene last night. Doc said it's a musical instrument, although I can't see where you'd blow into it."

"There was one in Ellen Dunbarton's room, too."

"There was?" He looked perplexed. "We didn't find it."

"Doreen did," Quill said a little guiltily.

"We aren't going to be able to prove she did," Davy said. "I don't think it's an official piece of evidence unless a real investigator picks it up."

"She could swear out an affidavit," Quill said, although she had no idea whether this was true or not.

"Where is it now?"

"In the junk drawer in the kitchen," Quill admitted. She forced a laugh. "Guess we broke the chain of evidence, all right."

"I guess so."

"You didn't find a triangle in the Gorge, where Fran's body was, did you?"

"If it's not on the list we didn't find it."

Quill wrote: *triangle*, *fire*, *murder* on the sheet headed FACTS and repeated them aloud. "What do those words have in common, Davy?"

He blinked.

"Cool," Dina said. Quill jumped. She'd forgotten Dina was there. "Sorry," Dina added, "should I shut up?"

"No, no, of course not."

"I like word association," Dina said.

Davy (who was clearly bewildered) said, "Hm!" in an authoritative way.

Dina winked at Quill and said. "Word association goes like this, David: triangle-fire-murder. What do those words make you think of? Well, the Bermuda triangle? Triangle trade route? The Bermuda Triangle, now," she said seriously, "a lot of people think aliens are behind the disappearance of those ships." She caught Quill's look. "What?"

"Aliens?"

"You never know."

"I'll tell you what I know," Quill said nicely. "I know that we may be getting tons of phone calls from people wanting to stay at the Inn this summer, and there's no one on the phones at the front desk. And in Times Like These—" She grabbed her hair. "Aaagh! I said it." She folded her hands on her desk and continued, more calmly, "In times like these where we could go bankrupt any moment, somebody should be out there, capturing any stray business that may float by."

"Me, you mean." Dina bounced up from the couch and headed for the door. "There's one more fire-murder-triangle thing. The Triangle fire."

"What about the Triangle fire?" Quill said.

"You know, those women that died at the Triangle sewing machine company?"

"Oh, dear. Yes. I remember. Ugh."

"Did they catch the perp?" Davy asked.

"There wasn't a perp," Quill said. "It was in 1911 or something. And it was an accident. I remember seeing a black-and-white picture of the bodies piled against the door in school." She shuddered. "Horrible. Now, say good-bye, Dina."

"I'll call you *instantly* on the house phone if there's the slightest chance of a booking."

Davy didn't seem particularly interested in decades-old cases, and to tell the truth, Quill doubted the relevance, too. Facts, Myles had said, not intuition. "Should we look for a triangle again in the Gorge, Davy? Your guys, I mean. I won't go near it, I promise. But it would be interesting to know why, in two out of three murders, we found an orchestra triangle."

Davy looked pleased at the prospect of achieving something tangible. Quill knew just how he felt. "I'll get a few of the boys right on it. You think it could be important?"

Quill threw her hands up. "Who knows? But it's an

anomaly, a recurring anomaly, and I don't think we should ignore it." Her in-house phone buzzed twice. Quill picked it up and said, "Quilliam, here."

Silence.

"Um. Hello?"

"Is that you, Quill?" Dina's voice. "You sounded sort of tough."

I'm feeling tough, cookie. Wish I had a cigar. "Sorry, Dina. Is there a problem? A tour bus filled with people who want to stay here for a month? An airplane load of tourists . . ."

"A fax just came in from Myles. Shall I bring it in? And Marge called. You want lunch or not, she says."

Quill looked at her watch. "Wow, it's eleven-thirty. Would you call her, Dina, and tell her I'll be there in about half an hour."

"I told her you were behind closed doors with the sheriff," Dina said primly. "And I wasn't sure when you'd be finished."

"You did, huh? What did she say to that?"

Dina giggled. "I'll tell you, if you really want to know."

"Never mind."

"I told her no, it wasn't Myles, it was our elected sheriff, and she was rude like she usually is and hung up."

"Call her back, tell her I'm on the way over. I'll pick the fax up on my way out." She hung up. "I've got to go eat lunch with Marge Schmidt, Davy. Thanks a lot for bringing these papers over."

"No trouble. But I'd better get on that search right away. Did you talk to the ladies at the hospital this morning?"

"I checked. They're playing canasta."

He shook his head. "When we catch this guy, I want to be alone with him for five minutes. Just five minutes.

And, pow!'' He smacked one hand into the other.
''Doesn't it beat all? Killing women who could be your
own mother? I mean, you have to ask yourself why each
one of those poor women was strangled, suffocated, and
burned. If he had to kill, why couldn't he kill quick?''

''We'll know when we catch him, I suppose. Do you
want a copy of Myles' fax for your files, Davy? We
should share.''

''Depends on what it says.''

The fax was hurriedly written, in Myles' gracefully
angular hand.

*Re: Smith: My old friend now works for a private
security firm out of Boston, details of current case to
follow, sweatshop abuses in manufacturing. Copies of
Vinge correspondence arrive by courier after five p.m.
Love to you, Quill, Myles.*

''I don't think we need a copy of that for the file,''
Davy said, reading over her shoulder. ''We find that little iron thing, I'll let you know right away.''

Quill crumpled the fax into her purse. So there might
be a connection between the triangles and the case after
all. She'd have to find Thorne Smith and talk to him as
soon as she could. ''Thanks, David. Dina, I'll just tell
Meg that I'm off to Marge's. If you need to reach me,
you know the number of the diner.''

Quill found Meg asleep on her couch in her rooms.
The television was on, the sound turned off. On the
screen, a very fat chef in a ponytail was slicing a rabbit
breast. Quill shuddered and turned it off.

Like her own suite, Meg's room had a balcony, but it
was hard to get to because of the amount of clutter.
Cardboard pots of seedlings sat in every windowsill and
on the floor near the bedroom. Cookbooks were stacked
in knee-high piles in front of overflowing book cases.
Meg loved bright, primary colors, and posters of apples,

cheeses, herbs, flowers, and kitchenware plastered the walls.

Meg had refused to install a kitchen in her rooms; she had a drip coffeepot, a small refrigerator, and a tiny cafe table, but that was it. The one professional framed piece of art in the room hung over this table, the first pencil sketch Quill had ever done of the two of them: Quill herself, at twelve, Meg at eight. Quill hadn't really looked at it for years. Meg stared out at her solemnly, her jaw firm, eyes bright. Quill had put herself in the background; by comparison she was indistinct, blurry, a cipher.

"You wouldn't draw it that way today," Meg said.

"I didn't mean to wake you up. Did you go to the hospital with Andy last night?"

"They seemed happier, once they got there. It was either Andrew's firm professional manner, the drugs, or Marge's 'buck up' smacks on the shoulder that calmed them down. I'm putting my money on Marge."

"I'm going there for lunch to discuss whatever it was the government types were discussing yesterday without us. Do you want to come?"

"Do I want to know my future, Madame Lasagna? Of course. Just give me a minute." She rubbed her eyes hard.

Quill said automatically, "Don't do that."

Meg grinned at her. "How's business?"

"Business sucks. I called around this morning to all our usual contacts. Nothing doing for the summer."

"That fifty grand isn't going to last too long, is it?"

"No."

"How long have we got? Before we have to do something dramatic, I mean."

"Dramatic like what? We can take out a second mortgage. . . ."

"Sand against the tide, don't you think?"

"Let's see what Marge has to say. The cavalry may be coming over the hill at any moment."

"I don't like having to wait on the cavalry any more than you do," Meg complained.

"Maybe we don't have to wait? Maybe Marge has some wonderful idea that's going to work fast, like Alka Seltzer. Come on, get presentable, and let's go."

"I'm presentable!" Meg stared down at herself. She was wearing baggy sweat pants, a purple T-shirt, and had bare feet. "Oh, all right. I'll put on chinos." She disappeared into her bathroom.

Quill walked around the living room, stepping over a stack of magazines from *L'Aperitif*, a pile of kitchen equipment catalogues, a file filled with scrawled recipes in Meg's spiky, hurried hand. There was nothing in this room to speak of a life outside a professional kitchen. Quill sighed. The Inn was her sister's life.

"There! Do I pass inspection?" The chinos were rumpled (Meg refused to iron) and the new T-shirt was clean but emblazoned with a full color silk screen of the Indigo Girls.

"You do. We have about twenty minutes. Do you want to walk?"

Outside, they discovered that the day was cool and overcast. Main Street, where Marge's Diner was located, was a fifteen-minute leisurely walk through the park. Max, bounding up to greet them, viewed the prospect of a walk through the park with an ebullience peculiar to dogs.

"You'd better get a license for him," Meg said. "That way, when he wrecks things, people will know to call you instead of Selena."

"He's going to be a good boy from now on," Quill said.

They walked the rest of the way in silence. Main

Street was quiet. Max bounded along the sidewalks, stopping to christen the white planters filled with geraniums, and the black wrought iron streetlights with obsessive attention. Most of the buildings in Hemlock Falls were cut stone; the few that weren't were white clapboard with black trim. Marge's Diner was cut stone. It had been a Laundromat in an earlier incarnation; goodness knows what before that. It was a very old building and could have been beautiful. Quill always suspected that the two large Laundromat windows in front were a significant factor in Marge's success. Hemlockians loved to sit and watch the world go by on Main Street. The other factor, of course, was Marge's cooking, which was excellent.

The diner was filled when Meg and Quill walked in, a sorry contrast to their own empty—and far more luxurious—dining room. Marge sat behind the cash register up front and looked up with raised eyebrows when they came in. "There you are," she said without preamble. "You didn't walk, did you? With this damn loony walking around burning women, the streets ain't safe."

"It's not a loony," Quill began, and then quit. Of course it was. "Never mind."

"C'mon back this way to my office. Betty'll bring us lunch in there." They followed her as she stumped her way through the tables to the back, shoving the customers aside with the assurance of a tank brigade come to relieve a beleaguered front line. She disappeared into a door marked PRIVATE! THIS MEANS YOU, then reappeared to beckon the two of them inside.

Quill followed her in, then stopped so abruptly Meg smacked into her shoulders.

"Doreen! What are you doing here?"

The housekeeper shrugged. "Marge gave me a call."

Marge's large metal desk had been shoved aside to make room for one of her Formica-covered tables. It was covered with a red-checked cloth, and a Mason jar of wildflowers sat in the middle. The table was set for four. Marge pulled out a chair. "Siddown."

Meg took a seat nearest the metal filing cabinet; Quill seated herself directly across from her, her back to a grimy window set high in the wall. Doreen settled grimly in the chair against the desk. Marge plunked herself between them, folded her hands and said:

"Now, girls. How much do you want for the Inn?"

CHAPTER 9

It was what she'd anticipated, of course. And now it was out in the open. Quill stared straight ahead. She'd expected Meg to jump to her feet, shout, "No way, Marge!" (or something worse) and make a grand exit. She wouldn't have been surprised if Doreen swept the Mason jar off the table and dumped the contents on Marge's head. Marge had endured more vehement attacks than that without a blink of her beady little eyes. She'd told them so last night, when they were trying to keep Freddie and Robin's spirits up.

What she hadn't foreseen was the overwhelming sense of relief.

"Sell the Inn?" she said—and images came to her, a series of paintings in the gallery of the past eight years.

Each corner of the massive building loved, labored over, wept over. The sound of the Falls in the evening. The way the moon looked over the koi pond. The kitchen with the massive fireplace, the wooden beams with Meg's dried herbs hanging from the rafters. Her own room, quiet, serene, with the French doors that led to her balcony—the late night conversations there with Myles, with Meg.

She wanted to sell the damn thing. Now.

It was the statistics. The bloody inexorable statistics.

Twenty-seven rooms, plus the bar and dining room filled with paying customers a minimum of two hundred days a year. Doreen had figured it out once: it meant cleaning 290 toilets; the washing, bleaching, and drying of 540 sheets, 1,080 pillowcases, 865 tablecloths; the scouring of 108 bathtubs and 172 showers stalls.

Not to mention the damn floors.

Then there were the customers: the yuppie couple that sued Meg over the runny scrambled eggs, the little boy that bit Quill twice because she didn't have any peanut butter, the numberless truly disgusting things people left in their rooms and on the carpets. The people who muttered, "They can afford it," and stiffed them with bogus checks, stolen credit cards, and even counterfeit cash.

Not to mention the lawn maintenance. The damn grass just kept on growing. The building maintenance, the gardens, the insurance, the waitress that stole a week's receipts and called three days later from Detroit for money to get home.

The bills—the remorseless tide of bills. Mortgage, insurance, workman's comp, wine, food, electric, gas. Taxes.

She never got any sleep.

She wanted out.

She took a deep breath. "Sorry, Marge. It's not for sale."

"You nuts? You really think you can make it in this economy?" Marge settled back in her chair with a grin, a warrior girding herself for a familiar and pleasurable battle.

"I'm not negotiating, Marge. I'm telling you a plain fact. Do you know what that Inn represents? My creative vision. Meg's creative vision."

Doreen cleared her throat in an ostentatious way.

"And Doreen's, too. The answer's no."

"Let me tell you what's gonna happen in Hemlock Falls the next coupla years. We got one of the prettiest parts of the U.S. of A., and nobody left to enjoy it. Taxes, no jobs, high prices—you name it, it's drove everybody out, down to the south. So what do we do? We fight it. This money from the government will give us a chance to drag people back up here for the good parts. The scenery. The lakes. The vineyards. We make it a good place to visit, but you don't have to live here to love it."

"It's our big chance," Meg said coolly, "finally. Why in the world does it make sense for us to sell just when we're on the verge of making a pile of money?"

"Here's Betty with the food. You wanna eat or talk?"

"Eat," Doreen said.

"Pot roast, crisped baked potatoes, new peas, and applesauce," Betty said. "Lemon custard pie for dessert." She banged the plates down, wiped her hands on her apron, and went away.

Meg took a forkful of pot roast and tried it. "You are a darn good cook, Marge. But Betty's better. This is terrific. And to answer your question, I'd rather eat, too, than have you try to skinflint us. You heard Quill, no sale."

"Hey," Marge's voice was tolerant. "Lemme lay out some facts. I eat at your place, I find out about the prices of the rooms, I do some rough figuring on payroll and maintenance, and here's what I figure. No way you can make it on the size you are now. You either gotta get bigger, so you can sell more rooms, or you gotta get smaller, so you can cut staff."

"If we get bigger, we just have to hire more staff," Meg said patiently. "Don't be ridiculous."

"One thing you can't do is hire more staff. You build more rooms, you work harder is all. Right now, you're operating at a loss even when you're full up, unless my math's off.'' (The likelihood of that, her tone implied, was that aliens lived underground in Roswell, New Mexico.) ''You gotta get the profit from somewhere, and where you get it from is the same amount of people servicing more rooms. The other thing you can do, is get smaller. Cut costs by maintaining less overhead. Point is, there is an equation where your business works, but you ain't at it.''

''We can get there,'' Meg said stubbornly.

''Hah! You two? And my gramma's from the moon. Meg—'' She leaned forward, her face intent. She tapped her forefinger on the table. ''You don't love money.''

''Sure I do.''

''Uh-uh. You like money, sure. Who doesn't? But you don't love it. I love it. I like to make it. I like to take what I made and make more of it. You got other things you love better. That Doc Bishop. Good food. Cooking. Your sister.'' She shook her head joyfully. ''No, you don't love money.'' She squinted at Quill. ''You said that place's your creative vision? Bullshit. It's pretty. The food's good. That location next to the Falls—perfect. But I don't see how you got the *nerve* to say it's your creative vision when you can't make the mortgage payment. It's creative failure.''

''This is weird,'' Meg said.

''What? Somethin' in the pot roast?''

''No. This conversation is weird.''

''People like you,'' Marge said, instantly defensive, ''you don't respect money either. You have names for people like me—and none of them very nice.''

''That's not true,'' Quill said gently. She thought she'd never heard anything more pitiful in her life than Marge's speech about the love of her life. ''I have a lot of respect for you, your skills, your expertise.''

''This conversation is weird,'' Meg said, as though

neither Quill nor Marge had responded to her initial comment, "because it makes so much sense."

"Thank the Lord!" Doreen said fervently.

Quill dropped her fork, tried to retrieve it, and ended up with peas on the floor. Marge regarded the peas, then said, "That damn dog still outside? Nah. We'll get it later. You were saying as about how I made some sense, huh?"

Meg took a deep breath and turned to her sister. "Quill? Do you know how many Rock Cornish game hen I've spitted and roasted in the last eight years? Six thousand, five hundred and fifty-seven. I counted."

"You're sick of it?"

"I'm sick of it."

"I'm seventy-two years old," Doreen said belligerently. "Ain't anyone gonna ast me if I'm sick of it? Well, I am. Stoke wants to retire and so do I."

"But what are we going to do?" Quill said.

"Have Marge give us this place." Meg twisted around and looked Marge in the eye. "It's a filthy mess and it will have to be gutted and then completely restored, and any deal we make will have to include enough money to do all that. But, Quill. Just look at it!" She swept her arm in the air. Cobwebs stirred on the window. "Can't you see how pretty this can be? I never told you this, but that boutique restaurant we opened—"

"And closed," Marge said.

"—was exactly the right size for a chef like me. I want to do dinners, only, six nights a week for no more than twenty people at a time. This place is perfect for that." She put both hands in Quill's. "You don't mind? Tell me you don't mind."

"I don't mind," Quill said. Then, quietly, "Yikes."

"So," Meg said, "now that we know where we are, we just need to establish a price."

The ensuing discussion was lively, profane—and on one occasion, Doreen did rise and threaten Marge with the Mason jar. Meg led the haggling—backed by a satisfying truculent Doreen. Betty brought in the pad of paper Marge did all her businesses with, then a second one when Meg stood up, shrieked, and tore the first into confetti.

The discussion lasted until four o'clock; Betty brought in coffee and shortbread cookies, reminded Marge that it was her bowling night, and Marge was on duty in the kitchen.

"Yeah, yeah, yeah. I'll get *on* it. So, Meg. You get the Aga, the big refrigerator, and that's it."

"Fine."

Marge licked the end of her pencil and made a note. Then she ticked off the contingencies under her breath. "You got too much," she declared. "I want the stove."

Meg rose to her feet for the fifth or sixth time and screamed, "*Sapristi!*" which disconcerted everyone except Marge. "That mean okay?"

"Freely translated? It means, hell, no!"

"*Sapristi?*" Quill asked. "What do you mean by yelling *sapristi*?"

"You don't think," Meg said with relish, "that I studied for two years at LeCordon Bleu and the Sorbonne for desserts without learning how to yell *sapristi*, do you?"

"Guess not," Doreen muttered.

"Them Frogs can cuss a treat," Marge said appreciatively. "Okay. We got seventeen contingencies and a basic agreement on price. Flip you on who gets Howie Murchison to write it up."

Quill, whose sole contribution had been to lay out the depressingly large list of their accounts payable, happily dug out a quarter. "Heads or tails?"

"Heads."

Quill flipped, slapped the quarter into her palm, and displayed it, tails up.

"Damn," Marge muttered. "All right, I got some bozo I use in Syracuse who ain't worth the fart it takes to get his attention. You get Howie. Let's close the deal ASAP, all right?"

"As soon as possible," Doreen said. "This agreement, you were talking, Meg, that I get maybe five thousand bucks?"

"Depending on the due diligence," Marge warned. "You guys got any debts you ain't told me about, we're back to the bottom on price."

"It's pretty close," Quill said. "The total haunts my dreams at night."

"And John . . . you said he gets a little bit more than me, because he has a few more shares."

"That's right," Meg said. "Do you want to call him and tell him?"

Doreen glanced sideways at Quill. "She oughta. The news oughta come from Quill."

"I'll call him tonight," Quill promised. "I think he'll be happy. He wrote off his shares in the company because of all the debt."

"He wrote off his shares on account of you," Marge said brutally. "Don't do to mix love and business. You girls remember that when you run this place."

"What are we going to call it?" Quill said. "I like Meg's Inn."

"Too cutsey," Meg said promptly. "And it's a restaurant, not an inn."

"Quill's Pen?" Marge suggested.

"Yuck." Meg shook her head.

"You got two artists here," Doreen said. "Call it the Palate."

"Not bad," Quill said. "Not bad at all."

•   •   •

Marge went into her kitchen, Doreen drove home, and Max got up from his post by the municipal garbage can with a "finally!" sort of bark. Meg and Quill stood outside the diner, looking over their acquisition. The overcast day had given way to a mauve-colored twilight. "The stonework's really beautiful," Quill said. "I wonder what the building was before some cretin turned it into a laundry?"

Meg stooped in front of the main door. "The cornerstone says 1828. It might have been a house."

"Miriam Doncaster should know. I'll ask her."

They turned to walk home to the Inn. Meg made a worried face. "There are so many 'pendings,' Quill. Pending inspection of the diner, pending due diligence. What if something goes wrong?"

"It might," Quill agreed cautiously. "But I don't think it will. Marge is a woman of her word." They walked on for a moment in silence. Then Quill said, "Why didn't you tell me you were tired of the Inn?"

"It seemed so important to you, Quill."

"It seemed too important to you!"

"I don't care where I cook," Meg said thoughtfully. "As long as I can cook. Are you going to tell Myles?"

"Of course. Why wouldn't I?"

"You never know with you two. Andy will be standing on his head for joy."

"Myles will, too," Quill said, although she wasn't entirely sure what his reaction was going to be. "And what do you mean, you never know with us? Our relationship should be perfectly clear."

"The only thing that's clear is that no one knows if you're going to get married or not." She eyed the engagement ring on Quill's finger. "It's been eight months since you put that on, and not one word about wedding plans."

"This case is keeping us both pretty busy," Quill said

evasively. They crossed Main and turned into the park. The lilacs were at their peak. The violet glow of the setting sun enhanced the purple flowers with an almost neon glow.

"Stop a minute, Quill. Look at how the Inn sits up there."

" 'Whatever walks in Hill House, walks alone,' " Quill quoted.

"Oh, come on. Most of the years have been wonderful and not haunted at all."

"That's true, they have." She narrowed her eyes. "Is that a Fed Ex truck? It is. Good. Myles said the Trenton P.D. was sending that correspondence. I hope it gets us a little further on the solution to the murder."

"You don't want to let the police handle it?" Meg said. "I mean, now that we've sold the Inn, or practically, we can give Myles back his money, and let Marge wrestle Burke."

"We can't quit now, Meg. We're just too close."

By the time they reached the Inn, the Fed Ex truck was gone, and Dina was folding up her laptop to leave for the day. Her greeting was a subdued "Hi, Meg, hi, Quill," as they came in the front door.

Meg put her hands over her head and danced a jig on the carpet. "Hey, Dina! We've got great news."

"Well, it's no use telling *me*," she said rapidly, "because the answer is no. No bookings. And Mr. Smith checked out, so there's only Mr. Pfieffer as an overnight guest, and he didn't want to eat in a dining room all alone, so he went down to the Croh Bar."

"Mr. Smith checked out?"

"Back to the Marriott. And I'm sorry, but I'm in the middle of checking the pond data on the cocophods for my thesis, and I just didn't realize."

"Realize what?"

"That his name isn't Max."

Max, hearing his name, went "woof."

"That his name isn't Max?" Quill said, bewildered. "Why should his name be Max? The dog's name is Max. Mr. Smith's name is Thorne Smith or Henry T. Smith, depending on what job he has at the—oh, no! You didn't!"

"What?" Meg hated it when people didn't let her in on the conversation. "Oh, no what?"

"The boiled rice, eggs, and bouillon?" Quill asked Dina. "And you wouldn't let him eat anything else?"

"Bjarne said he didn't know either. He said that Americans have very strange tastes and if that's what you said Max—I mean Mr. Smith—should have, that's what he'd make. Anyhow, I'm sorry. And he was our next-to-last customer, and I feel awful. You're going broke, and I'm shoving you right in the ditch!"

Quill put her arms around her. Meg rolled her eyes and said crisply, "Kiddo. Lighten up. Come into the kitchen and I'll pour you a glass of wine. We've got some good news."

"Like what?"

"Like, really good. But I want you to keep it to yourself for a while, okay?"

"Sure," she said disconsolately. "Quill, a package came for Robin, so I sent the Fed Ex guy to the hospital, okay? And David's guys found that thing you were looking for."

"You mean the third triangle?"

"Yeah."

"And the correspondence is at the hospital." Quill sighed. "Okay. It's part of the case that Myles and I are working, Dina. I'll have to go get it."

There were times when the three-mile walk to the hospital would have refreshed her and given her much needed exercise. But it was getting dark, and there was a bare possibility that Marge was right; there was an indiscriminate killer abroad, and Quill had never been fond of those heroines who persisted in going to the basement when everyone knew the killer was lurking behind the water heater.

She took her keys from the hook behind the reception desk and picked up her purse. Max, who'd appropriated a place on the hearth rug next to the cobblestone fireplace, looked very pleased at the prospect of going out.

"I think you should stay here."

He barked.

"On the other hand, if you stay here, you'll just get out again and go terrorize one of the farmer's chickens."

He looked ashamed of himself, but not enough, Quill figured, to keep him from a midnight foray.

"Okay. You're on. But there are rules to driving in the car, Max, and I expect you to follow them."

He didn't, of course, and Quill finally gave up and let him sit in her lap. It was a little hard to see over his head, but the streets of Hemlock Falls weren't clogged with traffic at any time, and especially on a night following three successive murders.

Quill parked near the emergency entrance to the hospital, left the windows partly rolled up, and told Max to "stay." He settled comfortably enough in the backseat, and after praising him lavishly, she walked through emergency into the hospital itself.

The hospital was small, with a total of twenty beds, and went under periodic review for closure by the five-county-wide hospital oversight committee. Somehow the clinic and the small O.R. managed to stay open year after year. It was located in back of the high school athletic field, and on warm summer nights, both patients and staff could hear the pleasant hum of baseball games.

Quill walked through the empty halls, her heels echoing. There was no one on duty at reception, so Quill slipped behind the desk and checked the room registry.

Freddie and Robin were together in Room Six.

She was a little concerned to find the empty chair that had been set for the young patrolman. When she walked in, Freddie and Robin seemed safe enough. They were sitting in the cheap plastic armchairs that somehow found their ways into every hospital Quill had ever seen. Selena Summerhill was perched on one of the two beds in the room. She was in the middle of a dog warden story, and Quill waited until she'd finished. "... and then, of course, I said, 'I am the dog warden, NOT the pig warden, and if I were you, I would call the butcher.'"

Freddie laughed until tears came to her eyes. Quill heard a tinge of hysteria in the laughter, and saw fear in the nervous way she moved. So Andy's drugs, whatever they were, weren't helping. "Where's the patrolman, Selena?"

"Out to get some food. I am a village official, I told him. I will stay here until he comes back. But now you are here, and I can go. I must get my Hugh some supper."

"Quill?" Freddie looked at her with fearful eyes. "You'll stay with us until he comes back, won't you? I told her that Sheriff McHale said a policeman, not a dog warden, but no one listened to me. And then will you ask the sheriff if we can go home? To Trenton?"

"Why, Freddie. Of course you can go home! You're not under arrest!"

Selena looked at Quill and smiled. "Ah, Quill. I have been trying to cheer them up, but Robin, too, says now they just want to go home. I smuggled in a little Summerhill red, which is very good for the nerves. Would you like to try it?"

"Not right now, thanks. Oh! I wanted to thank you for giving Max a bath."

"And so you should!" she said with mock indignation. "I could lose my job! But it gave us some time to become friends." She slid off the bed and stood up. "I will leave you ladies to your new visitor. And I will see you, Quill." She bent down and gave Freddie a quick embrace. Freddie screamed. Poor thing, Quill thought. Poor thing.

"Bah!" Selena ruffled Freddie's hair. "We will catch this monster. Perhaps I will do it myself. Don't worry now. Have a glass of our nice wine and relax." She whirled out the door, then popped her head back in and added, "And tell all your friends about the Summerhill red!"

She left in a wave of perfume.

"I wanted to pick up that Fed Ex," Quill explained. "And I was in such a rush, I forgot to bring you anything. Do you need some fruit? I know that Dr. Bishop takes excellent care of his patients, but it's a little different when you're just hiding out."

"We don't want anything more to do with this," Freddie said. "Go away, Quill."

"NO!" Robin said. "Don't leave us alone."

"It's going to be fine," Quill soothed them. "Now where's that Fed Ex? There. It slipped under your chair, Freddie." Quill picked it up and tore open the back strip. A sheaf of poor quality letterhead was inside. She pulled the stack out and flipped through it. The letterhead, the kind that can be created on any computer, read:

American Crafts and Kits, Incorporated
Office of the President

Robin Robinson
Treasurer
THE CRAFTY LADIES
Apt# 2E
561 Plank Road
Trenton, N.J.

My dear Mrs. Robinson,

Warm regards to you and your companions. I received your letter of Thursday, last, and will meet with you all the week of May twenty-second at the Inn at Hemlock Falls. I am looking forward with much pleasure to meeting you one by one to discuss activities past and present.

Very truly yours,

R.Vinge

R.Vinge

Quill stared at the signature for a long moment. "Revenge," she said slowly. She raised her head. Freddie's arthritic fingers played nervously with the fringe of her hand-crocheted sweater. "Revenge for what?"

"We haven't the least idea," Robin snapped. "We didn't even know this was a setup until—" She bit the words off. Her eyes darted toward the door where Selena's perfume still lingered.

"Until what?"

"We're not saying a thing until we have a lawyer." Freddie's eyes met hers and slid away again.

Quill had an excellent memory when she needed it. Sometimes it was a curse; she knew every single bill that was overdue at the Inn, and she'd told Marge the truth: the bills gave her nightmares because she couldn't get rid of the specifics. Sometimes it was a blessing: she never forgot a guest who'd stayed at the Inn, no matter how briefly. She wasn't sure which attribute to give her memory now, because—at last—the case was falling into place.

She slipped the letter back into the Fed Ex package. "Let's put some facts in order here." She took a moment to compose herself. Her heart didn't believe it; her mind told her nothing else made sense.

"The five of you have been—let's call it colleagues for years. Ellen was in the clothing business. Fran was a customs officer. You, Freddie, were an order clerk at Tracey's Department Store in New York. Mary Lennox was married to a travel agent. Mary was also a real estate agent who did 'a lot of business' in Queens. And you, Robin, worked as a paralegal in the international transfer department of a New York bank. The five of you have taken trips together for years: to Hong Kong, Singapore, Korea, Mexico, all sources of illegal immigrant labor. All places where the poor would do anything, anything, to escape to America and start a new life.

"You've been running sweatshops, haven't you?"

"Nonsense!" Freddie's cheeks were pale under her rouge. "How dare you say such things to us."

"It seemed so odd to me, that none of your families showed up to help you through this," Quill mused. "But they know, don't they, Freddie? I called your daughter, the attorney, and she slammed the phone in my ear. And I thought what you wanted me to think. That she's selfish, terrified of being trapped with your care. She's terrified of having to turn to you. I was willing to buy into the ungrateful young children spiel you all gave me. I mean, the five of you are—were—sweet little old ladies with the appropriate sweet little old lady hobbies, right? It's a good front. We're bigots in America, you know. We make assumptions based on the way people look and how they dress, and how old they are. Old people are sweet, to be respected. Nobody seems to remember that old people were young people once. Maybe criminal young people. Maybe crooks. Even murderers."

"I can't believe you're saying these things to us!" Robin said. "This is cruel! You've lost your mind!"

Quill gave her a steady, level look. "There's a very high-powered security officer from the Day Company here. The Day Company is the parent organization of

Tracey's, but you both know that, don't you? He's investigating deaths involving sweatshop labor in the garment industry for his employer. They are terrified, apparently, of the publicity that will be generated if it's discovered they've been selling clothing made by twelve-year-olds for a dollar a day in firetrap warehouses in New York. I know"—she leaned forward—"*I know* those deaths were by fire. Somewhere in those crappy buildings Ellen found for you, people burned to death. Trapped. Suffocating in the smoke. The murders of Ellen, Fran, and Mary all duplicated those deaths, didn't they? Trapped, suffocated, and burned," she repeated. "Trapped, suffocated, and burned."

"For God's sake," snapped Robin, "they were just a bunch of Mexicans."

"So the question is now, who's after you? Who's looking for revenge? That letter from the president—" She closed her eyes. The diction was familiar. The background fit.

Fran's snippy voice: "They all say they're Spanish."

Damn it all. Damn.

CHAPTER 10

She called the sheriff's office. And then she left. It was hard to breathe in that room.

The parking lot was deserted, except for the few staff cars parked in the rear. Someone was whistling, out of sight. The tune seemed familiar. Quill walked toward her Oldsmobile. The voice broke into song. *"Good-bye to my Juan /good-bye Rosalita,/adios mis amigos/ Jesus y Maria . . ."*

Quill knew the rest; a Woody Guthrie song, poignant, dreadful in its message to an indifferent commercial world: *They won't know your names/ when you fly the big airplane/all they will call you will be/deportees.*

Her Olds was parked under one of the halogen lights that illuminated the lot. She stopped and unlocked her car. Her hands were shaking. She couldn't believe she'd walked into the basement. Stupid, she thought fiercely, *stupid*! Max panted in the rear seat.

"Hola! Quill!"

"Hello, Selena."

She emerged from the darkness and stood under the light. She held a gun. "You have talked to the bitches?"

"Yes."

Selena's eyes glittered. "They have not yet confessed."

Quill eyed the gun. "We'll get them, Selena." She edged the door open. Max leaped over the seat and nudged her hand with his cold wet nose.

"No. No. You don't understand. Dunbarton, Lennox, Grrrrimbsy." She rolled the r's with satisfaction. "They have all confessed."

This took Quill a moment. Then she said, "You mean, have they expiated their sins?"

"You do understand! Redeemed by fire!" Her voice was high, strained, intense. Quill opened the car door a little further. Max barked, demanding to be let out.

"Max!" Selena smiled. She tapped her leg with her free hand. She held the gun steady with the other. "Come, *querido*." Max barked again, leaped onto the pavement, and wagged his tail happily. "Good boy. Good boy." She leveled the gun.

"No! NO!"

She fired. Max dropped. Quill's breath left her.

"Come now, Quill. Into the car. The shot will bring people. In New York? Where my sister died? Clawing at the doors that had been bolted from the outside to keep her from running away? No one would come in New York. But here, yes. In Hemlock Falls, people will come."

"Selena . . ." She heard shouts from the hospital. A door slammed. "I called the sheriff."

"Good."

"Quill?" Andy Bishop jogged toward them. He stopped. His mouth opened slightly. "Quill? What the hell?"

"MOVE!"

Quill got into the car. Selena held the gun steady and

got into the backseat. She nestled the gun barrel into the back of Quill's neck. "Start it up."

Quill turned the key.

"If you crash the car? I don't care. I died when she died. *Es verdad,*" she murmured. "*Es verdad.*"

Quill put her shaking hands on the wheel. She kept her voice calm. "Where to?"

"The Inn."

Quill drove onto Maple, then turned left onto Main. She glanced in the rearview mirror. Andy's Saab was half a block behind them.

Selena kept her eyes on the back of Quill's neck. "They are following? Good. They must bring the newspapers, the television, everyone."

"You want people to know you've done this?"

"You will see. Stop! Not in front, around to the garden shed. I have my things there."

Quill's stomach roiled. She recalled the burlap bag. "What things?"

"The phosphorous. The tape." Her voice turned ugly and guttural. "Stop, stop here. Open your door, but do not get out."

Selena was over the edge, but it was a cold, practical insanity that left Quill no chance to get away. Selena put her left arm around the outside of the driver's door, switched the gun to that hand, and got out of the backseat. She switched the gun back to her right hand and pulled Quill from the car. She nudged her to the garden shed, gun at the small of Quill's back. She made Quill pick up the bag, and tear off three lengths of duct tape. She taped Quill's hands tightly behind her back, then taped her mouth shut. She slung the burlap bag over her shoulder.

"Now," she said, "to the kitchen."

Quill stumbled back into the open air. The sheriff's car came up the drive, lights flashing. Quill wasn't a praying woman, but she prayed now: Get-out-get-out-get-out-get-out, all of you please, get-out.

The kitchen was empty. Quill, dizzy with the effort of breathing through her nose, almost fainted with relief. Selena dragged her by the sleeve and locked the back door, the windows, the door to the wine cellar and the pantry. She pushed her onto a counter stool and stood by her, facing the double doors to the dining room, the gun in her left hand, the muzzle at Quill's temple. "Now we wait."

Nothing happened for agonizing minutes. Then a shadow appeared at the window. Two shadows. Davy Kiddermeister and Andy Bishop.

"Come in through the dining room doors!" Selena shouted. "You hear me? That way is locked. You break in that way, I will shoot her!"

The shadows disappeared. Time passed; Quill didn't know how quickly. The blood drummed in her head, making everything dark.

There was a tap at the dining room door.

"Come in," Selena said.

The door swung open. Meg walked in. Quill cried out, the cry a groan, muffled by the duct tape. "*Buenos*," Selena said.

"Hey, Selena." Meg stood there, smiling, hands at her sides. "What can I do to help?"

"I want Hugh." The guttural, crazy note was back in her voice. Meg's eyes widened.

"Sure," she said briefly. "Hang on. The guys are outside, but you know that, don't you? I'll just let them know." She held both hands up, a plea, and backed through the swinging doors. She wasn't gone more than thirty seconds. Getoutgetoutgetout, Quill prayed. Meggie, please . . .

Meg came back. "They've got him on the phone now. It'll take about fifteen minutes. Can I fix you guys something to eat in the meantime?'' She edged into the kitchen, step by step.

Selena laughed. ''The dead do not eat, Margaretha. You will do this. You will call everyone. Everyone, do you hear? The TV people, the newspaper people, all of those *policía* hanging around out there. Everyone who will listen. I want them all in here. All, *comprende*?''

Quill's ''NO!'' was a strangled grunt.

''And then what?'' Meg said.

''Then we will wait for Hugh.''

''Hang on just a second,'' Meg said calmly. She pushed the door open and spoke to someone outside. ''Did you hear what she's asking? Good.'' She turned back to Selena. ''You haven't asked about Freddie Patch and Robin Robinson.''

Selena shook her head. ''They are pawns. I have made my point. It will be harder for them to live with what they have done, than die and be forgiven.'' She crossed herself twice rapidly.

''I see,'' Meg said, and perhaps she did. ''I don't know about the TV people, but we can probably get Axminster Stoker here. He's the publisher of the paper. If there's anything you want broadcast, he can see that the word gets out. That's what you want, isn't it? To make a statement.''

''That is what I demand!''

''No helicopter? No million bucks?'' Meg walked forward slowly, both hands extended. Quill held her breath.

''Don't be stupid! You will sit there, on the floor.''

''All right.'' Meg sank to the floor by the fireplace, squatting on her heels.

''And you will wait. We will all wait. Until Hugh comes.''

The silence was horrible, broken only by Selena's rapid breathing. Quill heard the sounds of vehicles coming up the drive, the cut-off whine of a fire truck, the slam of car doors.

People began to file in, one by one. Andy was first. He didn't speak, but sat by Meg, his hand on hers. Then Doreen came in, with Stoke. Marge Schmidt, Betty Hall, the mayor.

Tears trickled from Quill's eyes. Would she have walked into this kind of danger for friendship?

Selena broke the silence. "The police? Where are the police?"

"Surrounding the place, of course," Marge said. "Whaddaya think? We don't go for hostages in Hemlock Falls." A line, Quill thought, that would have been funny in any situation but this one.

"They are to be here," Selena commanded.

"I'll tell Davy," Betty said.

"You sit there, Betty Hall." Elmer Henry had been leaning against the wall facing the windows. He pushed himself away. "I got the authority here; they'll come in if I tell them to."

And they did. Denny the fire chief; Elmer, this time accompanied by Adela, the state troopers. Dina Muir slipped in, eyes wide.

"You are the little receptionist, no?" Selena asked. "Did they call you?"

"It was on the radio," Dina said in a hushed voice.

"Then where is Huuugh? Where is Huuugh?" Selena's howl made the hair on Quill's neck rise. Someone sobbed.

"Mrs. Summerhill?" Davy Kiddermeister walked in, holding Hugh Summerhill by the arm.

He was the most frightened man Quill had ever seen. His face was so pale it was green. His pupils were dilated. He vibrated with a fine tremor.

"And so you've come," she said.

"Selena, I . . . ." His voice was hoarse, faint.

"How stupid did you think I was?" she said, her voice conversational. "We meet, as if by accident, outside that warehouse. Accident?" She spat. "I don't think so. You saw me, didn't you? With my sister. The man in the shadows. You."

Hugh's eyes darted left, then right. "I don't know what you're—"

"Liar. You know how I know? That wine. The Pinot. No one else had it, but that bitch, that Dunbarton bitch. You gave it to her as a prize, did you not? You and your secret meetings. I knew there was someone else. Their president. And to have it be you, my Hugh. How funny." The gun in her hand wavered slightly. "I knew them all, all, from when I first came here, and after my sister died, I planned. The landlord, the one who pretended to be a lawyer to get us our papers. They didn't know me. I got them here, so I could get their confessions, one by one, and I talk with them and I look at them, and they don't know me. We look the same, we do. All the same. I drink their wine, your wine, Hugh, the wine no one but you and I had drunk. . . ." She didn't seem to notice the tears pouring down her face. "Come here."

He shook his head. Selena dug the pistol into Quill's throat. Davy pushed Hugh forward, and he stumbled and fell to his knees.

"Closer," Selena demanded.

He got to his feet and shuffled forward.

Selena bent down slowly, her right arm stretched up to keep the gun on Quill. She pulled the burlap bag off the floor, upended it, and the contents fell out: duct tape. A small knife. A black cartridge about the size of TV remote, wound round with wire. And a smaller cartridge with a homemade switch protruding from one end.

"You will tell them," she said to Hugh. "You will tell them what you have done."

He shook his head in a rapid, loose movement. It made Quill think of jellyfish.

Selena said quietly. "You will tell them how you made your fortune. By bringing whole families from Mexico. From Hong Kong. From Korea. All to that place in New York, promising them a future. You will tell them how you handcuffed them to their beds at night, so they couldn't run away. How you charged them for food, for shelter, so that they ended up with no money at all. Tell them."

"Yes," Hugh whispered.

"You will also say how you locked the doors, always, so they could not get out. And how you set that fire, because you were . . ." She began to breathe hard, pulling in air with great gasps. "Keeping. My sister. And they. Would tell me."

"I didn't . . ."

Selena pointed to the phosphorous bomb on the floor. "Whose is that?" she asked in a reasonable way. "Where did I find that?"

"All *right, dammit!*"

"Good," Selena said quietly. "I have to tell you all, because it is true, that I myself made that one. It is very small, not like the others. Pick it up, Hugh. Hold it. Show it to all these people here, what you have made." He didn't move.

Selena cocked the trigger.

Quill thought of Myles.

"Here, you." Doreen got to her feet with a groan, picked up the cartridge. Hugh backed away. Doreen put it in the pocket of his crisp blue shirt. "You all see that?" She turned to Selena. "He's got it now. He's holdin' his guilt. You let Quill go."

"Back away from him," Selena said. She held Hugh

to her, and pulled him backwards, step by step, until the thick oak frame of Meg's huge butcher's block stood between the two of them and the rest of the world.

And stepped on the trigger.

EPILOGUE

Rocky Burke stared at the remains of the kitchen. "It's not as bad as it looks," Quill said in what she hoped was a comforting way. "A lot of the damage occurred when people tried to get out of here." She looked at the floor. "She pulled him behind the butcher block. And the . . . the . . . device was small. I think she just wanted to get him. No one else."

He picked his way through the rubble and gave the splintered swinging doors a tentative poke with one finger. So far, he hadn't said a word.

"We haven't been able to find anyone here in Hemlock Falls who can handle the restoration of the floor, unfortunately."

Rocky poked the century-old flagstone with his toe. There was a hole the size of a twenty-five gallon stockpot. "Linoleum," he said. "Cheap, durable . . . you want linoleum."

"The worktable's in the worst shape." Quill regarded it doubtfully. "I don't think it's salvageable, do you? The preliminary estimate on that came from an antique dealer friend of mine. But that thick heavy oak saved a lot of lives. Hugh Summerhill was standing behind it when . . . um. . . . I guess I told you that already.'' She ran her hands through her hair. It was going to take a while to get used to having it short. The flames had seared it badly. The burns, Andy Bishop told her cheerfully, were no worse than those incurred by women who opted for laser resurfacing. Her skin would be pink and healthy in two weeks.

''Well,'' Rocky Burke said. ''Tell you what I'm gonna do, Cookie. I'll leave you a check right here, right now, based on a sensible repair to this place. All this old stuff—'' He waved his hand carelessly. ''You don't want to fuss with that, right?''

''It wouldn't do any good to leave a check with me,'' Quill said apologetically. ''We've sold the Inn, and we've assigned the claim for damages to the new owner. She's very interested in the costs of the restoration.''

''Somebody bought your inn?'' He looked hopeful. ''Well, now. If you just want to send me right on down to them, I'll leave a check for this damage and for Room 310, and that will be the last you see of me. Who bought it?''

''Marge Schmidt.''

The smile dropped from his face. ''Marge Schmidt!? That dragon-faced old bat? I mean, the woman who runs the diner?''

''Yes. Except we're going to be running the diner now, my sister and I. And Doreen Stoker, you remember her.''

''Yes,'' Rocky Burke said hollowly, ''I sure do.''

''She's going to be helping us. Part-time.''

''Marge Schmidt,'' he said.

Quill smiled at him. ''Rocky, it could have been a lot worse. No one was seriously hurt, just a few burns and a broken toe, but that happened when Adela and the mayor collided with each other trying to get out of the kitchen.''

"It could have been a lot worse, that's true. That fella and his wife—"

"The Summerhills? Yes. Both dead. Their daughter is with Hugh's parents."

"What about the old biddies who ran the sweatshop for him?"

"Thorne Smith's company is prosecuting them. They filed not-guilty pleas."

"Bet they get off. Jury looks at those sweet faces . . . I can hear the lawyers now, 'Would you send your gramma to jail?' "

"These grandmothers, I would," Quill said.

Myles had taken her to Canada for three days after the terrible events in the kitchen. The respite had been welcome, but she'd dreamed too frequently of Robin's malevolent face, and the hissing whisper: "They're only Mexican." She shook her head, to clear it. "Rocky, we hope to open the Palate in about three weeks, to take advantage of the tourist season this summer. We're going to need some liability ins—"

"No, ma'am. No, thank you. No way."

"I assure you that we don't plan on having bombers in for breakfast."

"What about that dog?" He pointed at Max, who was curled in his bed near the fireplace. "Da—I mean darn thing nearly took my finger off when I gave it a pat. You get rid of the dog, I'll think about insuring you."

"He's still recuperating from that gunshot wound," Quill protested.

"Yeah?" said Rocky skeptically. "Think his attitude will improve?"

"Well, sure it will," said Quill. "Mine has, now that this is all over. Will you excuse me for a moment? I have to make a phone call."

It had been ten days since the blast that killed Selena

and her Hugh. Marge had paid cash for the Inn, and the deal had gone through.

Quill wandered through the rooms. Marge had purchased most of the furniture; Meg, Quill, and Doreen had kept the couch in the foyer, the two large Oriental vases, and the rug. Their personal things would be put in storage until Quill decided on a house to buy in the village. Between moving into a new home, and restoring the little diner—now known as the Palate—it was going to be a busy summer.

She went into her office. The desktop was cleared of bills, invoices, shipping lists, tax forms, advertisements, laundry lists, business summaries—the lot. Quill ran one hand over the clean and shining surface.

She couldn't do it. Now that the cash was in Marge's hands, the furniture moved, the plans all set ... she couldn't do it.

She sat down, dizzy with the effort of breathing. Leave it all? Leave it *all*?!

"No," she said and picked up the phone. "Long Island, please," she said. "I'd like the number for the residence of a Mr. John Raintree."

MEG'S THRIFTY RECIPES

Meg had a hard time getting used to cooking on a budget, but she managed pretty well during the time that the Inn was in such financial trouble. Here are some of her recipes for gourmets on a budget.

LEFTOVER
SOURDOUGH BRUSCHETTA

Take all of the sourdough bread made for guests that never showed up and slice it into inch-long pieces. Melt one part pure unsalted butter to one part extra virgin olive oil in a sauté pan. Add several cloves of pureed garlic to taste. Brush on the bread. Do not clean the pan. Chop red peppers, green peppers, scallions, and pimiento very fine. Sauté lightly in the pan, for about forty-five seconds. Arrange the vegetables on the bread, sprinkle with Parmesan cheese, and broil until done.

FLAN QUILLIAM

1 cup heavy cream
1 cup whole milk
5 cups leftover brioche, broken into one-inch pieces
two tablespoons sugar
two eggs
raisins soaked in rum
dark rum, to taste

Beat the eggs to a froth. Add the sugar and beat to a cream. Add a dash of dark rum, an eighth of a cup if you made the mortgage this month, or a quarter of a cup if you made payroll on top of that. Mix in the cream and the milk until the mixture is smooth and uniformly colored. Add the raisins—two cups if you can afford it. Place the brioche in a casserole dish, add the cream/egg/raisin mixture. Bake at 350 for about thirty minutes, or until the cream is bubbling around the browned edges of the bread. Meg has a temper tantrum if she can't serve this with whipped cream, fresh raspberries, and a leaf or two of mint. But life's tough.

MARGE SCHMIDT'S BREAKFAST BAKE

Forget it. Meg would rather eat a rat.

About the Author

Claudia Bishop divides her time between West Palm Beach and upstate New York. As Mary Stanton, she writes young adult mysteries. She also writes for television. Her younger sister Whit is a gourmet cook. Both sisters like wine, gardening, and spend a lot of time on horseback. Claudia is at work on a new Hemlock Falls novel set at Meg and Quill's new restaurant, the Palate.

Welcome to Hemlock Falls...a quiet town in upstate New York where you can find a cozy bed at the Inn, a tasty home-cooked meal—and murder where you least expect it...

THE HEMLOCK FALLS MYSTERY SERIES
CLAUDIA BISHOP

with an original recipe in each mystery

__A PINCH OF POISON __0-425-15104-2/$5.99
When a nosy newspaperman goes sniffing around town, Sarah and Meg smell something rotten. It's worse than corruption—it's murder. And the newsman is facing his final deadline...

__A DASH OF DEATH __0-425-14638-3/$4.99
After a group of women from Hemlock Falls win a design contest, one disappears and another dies. Just how far would television host and town snob Helena Houndswood go to avoid mixing with the déclassé of the neighborhood?

__A TASTE FOR MURDER __0-425-14350-3/$5.99
The History Days festival is the highlight of the year in Hemlock Falls, with the reenactment of the 17th-century witch trials. But a mock execution becomes all too real when a woman is crushed under a pile of stones and the killer is still on the loose...

__MURDER WELL-DONE __0-425-15336-3/$5.99
Big trouble comes to Hemlock Falls when a sleazy ex-senator holds his wedding reception at the Inn. It's a success—until his body is found tied to a barbecue spit.

Prices slightly higher in Canada

Payable in U.S. funds only. No cash/COD accepted. Postage & handling: U.S./CAN. $2.75 for one book, $1.00 for each additional, not to exceed $6.75; Int'l $5.00 for one book, $1.00 each additional. We accept Visa, Amex, MC ($10.00 min.), checks ($15.00 fee for returned checks) and money orders. Call 800-788-6262 or 201-933-9292, fax 201-896-8569; refer to ad # 590 (3/99)

Penguin Putnam Inc.	Bill my: ☐Visa ☐MasterCard ☐Amex _____(expires)
P.O. Box 12289, Dept. B	Card#_____
Newark, NJ 07101-5289	
Please allow 4-6 weeks for delivery.	Signature_____
Foreign and Canadian delivery 6-8 weeks.	

Bill to:

Name_____

Address_____City_____

State/ZIP_____

Daytime Phone #_____

Ship to:

Name_____ Book Total $_____

Address_____ Applicable Sales Tax $_____

City_____ Postage & Handling $_____

State/ZIP_____ Total Amount Due $_____

This offer subject to change without notice.

Jane Waterhouse

"Waterhouse has written an unusual story with plenty of plot twists. Garner Quinn is a memorable creation and the book's psychological suspense is entirely successful."
—*Chicago Tribune*

GRAVEN IMAGES

A murder victim is discovered, piece by piece, in the lifelike sculptures of a celebrated artist. True crime author Garner Quinn thinks she knows the killer. But the truth is stranger than fiction—when art imitates life...and death.

__0-425-15673-7/$5.99

A Choice of the Literary Guild®
A Choice of the Doubleday Book Club®
A Choice of the Mystery Guild®

A POWERFUL NEW MYSTERY SERIES FROM
THE WILDS OF ALASKA

MEGAN MALLORY RUST

Dead Stick

Aviator Taylor Morgan can tolerate almost anything—last-minute wake-up calls for midnight rescues, sexist coworkers, and perilous travel through the untamed Alaskan wilderness. She's a pilot for LifeLine Air Ambulance, and saving lives is her business—and her pleasure as well.

Now that another woman flier has signed on, she anticipates a new comrade—and fewer jests from the all-male aircrew. So it comes as a horrible shock when Erica Wolverton, the new pilot Taylor approved for duty, fatally crashes her first flight. But as soon as this pilot turns PI, she begins to receive threats—and senses danger everywhere. Now Taylor must do her questioning outside of a biased investigation to find out the truth about the crash—before she too meets with a fatal "accident"...

__0-425-16296-6/$5.99

Prices slightly higher in Canada

Payable in U.S. funds only. No cash/COD accepted. Postage & handling: U.S./CAN. $2.75 for one book, $1.00 for each additional, not to exceed $6.75; Int'l $5.00 for one book, $1.00 each additional. We accept Visa, Amex, MC ($10.00 min.), checks ($15.00 fee for returned checks) and money orders. Call 800-788-6262 or 201-933-9292, fax 201-896-8569; refer to ad # 827 (3/99)

Penguin Putnam Inc.   Bill my: ☐ Visa ☐ MasterCard ☐ Amex _____ (expires)
P.O. Box 12289, Dept. B   Card#_____
Newark, NJ 07101-5289
Please allow 4-6 weeks for delivery.   Signature_____
Foreign and Canadian delivery 6-8 weeks.

Bill to:

Name_____
Address_____City_____
State/ZIP_____
Daytime Phone #_____

Ship to:

Name_____ Book Total $_____
Address_____ Applicable Sales Tax $_____
City_____ Postage & Handling $_____
State/ZIP_____ Total Amount Due $_____

This offer subject to change without notice.